IT STARTED
with a
HIGH TOP

IT STARTED
with a
HIGH TOP

LAYLAA KHAN

wattpad books

An imprint of Wattpad WEBTOON Book Group
Copyright© 2024 Laylaa Khan
All rights reserved.

No portion of this publication may be reproduced or transmitted, in any form or by any means, without the express written permission of the copyright holders.

Published in Canada by Wattpad WEBTOON Book Group, a division of Wattpad WEBTOON Studios, Inc.

36 Wellington Street E., Suite 200, Toronto, ON M5E 1C7 Canada

www.wattpad.com

First Wattpad Books edition: December 2024

ISBN 978-1-99834-155-9 (Paperback edition)

ISBN 978-1-98936-594-6 (eBook edition)

Names, characters, places, and incidents featured in this publication are either the product of the author's imagination or are used fictitiously. Any resemblance to actual persons (living or dead), events, institutions, or locales, without satiric intent, is coincidental.

Wattpad Books, Wattpad WEBTOON Book Group, and associated logos are trademarks and/or registered trademarks of Wattpad WEBTOON Studios, Inc. and/or its affiliates. Wattpad and associated logos are trademarks and/or registered trademarks of Wattpad Corp.

Library and Archives Canada Cataloguing in Publication information is available upon request.

151533290

Cover illustration by Amelia Schiffer

To the people who are searching
for peace; for growth; for adventure.

Chapter 1

ANNE

There is a poem that I read a few years ago that advised me to never date a man whom I can write poetry about; to instead date someone with clammy hands and a kind smile. Someone who is consistent and does not cause poetically tumultuous feelings.

The guy that I am in love with has both a kind smile and clammy hands, and his lips are currently planted firmly against a pretty, blond girl. Their bodies are pressed together, like two vines that have grown together for so long that they eventually mold into one.

How is that for poetry?

It would be easy to believe they are deeply in love. She holds on to him like she never wants to let go. Kissing Hunter must feel like those movie scenes; the way he'd hold me, look at me, and *want* me. It must be quite the experience.

The Earth could split open right beside me and I still wouldn't be able to tear my eyes off of them. I don't even know who the girl is. She is probably a senior, like Hunter. I've seen her at a few of my brother's parties, but I have never spoken to her.

My heart clenches inside my chest, like it is preparing to break apart at any second. Hunter slips his hands into the girl's soft, glossy hair. Hair that I have accepted I will never have without three hours of preparation. She leans into him, craving more.

I don't know why he does this with girls. He is at our house all the time because he is best friends with my brother, and he doesn't come off as a player normally. At least not as much as my brother does. But then he goes and does things like this, and ugh.

Having a crush on him feels like purposefully stepping into quicksand.

This isn't who he is or what he does. He needs a reason to get away from that gorgeous girl, right? I walk up to him, ever ready to help out a person in need.

"Hunter, we need to—" He lifts his hand and blindly presses his rough index finger against my lips to stop me from talking. *And that's the most action I am going to get today.* His fingers touching my lips—even in this unfortunate situation—leave me flustered. He pulls away from the kiss. His dazed eyes, the color of clouds rolling in before a storm, stare down at the girl with an intense desire. His expression seems conflicted between ending the kiss to talk to me or continuing what he was clearly enjoying.

"You okay?" he asks, his expression softening as he steps away from the girl. Now he is looking at me like he wants to kiss *me*. Probably just the aftermath. Although, having three brothers, I know that boys will kiss one girl and happily kiss another immediately after.

I need to get out of his line of sight before I turn completely red. "Yeah, yeah. Sorry. Don't worry. I'll—I'll talk to you later." I spin and scurry away before I can make a fool out of myself. I have a favor to ask Hunter. I could have asked another time, but he *clearly* needed rescuing from that kiss. I adjust my backpack, which is slung over my shoulder, and walk off in the direction of my least-favorite class—P.E.

I want him to convince his boss to hire me at the bakery he works at. I tried applying myself, but it has been three weeks, and I still haven't heard back. My mother has been taking so many shifts at the hospital. She barely has time to eat or sleep. She often sleeps on the hard plastic chairs inside the hospital. I hate it. It has been terrible for her health, and I never see her anymore.

I hear Hunter speak from behind me. "Annabelle?" I spent the first few years of knowing Hunter, wondering what his sexy accent was. The melodic cadence of his voice and the way his a's seem to stretch had always lead me toward the assumption of a British accent. He told me he is from South Africa, and while I have never been there, it is now my favorite accent.

I continue walking, pretending not to hear him. He knows that I hate it when he calls me by my full name. My parents named me after a cursed doll. It's not a coincidence. I asked my dad and he said he was a big horror movie fanatic when he was younger. *At least they didn't name me Chucky, I guess.*

Hunter quickly steps in front of me, waiting for a response. He plays with the white strings of his favorite dark green hoodie. Its hood is lifted to partially cover the dirty blond curls on the top of his head. I resist the urge to reach out and touch them. "You good?"

"We can talk later. I have to get to class." I step around him and pick up my pace, but he easily keeps up with me.

Holding on to my shoulders, he twists me to face him. His touch is gentle but firm. I look anywhere but into those eyes. If I meet his gaze for more than three seconds, I'll forget how to breathe. I've been daydreaming about what it would be like to trail my hands across his broad shoulders and down his chest. I don't think it would end well. "If you don't tell me, I'm not going to let you go."

I don't want you to let me go. "You have class, too." I have to keep my words simple and to the point around him, or else I'll start blabbering like an idiot. Like the time he asked me if I wanted to watch a music video that he liked, and I started ranting about the book that I am writing—how I wished people could be as easy to predict as characters in a story. The world would be a much better place if people couldn't hide their thoughts and intentions. He then asked me if I was hiding any secrets in my head ...

After multiple embarrassing moments like that, I realized that it was better to be quiet.

He pushes me backward until my body is pressed against the lockers. Somehow, he can be both rough and gentle. "What's your point?" he asks, grinning. His smile has always pulled at my heart. It is the kind of charming smile that draws people closer. It makes sense why he gets the attention he does from women.

His easy smile has always held my heart, from the moment I set my eyes on him. From the dimple on the left side of his cheek that I want to push my finger into, to the way his eyes scrunch up. *Man, oh, man.* There is little I wouldn't do to keep that smile directed at me.

His body is pressed against mine. My heart hammers inside my chest as he leans his arm up against the locker and dips his head down to watch me.

I take a chance and place my hand on his chest, a feigned attempt to push him away. I would have preferred to have my hands on the curve of his biceps—but what would my excuse for that be?

He smells like cinnamon rolls. He glances down at my hand, then back at me, a smile still playing on his lips like he knows all of my inner thoughts. "Were you at the bakery this morning?" I ask. Sometimes he gets awkward talking about it, as if a man who can cook is something he should be ashamed of.

"Don't avoid my question. What do you need?" *You.*

"Could you ask George if he will hire me at the bakery? Any job, even if I have to scrub the toilets. I tried applying already, but it's been three weeks and I still haven't heard back." My hands reluctantly drop from his chest.

"I'll ask." His face is inches from mine. There are small freckles dotted over his nose and cheeks.

"Thanks."

He leans in closer, which I didn't think was possible, and runs his tongue over his still-swollen pink lips. "Anything for you, Annabelle." He makes it so hard for me to not want more.

An arm suddenly comes between us. Hunter pulls back to reveal Daniel, my older brother. His dark hair is tousled like he has been working out. "Why are you two so close together?" he asks. His narrowed eyes move between the two of us. Neither of us answer. I'd put distance between us if I could. "If you touch my sister, I will emasculate you," he warns. One of the thousand warnings he has given Hunter.

Hunter and Daniel have been best friends since the fifth grade. Hunter accidentally hit me with a baseball ball, leaving a gigantic bruise on my thigh, and Daniel immediately took a liking to him.

I've always wondered who would win in a fight. They are both built similarly, tall and muscular, and it would not be fun to be tackled by either of them.

"What if she likes it?" Hunter reaches out and tucks my light brown hair behind my ear, doing it only to annoy Daniel. His rough fingertips brush against my skin, and I nearly lean forward.

There's a bright smile spread across his face as he watches Daniel's eyebrows furrow. "Do you like it?" Daniel asks me. His deep blue eyes bore into mine. His eyebrows are naturally angled to look angrier. If I don't answer this question, it will answer itself.

Daniel has—on multiple occasions—made it clear that nothing can ever happen between Hunter and me. The only problem is that if someone tells me I can click any button except the red one, all I want is to press the red one. Hunter is my red button.

"No," I say quickly, knowing hell will break loose if I give Daniel any other answer. "No, of course not."

"Good. Now get to class, you're late," he reminds me. A few people walking through the hallway wave at Daniel and Hunter. A group of guys stop near us, waiting to talk to them.

I turn and jog to my class. I'm already breathless by the time my overweight P.E. teacher is giving instructions to change and run five laps. If they say we should never trust a skinny chef, what would they say about this?

The boys in my class are already running. Their hair sticks to their heads with sweat. The sun is beating down, making the air hot and uncomfortable. I'm grateful Hunter isn't in my class. Physical exercise is not my strong suit. If he could see me write a History essay, however, he'd fall in love. I reach my changing-room locker, which has probably been broken since before my family moved to this town.

"Heyoo," a cheery voice greets. Clary is leaning against her locker, pulling her shoes off. She brushes her short red hair back behind her ear, but it only slips forward against her cheek again.

"I would appreciate it if you could tone down your happiness." I dump my backpack into my locker.

Clary is a really good friend. Safe to say, I don't have many friends, but I'd call her one. We pranked our teacher together in kindergarten by pouring apple juice into her Prada handbag, since she refused to let us take restroom breaks. When Miss Lieberbaum saw yellow liquid dripping from her bag, she didn't know it was apple juice.

"I heard Jaden Maddox is having a party next week Friday." She slips into her exercise clothes. "You should totally come."

The word "party" roughly translates to drunk, underaged people grinding against each other in the dark. Nothing unappealing about that. "I think I'm better off at home."

"Will your brother go?" she asks. There is a naughty glint in her brown eyes. She has hinted that she likes Daniel, but he has never shown the slightest interest in her. He is on a constant rotation of woman. Maybe that is why Clary and I get along so well. We both suffer from the aftereffects of unrequited love.

"Remind me why I am friends with you?" I tease as I pull my own clothes off. I am curvier than Clary, but it's one of the things I've learned to accept and embrace.

"Because I keep you entertained?" She ties her hair back into a small, tight ponytail that juts outward instead of down. Clary is good friend to have in a crowded room, because you could spot her orange-red hair from a mile away.

I roll my eyes and push my locker closed. It slowly pushes back open with a creek. I can't complain about it. Not when I am here on a scholarship.

My dad used to pay for our school fees, but he stopped once the divorce was finalized. My mom can't afford to send us to a private school. The privilege of most students here can be seen and smelled from a mile away, but the level of education we get here is significantly better than anywhere else in Tecumseh, Michigan. Daniel is here on a football scholarship, while I got in on a merit-based scholarship, and my two younger brothers attend a more affordable school in the next town, about a twenty-minute drive away. I go with Daniel every morning to drop them off—and have to deal with Daniel's horrid taste in music.

"So, what do you say?" Clary asks, stopping beside me so we can walk to the fields together. She nods and points her index finger at me like a mother scolding her child. "I will get you to this party, babe. I will show you the dark side and prove it's not all bad."

"I don't think so . . ." Being surrounded by people isn't something I enjoy. Even being here, at school, is daunting on most days.

She is about to argue, but the whistle blows, indicating that our torture is about to begin. We jog to the field.

•••

By the time the lesson is over, I am ready to collapse. Clary immediately finds her way back to my side. "I think our teacher enjoys torturing teenagers," she says. Her forehead is shiny with sweat. We walk into the changing rooms in silence.

"I think we need to go and get ice cream after class to make up for the trauma," I suggest, pulling open my locker. My heart starts racing in my chest, my mind switching to frantic mode. "Wait. Where is my other shoe?" I dig through my backpack. I take everything out until my locker is completely empty and I am certain only one shoe remains. "Clary, this isn't funny. If you took my shoe . . ." But she was with me the whole time. She wouldn't have had the chance.

"Your mom's shoes?" She frowns, dropping her things to come to my side. "You sure you wore them today?"

Am I *sure*? I wear them every day. Of course I'm sure! "Yes, yes. They were *here*." I point into the locker. "Someone took my shoe." This might be worse than if I lost my phone. My shoes hold much more meaning and more memories than my phone ever could. They are worth more to me than anything I own. I want to cry, but that won't get my shoe back.

"We will find it," Clary reassures me.

I'm going to make sure I do. It is not that someone wanted to wear them, or they would have taken both shoes. This is either a prank or something personal. They're easy to spot—turquoise blue with painted violets that I added on myself. I check the other lockers, which makes some of the other girls in my class scoff at me. The shoe is nowhere to be found. I turn to Clary. My heart is tight, in fear that I may never see it again. My mother's shoe.

"Why don't you come to the party. It'll give you a reason to approach people who might have wanted to, I don't know, get back at you or something. Everyone is going to be there."

That is not the worst idea. I narrow my eyes at her. "You want me to ask Daniel to pick you up on the way, don't you?"

She grins, framing the bottom of her face with her hands to feign innocence. Then, she drags her backpack over her shoulder. "Gotta go to my next class." She pulls me into a bone-crushing hug.

I melt into it, wanting to turn into a puddle. She is someone who understands how much these shoes mean to me. My mother's youth and the beginning of my parents love story is encapsulated in those shoes. She wore them all the time, until she gave them to me. They hold so many stories.

My parents have a rich history, meeting in Egypt where my mother was born. She was ostracized from her family for not wanting an arranged marriage. She endured a lot of struggles along the way. Each one of her struggles was combated in these shoes, all the way until she met my father and they fell in love.

My shoe can't be gone forever. Her story can't be erased that easily.

Maybe it *is* a prank. It could be Daniel or Hunter. They usually do these things to each other, but maybe they thought this would be funny.

Please, please, please.

I rush across the school to get to the football fields. Thankfully, most people don't notice that I am barefoot. Scanning the field, I spot my brother's mess of black hair. He is running laps around the field with the rest of his team. I wave to him and he immediately cuts across the field to come to me, ignoring his coach, who tells him to keep running.

He is breathless and disgusting, coated in sweat. "Hey, little booger. Are you all right?" He swipes his hand through his damp hair, pushing it away from his face. His chest heaves up and down.

"Daniel." My voice shakes and he can immediately tell I'm not all right.

He grabs me and pulls me into a tight hug. He is warm and sweaty, but at least he doesn't smell. "What happened?"

The hug is comforting. It's exactly what I needed. "Someone— someone took my shoe."

He pulls away, holding me at arm's length to assess my expression. He always looks serious, but with his eyebrows furrowed and his jaw clenched, most people would run. "Why would someone take it?" he asks. *Exactly!* They're not fancy or desirable. Even if they were, nobody would only need the single shoe. "Do you know anyone who would want to upset you?"

"Nobody comes to mind." I always keep my head down. I don't

IT STARTED WITH A HIGH TOP

speak to most people, aside from Clary, Daniel, and Daniel's friends.

"Unless . . ." He storms off past me and into the school. His coach blows his whistle multiple times, calling Daniel back. It goes in one ear and out the other.

I rush after Daniel once he has disappeared into the school. He is already the center of attention as he rushes past a few students. Naturally, everyone's gaze always finds him. He has someone's shirt twisted in his grip in an instant. "Was it you?" Daniel growls. The boy, whom I don't recognize, is already shaking his head. "Why'd you do it?"

"What—what? I did nothing!" He tries to escape Daniel's grip like a worm wriggling out of its hole. He swallows hard, his ears going red. Daniel drags him closer, until they are face to face. The boy looks like he'd rather be six feet under than in this situation. "Bro, let me go."

"Daniel, hurting him won't help anyone," Hunter says, walking up to us. He places his hand on Daniel's shoulder. "No matter how angry you are." Hunter is always the voice of reason at Daniel's side.

"I'm not going to hurt him," Daniel says. "Just getting answers." But he releases the kid's shirt. The boy immediately rushes off.

Hunter notices me. My cheeks immediately flush as he sends me a small smile. "Hey, Annabelle."

"Anne," I correct him.

His eyes trail to my feet. "Your shoe is missing." He winks.

I glare at him and, in my most sarcastic tone, I say, "Oh my, is it?"

"Some ass stole her shoe." Daniel almost seems more upset than I am. His hands are in fists at his side.

Hunter frowns and glances at me again. "Do you want me to drop you at home?" he offers.

"I can't, I'm here on a scholarship. If I skip without permission…"

That seems to alert Daniel. "Right, I should get back to the fields before I'm kicked off the team for bailing. We will find your shoe. Don't stress too much." He turns to Hunter. "Keep her safe, all right?"

"Always."

Chapter 2

HUNTER

"Such a good girl," I tease.

The only thing that convinced Anne to skip class was us going to the principal, explaining what happened, and getting permission to leave. He only gave her a pass because she started tearing up. I wish I could do something. She doesn't react at all to my words, which is unusual. She's almost always blushing, no matter what I say. We walk toward my motorbike in silence. Cobblestone crumbles under my boots. "What kind of music is a balloon scared of?" I ask, trying to fill the silence. Hopefully a joke will make her feel a little bit better. She looks up at me, with those caring brown eyes, and shrugs.

"Pop."

She snorts and quickly blocks her mouth. "Lame." Yeah, it was. She smiled anyway, which makes it a success.

We stop in front of my bike; a Ducati Multistrada 1200. It's an old bike, bought secondhand. I don't mind how old it is, because it's so comfortable to ride, especially with long legs. My father doesn't know about it, and I'd like to keep it that way.

I grab my helmet and carefully slide it over Anne's head. The smell of her soap, a warm violet scent—which I only know because I read the bottle label—fills my nose. "You wear it," she insists. Her small hands move up, onto mine, and she starts pulling the helmet off. She does this *every time.*

I push it back down and clip it, tightening the buckle so it fits her face. She narrows her eyes at me and tries unclipping it. I grab her hands in mine and pull them away from the helmet. We both look down at our connected hands. Her skin is soft and warm. She quickly pulls them out of my grasp, her cheeks red. It is adorable when she blushes. I have a suspicion that she likes me. Hopefully I'm wrong because I don't want to break her heart. Daniel knows how I am with girls, never serious, so he would never let me near his sister. I step back and straddle my bike. "Get on."

She throws her leg over the bike and sits behind me. Her arms slide around my torso slowly, as if she is trying to memorize the way my body feels against her hands. I shiver against her touch, my grip tightening on the handles of my bike.

I start the engine and drive out of the school parking lot, onto the road. My thoughts drift off to the girl I made out with earlier today. Tiffany. She offered to write my English paper for me if I kissed her. She was trying to make her ex-boyfriend jealous or something. I agreed because her favor would help me save time. I'll be able to take more shifts at the bakery, which means I'll be able to get away from home faster. Plus, it is a welcome distraction.

Wind blows past us as I drive. Trees and small buildings turn into a blur of warm Fall colors. The way the sunshine hits the leaves has always seemed ethereal to me. It makes me wonder, if something so simple can be so beautiful—what else is out there in the world, waiting to be noticed?

We reach Anne's house in less than ten minutes, and I park in the driveway. Anne climbs off after me, and I unclip the helmet, pulling it off her head.

"Do you want to come in?" she offers, as she quickly combs her fingers through her long brown hair, the blush back on her cheeks.

"No." I fix a piece of hair that she missed. "Go get changed. I'm going to grab my stuff and then we'll go to the bakery."

"For what?"

"To get you that job you want."

"Seriously?" Her eyes light up. She steps closer to me. "You're so great!" The excitement in her voice creates a warm feeling in my chest.

"Meet me out here in thirty minutes."

I walk over to my house, which is right next door.

The smell of cigarettes hovers in the air. Every counter is coated in dust. If my father could simply hire some help, we'd have fixed some of the broken light bulbs, we'd have a clean home, and maybe we'd even have a half-decent back yard. Instead, every time I walk in here, I feel nauseous.

"Hunter, is that you?" my father calls out as I shut the front door.

Damn it. "Yeah..." Who else would it be?

"Get your useless ass in here," he demands.

That is the reason I never bother to fix the lights or clean up myself. I'd rather find a way out of here and let him rot by himself in this dive.

I walk into the living room. He is sitting in his usual spot, in front of the television. He scratches the dark hair that trails up his belly. A lump forms in my throat. Seeing my dad in his boxers always manages to disgust me. There are empty glass bottles and takeout containers lying around him. It makes me want to get in the shower and scrub my eyeballs.

"Yes?"

His eyes search around. "Find the remote."

I pick it up from the coffee table, which is right in front of him. He watches me intently as I hand over the remote. He doesn't say a word, but his expression is full of disdain. "Get me a drink."

I walk to the kitchen and pull a beer out. When I walk back and hand it to him, he says, "You're a great waiter, you know?" A pause. "I've got a feeling that's all you'll ever be."

I'm so tired of this.

"I told you—I was promoted last year. I work as a baker. I'm actually good at it." This is something I've explained many times, but he never hears me.

He snorts. "Baking is for girls."

Pursing my lips, there are so many things I want to say to him. Mostly, I just want to record him and show the world how he speaks to me—so that I wouldn't have to hate him alone.

Going up to my room on the second floor, I pull out a white shirt and matching pants from my cupboard. George, my boss, told me that a white uniform is mandatory at work, but it has never made sense to me because white gets dirty so easily at a bakery.

My clothes turn into a pile on my floor. Staring at the reflection of myself, a million self-critical thoughts pop up. They're not true. But . . . why do I never feel like enough?

At least girls seem to like it. The acceptance feels good. Maybe it's the only thing that makes me not hate myself.

After pulling on my work clothes, I fall onto my bed and close my burning eyes. I went in to work before school this morning to prepare some extra pastries for the day and I'm exhausted. My eyes physically burn. I hate waking up early, but it has to be done. I want more than the life I'm living.

My room door slams open. "Why are you home? It's not after dark. Get out. Go do something useful. Or I'll put you to work here, boy."

Anger flares through me. I work hard every single day and it's never enough. He never acknowledges it. "Look who's talking!" I shout. He has let himself go completely.

"What the hell did you say to me?" My father pulls me off the bed by my arm. It hurts.

I push him away from me, which makes his face turn red with anger or embarrassment. "You heard me." I snatch my phone and wallet and rush downstairs, to the front door.

He runs after me and throws a glass bottle against the wall beside me. The sound makes me flinch. "You ungrateful piece of shit! Don't come home tonight."

I slam the door shut and walk over to Anne's house.

I force myself to stop on my driveway and I take a deep breath, refusing to let emotions affect me the way my father does. My heart is jumping like a horse on cocaine. I will not let my father have the satisfaction of knowing that his words and actions always affect me. I just need to knead some dough. It's the best stress reliever. All I want is to slam it against the table. Over and over.

My hands shake as I push Anne's front door open and walk in. This door is never locked, except at night. The house is very similar to mine, except they maintain it far better. It smells like polished wood, and I don't get a migraine every time I walk in.

I walk up the wooden stairs and into Anne's room. "Annabelle?"

She gasps, her hair dripping wet, and tightens the towel around her body. "Hunter, I thought I was meeting you outside. What are you doing here?"

The way she says my name makes it sound far more beautiful

it is. She speaks with a slight Arabic lilt, influenced by her mother, who comes from Egypt.

The towel hugs her curves, which are only emphasized by how tight she is holding it now.

I quickly twist around, my brain already imagining inappropriate things, like what might happen if she dropped the towel. "Sorry, I wasn't thinking," I say staring at the turquoise paint on her walls.

Her room is always well kept. She has a place for everything and has a way of making things beautiful.

People lie for two reasons: to protect themselves, or to protect others. I don't want to lie, so to protect myself I give a partial truth. "I couldn't wait to see you."

"Really?" she asks, as if that is unlikely. "You can turn. I'm done."

I twist to look at her, my eyes trailing over her body. She is wearing a dark red pants suit. The color contrasts against her golden-brown skin. Some people sit in the sun for hours to get the color she has naturally.

Looking at her feels like tasting sweet, fresh honey. "You know you're applying to be a waitress, right?" I ask, referring to her formal outfit.

"I dress for the job I want, not the job I have."

I walk closer to her. This would be much easier if she didn't smell so good. I want to wrap my arms around her, nuzzle my face against her and breathe in that comforting smell. "You don't *have* a job."

She laughs and shoves my shoulder. "Shut up."

She does have the job already. After Anne spoke to me this morning, I called George and he said that if I deep-clean the ovens and help him with some of his plumbing issues at home, the job is hers. Pure bribery, I know, but I care about him, and I'd do those things for free.

He has been a source of comfort for me, and someone reliable that I can count on. On days where I don't want to be at home, he opens the bakery up for me overnight so I can take out any frustration I have in the kitchen. Truly, he proves that family isn't always blood.

My hand grips on to her waist lightly. The material is velvety. "It's nice. Where did you get it?" I ask.

Nice? Out of all the adjectives in the world that exist, I chose *nice*. She's a writer, so I doubt she is impressed by such basic language.

She glances down at the outfit and runs her hands over the soft material. "Why, you thinking of buying one for yourself?"

"Yeah, I think red is my color."

"Ha-ha," she deadpans.

"Come on, it—" Anne places a finger over my mouth to shut me up. I frown. She slowly removes her finger, her brown eyes lowering to my lips. What is she doing, looking at me like that? "You're playing a dangerous game, Annabelle." She nods, her eyes not straying from my lips. "Do you want to kiss me?" I tease. Her eyes become wide and curious, as if she is waiting for me to do something. It makes me want—*need*—to do something.

It takes her a few seconds to come back to reality. "What? No." She shakes her head furiously, pulling away from me.

"Good." That's the answer I needed. "Let's go."

We walk out the house and toward my bike. I grab my helmet and slide it over her head.

She immediately pulls it off. "It's your turn to wear it. I wore it on the way home. You need to be safe, too."

She tries to put it on me, but she is a head and a half shorter than me and struggles to get it on.

I grab it and put it on her again. The soft click of the buckle finalizes my actions. "I promised I'd keep you safe." I'm a good driver, but there is no way to control what other people do on the roads.

Stepping forward, I close the space between us. There is something pulling me closer to her, making me want to protect her. Her eyes meet mine, and it takes a lot of restraint to avoid looking at her mouth—I know once my eyes fall on those lips that remind me of freshly picked berries, I won't be able to think straight.

I climb onto my bike, and she climbs on behind me. Her hands sliding over me like I'm a pastry she wants to savor. We drive off in the direction of the bakery. If she keeps touching me like this, I'm going to have to put her in front and make her hold the handles instead of my body.

We pass little old antique shops and small cafés, which make up most of our small town. People are walking around, making the most of the clear skies before winter comes. There is not much to boast about when living in a town like Tecumseh. It is, and has always been, a stopover town. There are never many people around. Anne seems to love it here. I think I'd rather live in a big city, where nobody would know my name or look at me twice.

Parking in my usual spot in front of the bakery window, we climb off my bike and walk to the entrance. There are lots of bicycles parked in what are supposed to be spaces for cars. The croissant-shaped sign on the front door reads OPEN. Anne pushes against the glass door, allowing the soft R and B music to flow out into the streets. The bakery has a warm glow to it, created by the dim amber bulbs and the various shades of nude used in the paint, the tiles, and the tables. There is a huge mural to the right of the bakery of different pastries and sugary foods—from croissants to cupcakes, with even a few attempts at baklava that don't look quite right. Most people don't look hard enough to notice them.

This place feels like home to me. A few pastries and baked goods I made this morning line the large wooden counter in glass jars and trays. Some customers sit at tables with drinks, or enjoying pastries that I made earlier. Sabrina, a waitress who also goes to our school, stands behind the cash register, placing an order for another customer. Anne sucks in a deep breath, inhaling the usual smell of cinnamon rolls—our bestseller—and coffee.

"Hey, kiddos," George greets us, walking out from the large swiveling kitchen door. He is clad in his usual corduroy pants and a black jersey. The kitchen door swings closed behind him, fanning the sweet aromas around.

George walks toward us. He has a friendly smile spread across his aging face. "Hunter, my boy." He softly slaps my back. He pushes his wire-framed glasses up the bridge of his nose to assess Anne. "Good to see you here again, Annabelle."

She turns to glare at me for a second. I am the reason why George calls her Annabelle. A smile finds its way to her face. It—no, I'm not thinking about how beautiful her smile is. "Thank you for agreeing to see me. I emailed my résumé to you if you would like to have a look at it. I'm—"

"You're hired," George says. There are a few pastry crumbs stuck in his graying beard.

I'm not going to tell her about the deal I made with George. Their family needs the money. Daniel works just as hard as me at the music store around the corner in order to improve their situation.

She glances at me, then back at George. "Really?"

He nods. "If Hunter says you're good, I'll take his word for it. Your enthusiasm reassures me."

George speaks so fluently that it would be impossible to tell that only a few years ago, he lived in India. The only telltale signs are his brown aging skin and the hundreds of stories he tells me about his past. He was awesome in his youth, traveling and exploring the world.

"Thank you so much." Anne shakes his hand again and turns to me with a big smile on her face. It warms my heart to know that glowing smile is because of me.

"Right, well, you can start on Monday. Let me get my notepad and we will plan what shifts you will take." George walks back through the kitchen door, disappearing from sight.

"Thank you for doing this for me," she says.

"Glad to be your knight in shining tinfoil."

"Tinfoil? More like parchment paper."

"Oh, a baking reference?" I unintentionally step closer to her again. "I think I like you even more now."

She averts her gaze, hiding her face behind her hair.

I hate to admit that when her cheeks turn red, instead of finding it cute, it comes as a reminder of my father's fuming face as he threw his glass beer bottle at me earlier.

George walks out from the kitchen and sits with Anne at one of the six tables. I walk into the kitchen to begin my shift. My eyes still burn with exhaustion, but I'd rather be here than at home.

The kitchen is small, lined with steel counters and large, noisy ovens. Flour and baking trays are scattered around from this morning. I didn't have time to clean up. After setting up the coffee machine and doing a quick clean, I slip on my apron and pull out all the ingredients I need to make more cinnamon rolls and some éclairs, which I know that Anne, and all the customers that come in today, will love.

As I am starting to mix ingredients, the kitchen door swings open and Sabrina strides in, her hips swaying as she walks. "Why is Anne talking to George out there?"

"Because she is going to be working here," I say, not bothering to look up from my mixing bowl. She scowls at the information. I've noticed from their few interactions that they might not get along.

She walks up to me and places a hand on my biceps, not-so-subtly squeezing it. She flutters her light blue eyes at me. "You are *so* sexy," she whispers. She presses her chest against me. Her perfume has a mix of roses and spice. "And kind and smart." She sighs.

I grin at her, opening up a little bit. I don't believe her compliments, but I am not going to reject them. It's nice to know that someone doesn't think I am a complete failure.

Her painted nail drags up the center of my neck, stopping at the edge of my chin as she tries to tempt me closer. But George is right outside, and he has an important rule here: no fraternizing with the co-workers.

Chapter 3

ANNE

The next day, I find myself sitting at the same table in the bakery, with my hands wrapped tightly around a perspiring glass of water. The cold droplets help ground me in the moment, instead of drifting into the thoughts of narratives that may work for the book I'd like to write.

Of course, I read too much. *Not at all* because I want to escape reality and find a life worth living. Especially now that my shoe is gone; something that sounds absolutely ridiculous to anyone else and that makes me feel even more alone. Now I am here, at a loss in more ways than one as I realize I have no right to write a book. Why are my words more important than anyone else's?

A wet cloth is thrown down in front of me. Sabrina starts aggressively cleaning the table. "Back off," she says.

I lift my glass up so she doesn't knock it over. It is my first day of work, and she has decided that closing time is the best moment to come over and make my day worse. "Sabrina, it's lovely to see you, too."

She narrows her eyes and leans closer to hiss at me. "I mean it, wacko. Stay away from him." She glances back at the kitchen doors.

"You want me to stay away from *Hunter*?" I scoff. "He is my brother's best friend and my neighbor. He practically lives with us. You know that's not possible."

Her sleek caramel-colored hair is braided, reaching all the way to her hips. Sometimes I wonder if she uses it to strangle her victims. "Then you better watch your back," she warns.

She has resorted to threats. That's classy. "Why?"

"Because Hunter is mine."

"Yours? Did you mark him?" I roll my eyes. She's always been unusually aggressive toward me, but it never crossed my mind that it could be jealousy over Hunter.

"Mark him with what?" Her eyebrows scrunch together. She forgets about wiping the table, her hands going to her hips.

"No, mark him ... like a werewolf—uh ..." Maybe I should stop talking.

It's almost a relief to know that I am not the only one suffering from unrequited love. In fact, I've seen the way girls look at Hunter and murmur about him when he walks by. I am definitely not the only girl in love with him, and I think he knows it. He never used to do anything about it, but maybe that is changing. I get up and walk into the kitchen. Sabrina rushes after me, likely assuming that I am going to tell him about her threat. I wouldn't, because I'm exhausted and I just want this day to be over without any more unnecessary drama. The kitchen is different from the rest of the bakery, containing simple metal counters and fridges, white walls, and no color whatsoever. Hunter is creating foam art on coffee. His eyes light up when he sees me. "Hey, Anabelle."

"I'm going to the bookstore," I tell him.

Sabrina's frown morphs into a smirk. Tilting her head, she watches me for a few more seconds before walking off to carry on cleaning up the empty tables.

He nods and slips on a pair of oven gloves. "I'll come and pick you up when I'm done here." He bends down to lift a tray out of the oven.

On my way out the bakery, Sabrina catches my eye. She is glaring at me, but I ignore it and walk the short distance to the small bookstore. It is a place where I can escape and recharge—and maybe focus on a little bit of research for my future book.

A tiny woman with thick red glasses and an oversize dress gives me a small smile as I walk in. She reminds me of Stuart Little.

I wave to her and walk to the back of the store, where all the conspiracy-theory books can be found. It smells like new books in here. I pick a book about the simulation theory and human consciousness off the shelf and drop myself down into a dark blue beanbag, choosing its color based on my mood.

The sound of pages flipping calms me. Tilting myself backward, I release a sigh. If I could spend all my time in here, I would.

•••

"There you are," a husky voice whispers.

Hunter's black boots stop in front of me and my eyes take their time trailing up to his face. He holds a plastic container in his hands. All of the theories I have been researching on consciousness make me doubt reality. Especially because there is no way that a guy like Hunter is real. I lift my hand and poke him in the thigh to check, and even though my finger comes into contact with his leg, I am no longer sure he exists.

He chuckles, his eyes scrunching at the corners. My oh my, he is a beautiful human. "Is this your way of trying to get me out of my pants?"

Would it work? I chuckle nervously. I would love to flirt with him, but what I fear more than rejection is that he would flirt back. What would I do then? Melt into the floor?

He holds out his hand to help me up. I take it. His hand is rough and firm. "What are you reading?"

We both glance down at the thick black book in my hands. "It's a book on the simulation theory. It questions reality and rationalizes that we might be living in an artificial simulation. It really, really messes with your brain."

He nods, genuinely seeming curious. "Tell me more."

"Really?" I bite my lip. He has listened to me rant about all kinds of theories over and over. Yet he always seems to be interested when I tell him something new.

"Yeah." He takes a seat in a yellow beanbag, and leans closer, his face the opposite of serious. "Convince me that I'm not real."

I smile and lean in, too. "There are endless theories on consciousness and reality. We might be coded into a realistic video game, or we could be nothing but brains in a vat. The human brain is incredible, yet so complicated that there's no way to understand everything it can and can't do.

"All of our senses, combined with other people's perceptions of us, make us believe we are real. We know our hands are real because we can feel them, we can see them, we can use them. If everyone we met told us we don't have hands, regardless of our senses, our brains would slowly believe that to be the truth. So, who is to say we aren't in a video game or some sort of controlled simulation where we are being tricked into believing reality based on what our senses and the people around us say?"

Hunter shrugs, uncertain. "Not necessarily true. If everyone told us we didn't have hands, but we are able to pick up a glass or throw a ball, then that means we do have hands, right? We back it up with proof. But if, for example, we were to say that the things we can't see or touch were not real, then I could accept that."

"Like God?"

"Or the stars. But that is why faith matters. Even for the things we can't see, we *need* to believe they're real. Some people wouldn't be able to be good without a Heaven to go to."

Say more.

"Close your eyes," he says. I do. Gently, his hand slides up my arm. "Can you feel me?" It slides across my shoulder and behind my neck, tugging me forward. My breath catches. His voice against my ear whispers, "Can you hear me?"

My lips part and, eyes still closed, I nod.

"It's our eyes that trick us the most," says Hunter. "We need to see it to believe that it's real. Imagine if news outlets only stated things without using images."

"But that's what I'm saying." His hand is still behind my neck. I can feel how close he is. "Those images can be manipulated. So, the simulation theory says that what we see with our own eyes could be manipulated, too."

"Is this real, Annabelle?" His thumb presses against my bottom lip.

My eyes fly open. *That's not fair.*

"Is it not the things we wish to be real that give us hope?" His eyes are on my lips. *Like kissing me?* "Do you want the simulation theory to be real?"

This is why I love telling him things. He asks good questions. He doesn't make me feel ridiculous, even when I know what I'm saying might be.

When I was younger, my parents never explained things to me.

Not only would they not tell me why stars existed or how caterpillars turn into butterflies, but they also kept me in the dark about their divorce and moving to America. It led me to come up with my own theories, which was more exciting than reality.

Sometimes the idea of what could be is more exciting than what we already know to be true.

He smiles and stands, holding out a container for me. "I made éclairs."

I gasp and take the container from his hands. "For me?"

"No, made them for the bakery."

We walk out the bookstore. A cold wind blows my hair away from my face. Streetlights illuminate the dark and empty roads. I pull the lid off of the container, and the sound seems to echo. "Thank you."

"No need, it was coincidental." He coincidentally made my favorite dessert. When I turn to him, his smile says otherwise.

"I could . . . kiss you." I shove an entire éclair into my mouth. That sentence should not have left my brain. It happens a lot: the speaking without thinking. At least I didn't say I love him.

"How does it taste?"

I moan. "Unreal. Out of this world. Extraordinary." Another reason I fell head over heels for him. "Can I take another one?" I ask, pointing to the container still in my hands.

"They're all yours."

My eyes widen. "All?" He nods. I take a second one out the container and bite into it. "This is definitely a simulation. There's no way these can taste this incredible."

"Thank you, Annabelle." His joy is palpable. That dimple is back. He always smiles the brightest when he is complimented on his talent for baking.

He holds his helmet out for me. Before I can try to reject it, he pushes it onto my head. "In my version of the simulation theory, I can't exist without you. Let's say that your reality is the only one that exists. That means if you die, I won't be able to live," he says.

That sounds almost romantic, but I know he doesn't mean it that way. "But we don't know *for sure*. What if you're real, but I'm not here? I could be coding or a figment of your imagination."

"Then I am grateful for my imagination, because it created you."

My heart swells like toilet paper dipped in water. He is flirting. I wish I was that playfully smooth. It would help if I didn't turn cherry red every time he smiled.

Click. "You don't have to clip the helmet for me every time," I point out. It's hard to be so close to him; to see every detail of his face, up to the soft freckles dotting his nose.

"Well, I don't have a car door to open for you." He climbs onto his bike, waiting for me to get on. His hands tightly grip the handles, causing the muscles in his biceps to flex against the sleeves of his white shirt. Oh man. Sometimes I entertain the thought of ripping his shirt off. "Plus, if I don't put that helmet on you, I know you won't wear it."

I climb onto the bike and this time I try to avoid touching him. I'm scared that if I do, I'll take it too far or say something stupid, giving away my feelings for him.

"You didn't—" He turns to look back at me, a strange look in his eyes. "Hold on, Annabelle," he says, his voice slightly rough.

The streetlights create a warm glow on the roads ahead as Hunter drives. My head starts spinning, contemplating how the houses and shops that we pass might not be there. I close my eyes, leaning my head against him to hide from the cold air. My heart is soaring with the speed he is driving at. It is such a simple moment, something we do all the time. I love it. I love feeling this way.

IT STARTED WITH A HIGH TOP

It might have been how I fell for him; that night when I got on his bike for the first time. The open night sky, the lights glowing in window shops, and the wind blowing my hair back. The roads were empty, like it was just me and him.

I wonder if he feels the same. Not to be in love with me, but to feel a sense of peace in moments like this. That would be enough.

When we reach my house, Hunter drives his bike into my garage. He keeps it at our house because his dad doesn't know about it. I walk out to the grassy patch next to the driveway and pull off my shoes. Nothing really feels the same without my high tops, for some reason. It feels like the world has turned upside down and I need to be grounded. I stare up at the endless stars above.

He comes to stand beside me, admiring the sky. "It's beautiful."

I nod in agreement.

He looks down at me. "Do you think they're real?"

"Giant balls of gas floating thousands of light years away, in an endless darkness." I pause. "I hope they're real." We can hardly understand our own brains, there's no way we're close to understanding the universe.

"Me, too."

"Are you staying over tonight?" I ask. Hunter sleeps at our house all the time, he even has clothes that he leaves with Daniel so he doesn't have to continually pack. We're his second home and I wouldn't want it any other way.

"Yeah." He turns to walk toward the house and I follow him inside.

"I don't think Daniel is home. His car isn't here."

"I texted him. Said he'll be home later." He is probably on another date. "I'm exhausted, so I'm going to shower and sleep."

That works out perfectly for me, because I want to be alone. I have interacted with too many people for one day. I may have also procrastinated finishing an essay that's due soon. We part ways and I trudge up to my room.

My room stays neat, my bed neatly made and nothing on the floor, as my mom taught me. Her typical "a place for everything and everything in its place" motto. I respect it, because I know that she needed it in a time where her world was falling apart, and the only thing she could control was the cleanliness of her home.

My desk is the only untidy space, with papers scattered holding rough ideations for my book.

I sink into the soft seat in front of my desk, my head and heart feeling like the few crumpled balls of paper tossed into the trash can. Even though it was a successful day, and I now have a job, I feel like I have lost so much. Whoever stole my shoe did it to hurt me, and they succeeded. My mom would be so upset too, if she knew my shoe was stolen. I want to hunt down and find my shoe.

Using that anger, I start to write.

•••

The following school day goes by in a long, draining blur. The same routine, the same people, the same building. At least it is new information. I walk out of my last class for the day and toward Daniel, who is leaning against his locker. His friends stand around him, talking about their next football match.

"Hey, beautiful," Daniel and Hunter's friend, Elias, greets me. His blond hair is parted in the center.

"Hey . . . you."

His clear blue eyes scan over me. "I like your outfit."

I'm wearing a shirt with a bunch of cartoon characters on it and faded light blue jeans. It would have gone well with my high tops. I still have the one shoe in my backpack in case I find the other. I'm not letting go of that hope. "Thanks. I like your face."

Elias will flirt with anything that moves. He has never said no to a female before. No matter the request. Once, he retiled a girl's restroom (badly).

It is easier to flirt with Elias, because there are no feelings behind it. That's why Hunter's flirting scares me, because he might feel nothing and that's why it comes so easily.

Daniel watches the two of us intently, making sure that Elias doesn't touch me. He lifts his bag from the ground and hooks it over his shoulder. His backpack seems light, nearly empty, which is unusual for someone in their final year. Sometimes I really get concerned for him. "Ready to go?" he asks.

I nod.

"Cheers, guys." He guy-hugs every single one of them. They all chorus in their goodbyes as we walk off. "How was your day?" Daniel asks, lazily throwing his arm around my shoulders.

I want to say "long and hard," but I know he will make a dirty joke out of it. Mom needs to take him and dunk him in some holy water. I decide to talk about Art and History, the only subjects that give me energy. We walk through the parking lot and toward Daniel's black Audi. He received it as a sixteenth birthday present from my dad. For my sixteenth birthday, my dad bought me an expensive pair of red-bottomed high heels. Clearly, he doesn't know me.

"I'm sure your brain hurts, learning about all the atrocities that happened only a few decades ago," he says, climbing into the driver's seat. The seat of the car molds against me. The black leather is unbelievably comfortable. He has a vanilla-scented air freshener hanging from the rearview mirror.

Studying history makes me deeply doubt humanity; when we look at what people become when they are put in positions of power or suffering. It makes me walk through everyday situations wondering what the people I pass would become in those places. That is why I enjoyed *The Hunger Games* so much.

It only takes a few minutes to get out of town and to the shopping mall. It is the only shopping mall for miles, but it has everything. That is why Daniel brought me here to buy me a new pair of high tops. I didn't bother pointing out that replacing the old shoes with new ones is not the same. It is like taking someone's cat and replacing it with an identical one. The soul isn't the same.

Daniel parks the car. "We still need to fetch Adam and Haiz from school. Meet me back here in thirty." He hands me his card.

Wandering through various stores, I look out for something that captures my attention. The only thing I notice is how malls are designed to make me feel like I will never have enough. Maybe that's only because I am looking for one thing—a pair turquoise-blue high tops with little purple violets on them that I painted on two years ago. My gaze shifts to the footwear of people passing by, as if somehow I'll catch someone wearing *one* of my high tops.

Taking a break from my search, I stop at the cinema and get myself a gigantic box of popcorn. Daniel is not going to be happy about this, but at least I found something I like in here.

The popcorn—my only source of happiness in this long and painful day—falls from my hands when I notice Hunter and another girl standing at the self-checkout. I've overheard Daniel tell Hunter to take a girl to a movie and she'll be more likely to kiss him. I never thought he would. Is he dating now?

It feels like a rejection, even if it isn't one.

He must have a thing for blondes. *Great.*

My popcorn is all over the floor. *Double great.*

A candy-sweet voice speaks from behind me. "Ew, why are you here?" Sabrina takes a long sip of her Slushee, her judgmental gaze trailing over me. *Triple great.*

"Did you forget your GPS at home today? You must have taken a wrong turn on the way to the zoo," I say. A buzz of conversation starts. Students pour out of one of the cinema doors.

She barely blinks at the insult. Probably because it was a bad one. I can barely think with Hunter's arm brushing against that girl.

Why is Sabrina even in the line if she already has her Slushee? "I want my shoe back," I demand. I have a feeling that she took my shoe. She's the only one who seems to want to make my life miserable.

Her face scrunches with disgust. "I wouldn't touch your shoe even if I had a hazmat suit on." The slurping sound as she drinks drives me crazy. Worse than when someone bites on a fork.

I don't believe her.

There are many benefits to a small town, but the major downside is constantly running into people you don't want to see.

Sabrina's gaze goes behind me, and I turn, wondering what caught her attention.

Hunter and the girl. They haven't noticed us, which means he isn't doing this for show. He wants her. He can't drag his eyes away. It is the way he looks at me when we are alone together. He is good at this; making people feel like they matter.

Pulling roughly at the bottom of my shirt, I remind myself that I can't be jealous or upset. I can't ruin what we have. If I hold on too tight, afraid of losing something, then it will shatter in my hands.

Breathing slowly and deeply is supposed to help, but it doesn't.

"You're upset. Your face is red."

"*Your* face is red." My insults are lacking today.

"Go drop this on her." Sabrina holds out her Slushee. My hand gestures indicate that I want her to simply leave. She is only adding to the aching feeling in my chest. "Come on," she urges. "It'll show Hunter what that girl's true colors are, and it'll make him more protective of you."

"That's manipulative."

"In this world there are only two kinds of people: the manipulative and the manipulated. Which one are you?"

"I don't believe that."

"Yet you believe the simulation theory?"

"Just—just . . . why do you even care if I go up there?"

She shrugs. "Less competition."

"I'm not going to. If you care so much, you do it."

She steps closer, lowering her voice to a near-whisper. "Do it, or I'll tell Daniel about how you feel about his best friend." The look I give her is one of disbelief. This is why I am convinced she has my shoe. She basks in other people's pain and embarrassment.

I guess she has chosen to be in the manipulative category.

I snatch the purple drink out of her grasp, leaving the straw dangling between her lips. She narrows her eyes at me.

Turning, I rush up to Hunter. "Oh, Hu—" I pretend to trip, causing the Slushee to coat the girl's pretty yellow dress.

The girl, who was previously playing with the strings of Hunter's gray sweatpants, jumps back. Her clothes are covered in the purple drink. She cringes, not knowing what to do with her hands. "What the hell?" she shrieks.

The insides of Hunter's eyebrows push together, making him look like a lost puppy. "Annabelle?"

"I . . . I'm sorry." I am mortified. This is exactly why I don't like going out in public. None of this would happen if I stayed in bed. "At least purple and yellow are complimentary colors . . ."

I didn't expect it, but a laugh bursts out of him, his smile growing wide. He looks down, gesturing to the stains. "Do you like it better now?"

Oh my gosh. I am sweating in places I didn't think I could sweat. "N-no." I rapidly shake my head.

He turns to his date. "I don't like those stains, either. I think I'm going to have to take you home and get that dress off." The girl he is on the date with sucks some of the purple slush off her thumb and nods, batting her eyelashes at him.

He flirts under his breath, his voice deepening. His hands lift to her arms, to her shoulders, exploring.

It reminds me of last night, his hand behind my neck, pulling me in.

The low rumble in his voice makes me need more air than my lungs can handle. I cross one leg in front of the other.

I'm getting turned on while he flirts with *another girl*. What is wrong with me?

I slowly back away, tears threatening to leak from my eyes. Maybe I'm that pathetic—that the reason I want him even more, is because he barely notices me.

He flirts sometimes, but moments like this show me that it truly means nothing. That I truly mean . . .

As soon as I turn to walk away, he calls out my name. "Where are you going?"

Where am I—? "What, you want me to stand around and watch?"

He shrugs. "Well, you seem to enjoy it. You do it quite often."

Mortified. I am mortified. A playful smile forms on his face as he notices my expression. Is he really teasing me right now?

I storm up to him, pressing my finger into his chest. "You know what, Hunter?"

He raises an eyebrow. His tall form making him have to tilt his head to look at me. "What, Annabelle?"

"You—"

He tilts his head, still playful. "Are you going to ground me for flirting with my date?"

"Men are just . . . dogs." It's true. I'm sure Daniel is waiting for me in his car, texting three different women at the same time. I'm sure my father used to do that, too.

The only hope I had for men was Hunter. I held on tight to the idea that when it came to it, he would choose to be with one girl.

"Meow."

The heat rising to my cheeks makes me frustrated. "Did you just meow?"

He shrugs. "Just saying." I bite down on my lip. As much as I want to laugh, the painful ache in my chest holds it in. Being human is such a strange thing.

He sighs when he realizes I'm not going to laugh. "Look, I'm not going to sleep with her."

That puts a dangerous feeling of hope in me. My eyes light up and I turn to look at the girl who is rather patiently waiting. She must really like Hunter if she's still here.

"Why not?"

"Flirting is fun, but the rest? That's more Daniel's thing." He runs his hand over my hair, probably neatening a few baby hairs that are standing up. "You know?"

Yeah, I do know. I know because I've seen it. He must have the self-control of a freaking monk, and I can't say anything about it because then I'd be contradicting myself.

He leans in closer in the hopes of a reply. If he could kiss me, that would be really, really nice.

"What's my thing?" Daniel asks, lazily striding up to us. Why is he always here, interrupting?

"Sex," Hunter states.

"You know, I like other things, too. I am a complex and layered human being."

"So you're saying sex is not your thing?" Hunter asks. His playful side is one of my favorite things. I could see him being old and happy, because of that light inside him.

Daniel and Hunter bring out the light in each other. There is no way I can ruin their friendship by getting in the middle of it.

I *can't* be the reason for them losing that. I love them both too much.

"Oh, it is most certainly my thing. But you know, it would be nice if a girl would write me a poem for once. Something romantic." He gestures grandly with his hands.

Hunter's date giggles, but Daniel doesn't even look her way, following their "bro code."

"We have to go, little booger. Adam won't stop calling me." He holds his phone out to show that his phone is, in fact, buzzing with a too-close-up photo of Adam's face on the screen.

That's my opening to run as far away from this situation as I can, and I take it.

Chapter 4

HUNTER

Anne has been avoiding me for almost two days. When I try to talk to her, she gets very quiet or comes up with an excuse about why she needs to leave. She's behaving like I was the one who spilled the Slushee on her.

She might still be upset with the way I behaved at the mall. Flirting is for fun. It makes me feel good. It makes me forget about other parts of my life. I shouldn't feel bad about it. I just want light and easy and . . . an escape.

Anne might be noticing. She sees me too clearly. If I'm not careful, she will start to notice why I avoid going home; she might notice why, on some days, she is my only escape route—with her strawberry lips and violet scent.

She is currently standing on the blue metallic bleachers that line the football field, cheering on Daniel as he tackles a player on the other school's team.

"Hey." I walk up beside her. She stays silent, refusing to meet my gaze. "Don't ignore me. I won't allow it."

"I won't allow it," she says in a low-pitched tone, doing a terrible imitation. "What are you going to do?"

She—*mmmm*. My jaw clenches. Sometimes I consider pushing her up against the wall, pinning her arms up above her head and making her quiet. *Very* quiet.

Because she never is. She always has something to say, and ninety percent of the time it is sarcastic.

I sit in a sunny spot beside Anne. It is Fall and the days have started to get a bit cooler.

The bleachers are full of rowdy students. Everyone is dressed in the school colors: royal blue and white. Our principal played football when he was younger, so football games are a big event at this school. There's one every Friday.

I have no idea how Daniel manages. He has tried to convince me to join the team, but I wouldn't have time for it with my job and school. He gets a lot of fans, specifically of the female species, for being the captain of the team.

"Hi," a sweet, soft voice greets us. Two unbelievably hot girls stand in front of me, smiling. They've both got blue and white paint smeared across their cheeks. "You're Hunter. You're friends with,"—the brunette turns to the field and points at Daniel—"him, right?"

"Yeah . . ." They probably want his number or a date.

"Can we go on a double date?" the other girl asks. She twirls her ebony hair between her fingers. Anne goes still and silent, no longer cheering for her brother.

"Let me talk to Daniel before I give you an answer."

They giggle and the brunette holds out her phone. Her phone case is in the shape of a pineapple. "Give me your number. I'll text you and we can set it up." Straightforward. I type my number into her phone. "My name is Astrid, by the way. This is Aaliyah." I'm not good with names. I'm definitely going to forget.

Once they walk away, I turn to Anne. "I wonder why they wanted a double date."

She scoffs. *"All right."* The light from the sun turns her hair golden, and emphasizes the outline of her figure. I shift in my seat, staring too long at her legs and the short, checkered skirt that she chose to wear today.

She folds her arms across her chest, pushing her cleavage up.

"What?" I ask.

"You're one of the most popular guys in this school. Don't act like you don't know that girls are attracted to you."

Yes, I have noticed that girls are attracted to me. I simply don't know *why*. Most likely because I am best friends with Daniel.

I slide closer to her and put my arm around her shoulders. "Are you?"

Her dark eyebrows scrunch up in confusion. "Am I what?"

"Attracted to me." I said I wouldn't flirt, yet here I am ...

"No," she says quickly. She turns a deep shade of red. It's starting to become my favorite color.

She quickly stands up and cheers Daniel on, louder than everyone else here.

Even though Anne hates attention, she's never too scared to be the loudest at his football games. I admire that about her. It almost makes me wish I had a sister, but then I remember how my dad would break her if I did.

At half time, the referee blows the whistle and the players all scatter. Daniel reaches down to snatch his water bottle, and then strides over to us, using the hem of his shirt to wipe the sweat off his face.

A few girls swoon. Their eyes don't leave him. "Imagine him bringing flowers to your front door," a girl beside me says to her friends.

They all chime in with sounds of excitement. "I'd like to pour chocolate sauce all over his body and then slowly lick it off." He'd love that.

"He could sweat on me and I'd say thank you." They giggle. I stare at them, causing them to go silent. Put that on the list of things I wish I could un-hear.

"Are you staying over tonight?" Daniel asks me, stopping in front of us.

I'm avoiding my father after what happened the other day. "Yeah."

"I'm bringing a hun over, so Anne will have to entertain you," he says. Anne watches me, her cheeks still slightly pink.

"You better change the sheets afterward or I'm not going near your room," I say. Maybe I shouldn't say that in front of his little sister.

He sticks his tongue out to lick the air slowly, revealing his venom tongue piercing.

The coach calls all of the players back to the field. Daniel grins at me and Anne before running to the center of the field, where other players are huddled together.

The setting sun turns the sky into a canvas of pink and orange. Anne pulls a packet of salted caramel chocolates from her backpack and tosses them to me.

I immediately tear the packet open. "You bought these for me?"

"No, I got them for myself. You got lucky." She bought my favorite sweet for herself, by chance? I know she is teasing me for Tuesday, when I said the éclairs were for the bakery.

The wrapper crunches as I pull it off. On the outside it looks average, but it is mind-blowing when you put it in your mouth—like me. The sweet caramel bursts from the center, melting on my tongue. I want to learn how to make these. "Thank you, Annabelle."

She hits me with the back of her hand. "Stop calling me that."

"Can I call you mine?" She goes quiet and fiddles with her fingers. Flirting with her is dangerously fun. "What do you want to do tonight?"

She shrugs. "We could watch a movie."

"Horror?" Luckily, I have the evening off. George told me I've been working too much and warned me that he would lock me out if I went to work tonight.

"As long as there's lots of snacks and blankets to hide behind."

● ● ●

The football game ends with a score of six to two, to the other team.

With his shoulders slumped and his hair drenched with sweat, Daniel walks up to us. "Will you bake a cake to make me feel better?"

"Sorry, mate. Only winners get cake." He laughs and chucks his empty water bottle at me. My arm flies up to block it.

A lanky, doe-eyed girl walks up to Daniel and places her hand on his large biceps. He gives her a once-over, admiring the soft blue dress that is wrapped around her.

Daniel grins at me and then turns to Anne. "We'll be home after dinner. Call me if you need anything. Promise?"

Anne rolls her eyes. "Yes, *Dad*. Don't worry about me."

Daniel shares a look with me. *Take care of her*. He knows I will, but I am glad that he trusts me alone with her.

"All right. See you later, little booger."

"Use protection. I don't want to become an aunt," she says. The girl beside Daniel laughs as he leads her away.

I pick up Anne's school bag and carry it on my back. She latches on to the back of it. "I can take my own—"

"Shh."

She gasps. "Excuse me? Did you shush me?"

"You heard me."

"I will not tolerate this disrespect."

"What are you going to do?" I narrow my eyes, leaning my face closer to hers. She tries to grab her bag from me, but doesn't succeed.

"This is unfair. You're at an advantage."

"How?"

She pokes my biceps. "You've got muscles."

"Survival of the fittest." I turn and walk toward the parking lot.

Anne follows behind me, not letting go of her bag. She is unbelievably stubborn.

Once we reach the parking lot and my motorbike comes into sight, I roughly spin with her bag still over my shoulder. It causes her to fall forward against my chest.

Her breath catches, her eyes momentarily lowering to my lips.

"Do you . . . want to kiss me?" I ask. I've asked her this before. A few times. It's the tactic that I use to get her to back off without turning her down. Because she always gets red, and always denies it. There have admittedly been some moments where I wanted to slide my hands along the curves of her hips and then tug her closer. To curb my curiosity and find out if she tastes as good as she smells. But I've never been one for impulsive actions. I've always watched my step, always thought about my words and my actions—maybe because my father thinks so little about his. I don't ever want to be like him.

As expected, Anne backs away, completely forgetting about her backpack or her insistence in doing things on her own. I don't know why she does that. I want to help her; I care about her.

Maybe it is a good thing. I think if she softened, if she let me take care of her, I'd get too protective. I'd fall. Hard. She's so lost in her own thoughts that she doesn't even put up a fight when I slide my helmet onto her head.

•••

We reach Anne's house in a matter of minutes. My bike fits perfectly in her garage. "You make the popcorn and get the blankets; I'll set up the movie," I say.

We walk into the house. "No cult horrors, please." She heads into the kitchen. I go to the living room and choose a horror about the suicide forest in Japan.

The scent of warm, buttery popcorn wafts into the room. As I close the curtains and turn off the lights, my eyes stay on Anne. I can see her from here. She sways in front of the microwave, humming an unknown song.

What would happen if I walked over and stopped ignoring those glances at my lips—if I kissed her?

No. I will fight that thought with everything that I have. I quickly move away from the curtains and distract myself by fluffing the cushions that decorate the brown leather couches.

Anne walks into the living room a little while later, looking like the Loch Ness monster, with layers of blankets over her shoulders and popcorn in her hands. I lift the blankets off her and drop them onto the couch.

She sits at the far end of the couch, putting as much space between us as possible. "What movie did you choose?"

"You'll see." I shift to sit beside her, getting close enough to make her uneasy. I love her reactions when I tease her.

The room falls silent. Anne shifts closer and pushes some of her blanket over me, even though there are a few other blankets I can take.

Eerie music starts playing and before long, Anne and I are pushed back into the couch. She covers her face with the blanket, dragging it off me.

Pulling her legs to her chest, she whispers, "Why would you choose this movie?"

"It's not that scary." Okay, maybe there is a part of me that is trying to sound tough so that she'll lean over and let me hold her.

Her breathing gets slightly ragged and her hands shake. I put my hand down beside hers. She stares down at it and then up at me.

Pretending not to notice, I keep my eyes on the television screen.

She shifts her hand closer to mine so our pinky fingers touch. Time seems to slow down. *Are we doing this?* Taking a deep breath, I graze my pinkie against hers to let her know that I am aware of what is going on.

Her skin is as soft as rose petals. My chest tightens in fear and excitement. She slides her fingers over mine, trailing them against my skin.

A few moments pass and I intertwine our fingers. My heart starts thrumming against my chest. This is a bad idea. A horrible, terrible idea. Daniel trusts me not to do this.

Her fingers gently close over my hand. We both stare down, not sure what to do next; not wanting to let go.

Screams come from the television. The music becomes louder and more dramatic as a woman weaves between the trees.

Nervousness washes over me. I tap my foot against the floor. I'm holding Anne's hand.

She's still staring down at our hands. The curiosity in her eyes pulls me closer to her. Her usual smell of violets drives me crazy, making it almost impossible to resist grabbing her. Those soft, caring eyes. Those rosy cheeks. Her wavy brown hair. This is Anne in front of me, not any other girl.

I quickly pull away and stand up. "I'm— I'm going to get water." I clear my throat. "Do you want anything?"

She stares up at me. She blinks once. Twice. "What?"

"Do you want anything from the kitchen?"

"No."

I walk to the kitchen and pour myself a glass of water, thinking about Anne's opinion on the theory that the fluoride in water is slowly brainwashing us. I wouldn't mind being a mindless zombie. What would brains taste like? They must be squishy and hard to chew.

Anne sits in her spot at the far end of the couch with the blanket wrapped around her like a burrito. Her body shakes.

She almost jumps out of her skin when I walk back into the room. I turn on the lights. "You're shaking. Do you want to watch something else?"

"No, I'm okay."

I hesitantly turn the lights off again and sit on the couch. Our thighs brush against each other. Her chest rises and falls rapidly. "Stop staring," she whispers.

I lean closer and wrap my arm around her. She leans into my body, intertwining her hands as if she doesn't know where to put them. *I know where I want her hands.* I tug a blanket over my lap so she won't notice I am getting rock hard.

Right before a jump scare, she turns and puts her face against my hoodie, pulling me impossibly closer to her. A warm feeling bubbles in my chest.

What are the warning signs of an impending heart attack? I think the rate of my heart might be dangerous. We really shouldn't—

I hold her tighter in my arms. "It's not real," I remind her. I brush my fingers over her hair, tucking a few stray strands behind her ear.

The front door clicks open. Anne and I jump away from each other like we're doing something illegal.

Daniel shuts the door and walks over to us. The girl he was with earlier is at his side. As he switches the lights on, his eyes narrow. "Six feet apart at *all* times and the light stays on," he demands. Anne and I shift farther away from each other. "Good. When I come down, you'd better be in the same place."

"Yes, Dad," Anne grumbles.

"Go up to my room. It's the first door on the left," Daniel says to the girl. She whispers something in his ear that makes him grin like the Cheshire Cat, then follows his instructions and makes her way up the stairs.

Daniel walks over to Anne, turns so his back is facing her, and releases a thunderous fart. He uses his hands to push the air toward her. "I've been holding that in all night. I ate an extra taco, just for you."

My body shakes with laughter. I lift my shirt to protect my nose from the smell.

Anne jumps to her feet and violently slaps his head. "You're disgusting!"

He pouts and holds his head in his hand. "That hurt, little booger."

"Stop farting on me."

"Never." He makes a heart shape with his fingers and leaves up the stairs.

Anne sits back beside me right as a woman is brutally murdered on the screen. Blood splatters everywhere. Loud screams and the crunching of bones fill the silence. Anne's eyes go wide and she doesn't move.

"Do you want me to put on a Disney movie?"

"Yes, please. I'll go get my notebook." She runs up the stairs. The thumping of her feet against the wood echoes through the house—or maybe that is Daniel.

I switch to one of the "romantic" Disney princess movies. Anne comes back down, with her turquoise notebook and a pen. The notebook has a sticker of Stitch from *Lilo and Stitch* on the front.

She takes a seat at the far end of the couch and watches the movie with such focus, only looking away to write notes every few minutes.

"You're studying it?" I'm used to her studying people and theories, but this is a first.

"Mmm." She doesn't take her eyes away from the screen. "My book. It needs some romance scenes and I'm taking notes."

That explains why she is still single. Her ideas of romance are based on Disney movies. "Anne, you do know this isn't reality?"

She turns to me, her face scrunched with frustration. "I know it's an animation, but the stories could happen . . ."

"Oh, you think you're going to lose your shoe at a ball and then a prince will come and find you? There's no way he could possibly find you! You're not the only size six in all of Michigan."

"*I* lost a shoe." *There's no Prince Charming here, Princess.* Reading my mind, she adds, "I don't need a prince. I just . . . I want to be able to describe kisses, and acts of love—like when Eugene in *Tangled* takes Rapunzel to see the lanterns for her birthday. He wanted to make her happy. That is love, right?"

I don't know.

"Okay, but a notebook? Really?" I lean closer to see. "What did you even write about kissing?"

"Why? Are you going to give your expert opinion?" she teases, turning her notes away so I can't read them.

"Yeah." I lean closer, making her close her notebook. From this close, I can see the length of her eyelashes and the tiniest dip in her bottom lip. "When the kiss is getting so good that you don't want it to end, pull away. It'll drive the guy crazy."

She nods, glancing away. Giving her advice on kissing isn't breaking any friendship rules, right? It's for her research. For her book. That's all.

"And if you really want to tease . . . ask him where he likes to be kissed, aside from his lips." I doubt Disney will teach her that little trick.

Her eyes fall to my lips again. An unknown force pulls me closer to her. "Hunter," she whispers breathlessly, the tone of her voice higher than normal, like she is trying to stay back and pull me closer at the same time.

"Mmm?"

"Are friends allowed to kiss?" she asks. "For research."

"I don't think so."

Her face falls and she leans back. "I didn't think so."

I lean forward to close the gap she created. "But that doesn't mean that I can't explain what I *would* do . . . for your research."

She looks around, not knowing where to look or where to put her hands. "Should I, uh—?"

I get up and hold my hand out for her. Suddenly she is standing flush against my chest. Not good. "Well, I'd start by finding a way to get closer—as close as possible. Then I'd, um . . ." My hands slide along the curves of her waist.

Her lips part. Her chest presses against me every time she takes a breath.

"Every person kisses differently, leans in a certain way, or has things they don't want."

"What do you like?"

"Teasing turns me on. I love not being able to have something that I want."

She nods, her big brown eyes telling me to do something I shouldn't. She gently places a hand against my chest. When she looks at my lips, she bites hers and asks, "Is this good?"

Is this good? This is stupid. I can't hurt Anne—she's too soft and loving. I wrap my hand around her wrist and pull it away. "No." Her face fills with confusion and longing. After high school, I am getting far away from this town. It would hurt her if I left her, so it would be better to avoid starting something unnecessary. "Ask someone you like. They will kiss you."

"Come on, Hunter. That only happens in Disney movies." She takes her journal and sits back on the couch to continue her movie.

Chapter 5

ANNE

I could see it: Hunter was looking at me like he *wanted* to kiss me.

But that was a week ago. And we haven't brought it up since, so maybe it was nothing.

Maybe I should start moving on, finding something else to pass my time with because this whole love thing is seriously confusing and painful.

"Anne! Get your ass down here now or *sa'neehak*!" Daniel threatens to end me. He has started practicing his Arabic more, because my mom wants us to keep our Egyptian roots strong. Unfortunately, he uses it for threats instead of for good.

Downstairs, on one end of the kitchen counter, Haiz and Adam are playing a racing-car game on their phones. Daniel and my mom sit on black stools on the other end. I run over and give my mom a bone-crushing hug from behind. Her perfume smells of jasmine.

"Hi, baby." She turns on her stool and kisses me on the cheek, probably leaving a brown lipstick mark.

"Hi, Mama." I have so much to say, so much to ask her, but she's never here for long enough to talk. "Do you have any time off from work today?" I ask while grabbing an apple from the fruit bowl and leaning against the island.

It is rare to see her at home. By the time she gets off work, it is already the early hours of the morning—not the best time to talk—and that is when she comes home at all. Her work environment is terrible, but her responses is always "That's life."

She laughs like I said something hilarious. "They would never give me time off on a Monday. I will go to the hospital soon, but I wanted to spend a little bit of time with my babies first." She looks different. Her skin is softer and slightly saggy in some places. There are freckles spread across her nose that are noticeably darker than her light brown skin.

"How is work?" I ask my mom, trying to make small talk. The bags under her eyes are more sunken than I remember. It hurts to know that she is growing old. It makes me want to cry, and hold on to her, and tell her everything that I never got a chance to. I desperately want to tell her about my shoes, because she is the only one who will understand how I feel about losing them, but I have no idea how to bring it up.

"The hospital is struggling with funding. Small town, not important enough for a big investment opportunity. A lot of people have been fired recently. I must prove they need me, or I will be fired, too." Trying to be indispensable in a hospital that doesn't even pay well must be hell.

"What? Why didn't you tell me?" Daniel asks, holding his bowl of cereal with the spoon halfway to his mouth.

He usually doesn't make breakfast, either. He is probably doing it to show my mom that he can be a half-functioning human.

She makes a brushing away gesture with her hand. "It's not a big deal. I will just have to work more than usual."

Daniel nods and places a hand on my mom's shoulder. "Everything will be okay, Mama."

"Thank you, *hayati*." She smiles adoringly at him and then turns to me, raising her eyebrow.

"What did I do?" The apple almost falls out of my hand. She is always comparing us, so I immediately assume that is what she is doing now.

If she knew half of the things that he did . . .

I wanted to tell her that I got a job, but suddenly I feel closed off and unable to say anything. I'll leave Daniel to the parent-pleasing.

Haiz and Adam nudge each other in the ribs as they play, trying to make the other crash in their game. "Nooo!" Adam shouts and lowers his head in defeat, his dark brown hair falling forward, almost touching his eyebrows. He pushes it out of the way. Haiz grins and holds his phone high up in the air, singing "We Are the Champions" by Queen.

My mom glances over at the clock hanging on the wall. "Quarter past seven. I should go." She ties her thick, light-brown hair into a ponytail and comes around the table to kiss each of us goodbye. Her hands are gentle on my face. Her head barely reaches my shoulder when she stands next to me. "Stay safe. Please do the dishes and neaten up the house a bit when you get home from school." Grabbing her handbag, she rushes out the door.

After eating, I pack the dishwasher and head to the garage. Daniel's shiny black Audi waits for us.

Daniel reverses out, onto the street. His heavy metal music blasts through the car. When I try to lower the volume, he slaps my hand away and makes it louder, screaming along and nodding his head to annoy me.

The car stops in front of a large open gate. Students are walking in or standing to the side and talking. All of them are in a green-and-gray uniform, and even though it is a stange color combination, it must be much easier to not have to worry about what to wear every day.

The twins' "goodbyes" are barely audible as they climb out of the car. Daniel waits until they reach their group of friends before making a U-turn to drive to our school.

When we reach our school, there are students all over the parking lot. They will do everything in their power to stay outside the school for as long as possible. A few students in the back stand huddled together, smoking in secret. Most of them are Daniel's friends. His taste in friends is like his taste in music. Except for one curly-haired friend who left our house early this morning to go to work. He walks up to us, greeting Daniel first.

When Hunter approaches me, I can smell the warm scent of bread and cinnamon left behind on him. He ruffles my hair and pulls me in for a hug, not knowing the effect that his fingers running through my hair has on me. Those same fingers were tangled with mine a week ago. My head presses against his chest, his other arm wrapping around me. "Morning, Annabelle." His chest vibrates as he speaks.

Even though I know the hug won't last forever, I bask in it. He holds me a bit longer than usual, but not long enough for Daniel to say something.

As we make our way toward their other friends, I notice Sabrina standing alone. Even though it's a terrible idea, I go up to her.

Why? Because . . . "I know you have my shoe."

I need it back. The other one still waits in my backpack, ready to be worn again. If she wants to bargain, fine, but I need it back. It is a memory and token of my mother's life and my parents' love.

There are a lot of things I need to do, with a new job and ideas for my novel. Yet, with my shoe gone, I feel like I don't want to do anything else.

Sabrina sighs, tilting her head. "So, what if I do?"

What? "Give it—! *Please*, give it back." Getting frustrated is not the answer. Not now.

"If we make a deal." She pulls the end of her braid over her shoulder and plays with it.

I've realized yesterday that the deals she makes are never fair. Still, I'm desperate. "What deal?"

"Get Hunter to ask me out."

She's making me choose between my shoe and my feelings for Hunter. Glancing over at Hunter, his smile is bright as he seems to be messing around with one of his guy friends. He is always playful and kind. It makes me like him so much more because I can imagine a future with him that would always be filled with curiosity and games.

"Why can't you do it yourself?" I am asking questions that I know she will not directly answer.

"Do it, and you'll get your shoe back."

The pain starts as a burning behind my eyes as tears threaten to fall. My lungs feel like balloons trying to inflate inside a box, resistance coming from every side.

"Fine," I agree. "One date with Hunter, and you'll give me my shoes back?" I have to choose my shoes. One day, maybe I'll find a man with the same kindness, gentleness, and playfulness as Hunter. But my mother's shoes will never be replaceable.

"Great, I'll—" The bell rings, cutting off whatever she was going to say. It's almost satisfying, seeing her being interrupted.

I turn, not wanting to hear her voice for a second longer, and head to my biology class.

•••

The lab is filled with the chatter of my classmates. Motionless frogs lie on trays at each two-person station. It smells like death and detergent. Mrs. Wessel sits in her plush black swivel chair, watching everyone's reactions to seeing dead frogs. There's a glint of amusement in her eyes.

I cover my nose with my shirt to protect myself from the smell. It's almost worse than the smell of Daniel's farts. *Almost.*

"All right, everyone, take your seats," Mrs. Wessel says. "I'm going to be assigning you a partner for this frog dissection." Everyone grumbles in protest. She assigns a number and a table for each person.

I make my way to the table I'm assigned to. A scrawny, dark-haired boy sits with a scalpel in his hand, ready to start the dissection. At least he doesn't seem like a slacker.

His name is Jaden, I believe. I have never spoken to him before, but I have seen him in class every day since the beginning of this year.

Jaden's gaze shoots up from the frog and he looks me over, through his thick red-framed glasses. His eyes widen. "Oh, you're Daniel's sister!"

"Really? I had no idea." So he doesn't know my name. He must recognize me as Daniel's sister because I sit with Daniel and his friends at lunch every day—not by choice. Daniel always offers, and Clary always agrees for the both of us. "Anne," I grumble, my mood still low after speaking to Sabrina.

"You're beautiful. Where are you from?" He pushes his glasses up his nose. For some reason, I dislike the question. Nobody ever asks Clary that, and she has been in this town for as long as I have.

"I've lived in Michigan since I was three, but I am from Egypt." It's been a huge change, especially seeing my mom having to get used to the norms here, but this is what I am used to now—the funny ways of talking, the cyclists everywhere, the camping holidays as a kid. But I never learned to cycle here. My parents were too busy going through a divorce to teach me and my brothers how.

"That's amazing." He shifts closer to me, completely forgetting about the decaying frog lying on our desk. "What is it like there?"

"I haven't been there since I was three." All I have are my mother's stories to paint a picture of how beautiful it is; the friendly, generous people, the history behind everything, and the melodic language. "But I know that Egyptians are very passionate about everything that they do."

"Well, I am half German. We aren't the most . . . passionate, but we are always on time."

"Oh, nope. We would not get along." I shake my head. "I don't think my family has been on time for a single thing in the past sixteen years."

He shrugs one shoulder, continuing to lean in farther. "I think we'd get along just fine." I am no expert, but I think he might be flirting with me.

•••

By the end of the day, I can barely stop my feet from dragging through the school hallways. Today felt longer than usual, but it isn't over yet. Aside from talking to Jaden, my day has been the same as most school days. I have no idea how other people handle long classes *and* have time for extra-curriculars *and* have a social life *and* maintain their mental health. It doesn't seem logistically possible.

"Hey, little booger." Daniel throws his arm over my shoulders and shakes me. "Let's go get ice cream, yeah?" He smells like cologne and cigarettes. See, that right there, is how I maintain my mental health—by remembering that I have a great brother and sugary cream available.

Right now, all of my assignments are in order, but I want to get ahead of some upcoming deadlines. "I was thinking of staying in the library and finishing my homework."

"*Or* . . . you could get ice cream." He tilts his head and grins. "They have little chocolate fudge pieces that they can add for only two dollars more."

How can I say no to that? He knows my weaknesses. Maybe too well.

We leave the school and walk across the road to the ice cream shop. My favorite part of this place is the textured wall they have made out of fake sprinkles. Cold air is circulated through the vents inside.

Daniel and I get our ice cream and take a seat at a small booth. A few younger girls turn in their seats to look over at us—at Daniel, more specifically. They immediately start whispering to one another and subtly grooming themselves to look better.

"How are you finding the work life? Excited to go in today?" Daniel asks.

"I am realizing that I am not exactly a people person."

"That's an understatement." I kick him under the table and he winces. "You just proved my point. Please avoid kicking your customers, okay?"

"I make no promises."

He takes a lick of his ice cream. I wonder how it feels to lick ice cream with a tongue ring. It must be weird. "I'm proud of you," he says.

"Really?" He has no reason to be.

"Yeah, man. You're growing up so fast. I want you to stay tiny forever." He holds his hand out to the size he wants me to remain, which I have passed several years ago. "It isn't easy being born to immigrant parents, and having to work from sixteen, but I want you to know that I have got your back and I am so proud of you."

"You sound like Ammeh when you say that. I'm only *two years* younger than you." Ammeh is the name we use for our uncle.

"You're still *two years* old in my mind. The annoying, tiny thing that followed me everywhere and stole sips from my juice boxes when I wasn't looking."

I hold up my hand. "I solemnly swear I will always steal your juice."

"By the way, Dad called me last night."

My mood falls. I push my ice cream away. That's one way to get me to lose my appetite. "What did he want?"

"Since we haven't seen him in a while, he wanted us to go away together. I told him we could go next weekend."

"You told him what? Why would you say we can go? Where are we even going?"

"He booked for us to go to Toronto."

"He is so full of it. I'm not going." My mom fell for him, his charm and good looks, until he became arrogant and wealthy. His ego told him that at forty, he could get a better woman and family than the one he had.

Without telling my mother, he found a woman and then left without warning.

"I know, but Mom said we 'have to' go. She said we should have fun and enjoy it, because we probably won't have a chance to go on a vacation like this again for a long time." His vacations involve a lot more money.

Sometimes I hate how rational my mother is. Other times, I wish my dad could see these good qualities that she has and fall back in love with her. Unrealistic, stupid dreams.

If I go on this vacation, if I start accepting the new woman as something real, then what will happen to my parents? Will my father think that the way he behaved is okay? Going on island holidays while my mom works tirelessly for us to have food on the table doesn't sit right.

The door to the ice cream shop swings open, causing a tiny bell to ring. Hunter walks in. The group of girls stare at him. He smiles and gives them a small nod, causing them to giggle.

I still have to ask him to go on a date with Sabrina. Maybe I should do it now, in front of Daniel, to prove to Daniel that nothing is going on between me and.

"Hey," he greets me, sliding beside me in the booth. His thigh presses up against mine. And suddenly I'm remembering how his fingers felt intertwined with mine, his skin warm and rough.

He casually leans his arm against the back of the booth. It makes me freeze. If he were to lower his arm, he could wrap it around my shoulder and pull me into his side. He could hold me close and I could breathe in his—no, we wouldn't hear the end of it if he did that in front of Daniel.

He drops his head back against the booth.

"You have ice cream on your mouth," I say and, without thinking, I brush my thumb across his lips. The air is sucked out of my lungs. They're so soft.

My entire body goes still. Daniel notices our proximity. "Distance now, or I am coming to sit between you two," he practically growls. Hunter's words from before run through my mind: *I love not being able to have something that I want.*

My heart is flipping and spinning like an acrobat in a circus show. There is a strange buzzing sensation in my body. Excitement? The feeling of Hunter's lips . . . oh, man.

Hunter defiantly shifts closer. "Calm down, Danny boy. It was a harmless mistake." He pushes his shoulder against mine. "Right?"

"Of course. It's not like I wanted to touch his lips . . ." *Cringe.* Maybe I should just keep my mouth shut. I'm making this worse.

Daniel's expression shifts, his eyebrows furrowing, and I know he is about to go on one of his rants again about Hunter and me and the rules that we must follow—no touching unnecessarily, no flirty comments, and most definitely no wiping ice cream off mouths.

But his phone begins to buzz. Bless whoever is calling him. Daniel emits a low rumble as he checks his phone. "I have to go."

"A date?" Hunter asks.

"Nah. Coach wants to meet with me. Apparently, there is going to be a scout at Friday's game." He takes the last bite of his ice cream then slides out of the booth, answering the call to claim that he is on his way.

Holding my breath, I say, "Hunter, I need a favor."

His head tilts, his gaze making my skin boil. A few curls fall against his forehead that I want to gently brush away.

My fingers ball into fists. *Okay, this is for my shoe.*

"IneedyoutogoonadatewithSabrina," I say, sucking in air like I have been dunked under water.

He grins, running his tongue over his lips. That cute little dimple pops up on his cheek again. "What is she holding over you?"

I nearly knock my ice cream off the table. "Huh?"

"Come on, it's not a secret. You don't like her. I don't think she is a fan of you, either. So, what is she holding over you?"

"She has my shoe," I say, deciding to be honest. *She also knows that I am deeply in love with you.*

"Your shoe," he repeats. He looks away, seeming to consider it for a moment. Shifting closer, so his leg is completely pressed to mine under the table, he asks, "You want me to ask her out?"

Of course not. It feels hard to look into his eyes. There's an underlying question there, but I don't know what it is.

My chest seems to completely close up, to stop me from responding for far too long. "Yes," I breathe out, hating every second of this.

Hunter moves across the table to sit where Daniel was sitting. I was hoping he would move closer to me, not farther away.

"I'll do it," he says. Again, something that a part of me was hoping he wouldn't do.

He barely even thought about it. "Oh." I can't tell if I am happy about this. It does mean I'll get my shoe back, but . . .

"Hey." He reaches across the table and takes my hands. My wide eyes meet his, then go back to where he is holding me. *Stop, stop, stop.* This needs to stop. My feelings need to stop. "I said I am agreeing to what you asked. You'll get your shoe back."

I nod, forcing my mouth into a smile. "Thank you so much." I squeeze his hands lightly. "I'm grateful." And that is the truth.

My smile doesn't seem to last long. Forcing it onto my face only makes me want to cry. Pulling my hands away, my focus goes to the cup of ice cream in front of me, hoping it will distract me.

"When would a banana need medication?" he asks.

I glance up at him, waiting for his lame response. He always does this, especially when he is feeling awkward.

"When it doesn't peel well." I hide my smile with my hands. He is such a dork sometimes. Rising from his seat, he says, "We should go. I want to get to work early, so I can show you what to do."

Hunter smiles at the group of girls on our way out.

"Why do you do that?" I ask as we step outside into the fresh Fall air. He's not like Daniel—he doesn't want sex.

"Because." He steps closer to me, brushing the back of his index finger gently against my cheek. "I like making pretty girls blush."

So that's what this is. The flirting. It's some sort of affirmation for him. The small touches, the hand-holding, the cute comments. They're just an ego boost for him. It turns out he's just like every other guy.

Hunter's bike waits on the curb. Its red and black colors make it look fierce and intimidating. He slides his helmet onto my head.

I try to duck away. "You—"

His index finger presses against my lips to shut me up. He's touching my lips. How do they feel to him? I stare up at him with wide eyes. "*Basta*. Wear the helmet," he demands.

His finger drops from my lips. "Basta? When did you start learning Italian?" I ask.

"We learned it in our Spanish class. It's both Italian and Spanish, originating from Latin. Languages are actually pretty cool."

"Yeah? What else do you know in Spanish?" I make it seem like I am just curious, but really hearing him speak Spanish is making me feel really...warm.

A smile tilts one side of his lips upward. *"Estás como me lo recetó el doctor."*

So badly, I wish he was my boyfriend. Right now, all I want is to pull him closer and have his lips on mine, his hands tangled in my hair.

"That one I did not learn from Spanish class," he jokes. I don't even know what it means, but I laugh anyway.

He straddles his bike. I climb on behind him and place my hands on his head. "What are you doing?" His curls are so soft.

"I'm your helmet."

He places his hands over mine. "I like this helmet much more than my old one." Taking my wrists, he lowers my hands, wrapping them comfortably around his torso. I melt against him, pressing my cheek against his back. "Now you're a seat belt, too. A multifunctional friend."

The bike roars to life, drowning out the word friend from my mind. People walking along the street turn to watch. It makes me feel like I'm in a movie. The sun shines, bringing out the golds and browns of the leaves as we drive along the road. It's tranquil. Many people are walking their dogs or holding the hands of their loved ones, enjoying the beauty, too. I imagine myself walking down the street, holding Hunter's hand one day. A day where I will say "I love you" and he will say it back. A day where pulling him closer and kissing him will be normal. I wrap my arms around him a little tighter. That day will never come, so I might as well enjoy this moment where I can be close to him.

I adore this town, but Hunter wants to leave. I can tell from the way her talks about his future to Daniel. He wants to move to a big city, with lots of things to do and people to know. He might even leave straight out of high school. I prefer being in a town where nobody is in a rush. As a girl, I feel safe walking alone here. I love the boutique stores and friendly, familiar faces. This is my home.

We reach the bakery. Sabrina sits at one of the wooden tables inside. There are no customers. Soft R and B music plays, creating a warm and calming atmosphere.

"Have you found your shoe yet?" Sabrina asks. She has no idea that I told Hunter about our discussion. The look that she gives me feels like a threat.

I snatch a mini croissant of out a basket that sits on the giant wooden counter and stuff it in my mouth, subtly shaking my head *no*.

She runs her fingers through her straight, caramel-colored hair. "Well, good luck."

Hunter turns to me and places his hand on my lower back to direct me toward the kitchen. The gesture feels slightly protective. Butterflies form in my stomach. There are few places I wouldn't let him put his hands. "Let me give you a small tour and show you how things work around here."

The bakery is modest; there's a main seating area, a kitchen in the back, and George's office, which nobody is allowed.

After giving me a breakdown on the cash register and the strange, futuristic coffee machine, Hunter wraps his fingers around my wrist and pulls me into the kitchen.

"You've already showed me the kitchen."

The door swings closed and he pushes me up against it. His forearms come up on either side of my head. I suck in a breath. "I know, but there's one more rule you should know." His lips are barely inches from mine. A storm whirls in his eyes.

"What?" I'm conflicted between needing to move away and needing to pull him closer and let him kiss me. The thought of him kissing me makes my knees weak all over again.

The hidden tattoo on his inner biceps peeps out of his sleeve. It's an upside-down image of a man with ten swords in his back. The reversed Ten of Swords card. He has never explained what it means to him, but a quick online search has told me it signifies endurance.

"No fraternizing with coworkers."

I sigh animatedly. "Well, there goes my chance of hooking up with Sabrina." Although he might be the one who ends up hooking up with Sabrina now.

Hunter bites his lip and presses forehead against mine. His eyes soften. Sometimes his actions indicate that he wants me, but then his words end up proving otherwise.

"What are we doing?" I ask.

Clearing his throat, he steps back. There is a long pause. "I'm giving you a tour."

Walking forward, I close the distance between us again. His eyes flicker to my lips. My heart pounds so hard that it almost takes me off balance. This could happen. I could kiss him.

Sabrina walks into the kitchen. She glances between the two of us, her eyes filled with anger and frustration. "I'm going home for the day." Before anyone can disagree, she turns and leaves, letting the kitchen door close behind her. She is not going to be happy about this, and I can guarantee she is going to take it out on me.

The day ends up being very anticlimactic. Except for an old couple and one woman who ordered three cups of coffee and drank them all in one go. She was very much a Lorelai.

I busy myself by organizing the pastries on the counter. It amazes me that Hunter can make all of these treats by himself. He is going to be famous for it one day. I know it.

A man, clad in a linen navy-blue suit, walks in. His loud voice booms through the small space as he chastises someone on the other end of his phone call.

I silently lead him to a table. Pressing his phone to his chest, he says, "Get me a vanilla milkshake. Make it fast."

I nod and scribble it down on my notepad. Walking into the kitchen, I stick the order onto the wall the way Hunter showed me to. "There's an order for one vanilla milkshake. He asked that we 'make it fast.'"

IT STARTED WITH A HIGH TOP

Hunter rushes to make the milkshake, adding in a whole lot of vanilla ice cream. It's fun watching him in the kitchen; seeing how focused he is. When he is in his own world, he bites down on his lip without realizing.

To top of the milkshake, he adds a bright red cherry and then gives it to me. "This looks amazing."

He beams at the compliment in a way that makes me want to keep complimenting him, to keep that brightness in his eyes.

I hand the man the drink and pivot to join Hunter again in the kitchen. "Have any mo—"

There's a loud crash in the seating area and I push the door open and rush out.

The milkshake is spilled all over the veneered wooden floors. The cherry looks sad, sitting in the mess of glass and liquid.

"Eh—sir—uh." I look around, as if some imaginary person is going to tell me what to do. "What happened?"

"This is the absolute worst milkshake I have ever tasted! Who the hell made this?"

The door swings open behind me and Hunter steps out. The situation is so unexpected that I am frozen in place, not able to look back at him.

"I made the milkshake. If you don't like it, I could—"

"Did you take this out of the garbage and put it back into a cup? That's how it tastes! Come on, I give this place a chance for the first time—" He clicks his tongue. "You know, I knew I should never trust an empty bakery. Bad service, horrible drinks: that will be your review!"

He steps around the mess and walks out, the little door chime ringing as he goes.

My heart tightens at the insult. I did a bad job. Even as the kitchen door closes, I can't stop staring at the floor. People truly behave like spoiled children; as if we're not all human.

Hunter comes back out with a mop and bucket and an empty black bag. He steps into the creamy mess and starts picking up the bigger pieces of glass.

His gaze is hardened and distant. There is a tightness to his jaw. Over and over, he picks up pieces of the broken glass and roughly throws them into the bag.

Snapping out of the shock, I take the mop and bucket, ready to start helping him clean. As soon as I dip the mop inside the mess, Hunter says, "Just—please. Sit down."

"Hunter, I'm—" Trying to help.

"Not now. Just sit down." He's upset. This is my fault. I should have been out here, so the customer could tell me what the issue is. I wasn't here—that's why he threw it on the floor.

Not wanting to cause more problems, I listen and sit down.

He puts the bag in the trash then forcefully starts mopping the floor. It hits me suddenly that he's not upset because of me.

It was his smile; his excitement when he had made that milkshake. He was like a little kid that did something correctly by himself. He was proud of it.

That rude man hurt Hunter's pride.

Kneeling down, however disgusting it is, I stick my finger in the mess and put it in my mouth.

"Annabelle, what the hell are you doing?" The tone of his voice is hard, cutting. His frown deepens. He leaves the mop on the side. "You're going to get sick."

I slowly step closer to him, pulling my index finger out of my mouth. Suddenly his eye contact feels like too much.

"It's good. *Really* good."

He shares a small half-hearted smile and looks away. "You don't have to lie. I'm fine."

"Hunter, I'm serious. It's delicious." My hand reaches out to hold his arm. "I mean it."

He nods, still not meeting my gaze. "Thanks."

He doesn't believe me. I don't know what I could do to make him see the truth. My hand lifts to his jaw, feeling the stubble that he will have to shave again for school.

He leans into the touch, tilting his head. Maybe I don't have to feed his ego. Maybe I could just give him a hug.

Slipping one arm behind his neck, I press my body against his. The usual bakery smell on him is dulled out by the stronger smells in the bakery itself, but I nuzzle my head into his chest and breathe him in anyway.

"Change the narrative," I say.

It's something he'd always say whenever I got sad or irritated. 'Find a way to remember today the way you want to. Change the narrative.'

He pulls away from the hug slowly, and I let him. His hands don't move away. His breath brushes against my cheek, but I feel it on every part of my body. It makes me nervous.

"How?" he whispers in my ear. He pulls away a little more, only to look at my lips with a hunger in his eyes.

I'm not bold enough to tell him to kiss me. Instead, I grab a fistful of his hoodie and pull him a little bit closer to my lips.

His hand slips behind my neck. "How?" His voice is a little bit more restrained and hardened.

I can't say it. I can't tell him. A part of me fears that if I say anything, if he hears my voice, he'll come to the realization of who he is about to kiss.

But I can't do this, can I? He is hurt. Searching for attention and approval from women—any female at all—is what he does when he needs an ego boost.

That's all this is.

I can't let that be the reason he kisses me. With a lump in my throat, and a tightening sensation in my heart and between my thighs, I put some distance between us.

It seems to snap him out of it, too.

He clears his through. "I—"

"Maybe you could teach me how to make a milkshake?" I ask, trying to stop him from having to make up an excuse for what just happened.

He grins, his playful mood returning. Reaching out, he ruffles my hair. "I can teach you whatever you want, Annabelle. That's what friends are for."

Ouch.

Chapter 6

HUNTER

I knock on George's front door. I offered to help him with some of the repairs he needed done in his apartment. My father taught me how to fix a lot of things, thinking it would make me more "useful." I guess he wasn't wrong. According to yesterday's incident, he has not been wrong about my talents, either.

The door swings open, revealing my favorite short old man. He is wrapped in a cozy gray sweater. George waves his hand to beckon me in. A low wheeze leaves his lips before he speaks, concerning me. "Thank you for helping me out, kiddo. It's hard maintaining a house and business when all I want to do is nap every second of the day."

I've helped him with small things around his house before. I love being here. I'd much rather be in this cozy, warm apartment than in a house that makes me feel empty. I roll up the sleeves of my navy-blue hoodie. "Any time." Considering everything he has done for me, this is nothing.

George gave me a job when I had no qualifications. He has given me meals when I didn't want to go home. He has been open and kind and has made me feel like I am not a complete waste of space. If I hadn't found my passion for baking at George's bakery, I don't know where I would be. I don't know who I would be.

"Well, can I make you some tea before you get started?" he offers.

My eyes scan the apartment. It is cluttered with books, souvenirs, and boxes that he never unpacked. "Tea sounds good."

I've been through some of his boxes before, out of curiosity. They're mostly filled with intricate items from India—jewelry from his late wife, lamps, clothes.

"How are you doing? We haven't had a good old chat in a while," he asks.

I trail him into the kitchen. The only thing that divides the lounge and the kitchen is a granite counter. He pulls two mugs out of his cupboard and pours water out of a bottle into the kettle.

"I'm surviving." *That's all I need to do.*

"Surviving? That doesn't sound good. You should be living your best life!" he exclaims after dropping the teabags in the mugs. "You should be getting over your fears and getting under girls." He coughs slightly and pats his chest.

I lean back against the counter. "I'm not as cool as you, *Grandpa*," I tease. George adds two teaspoons of sugar to my tea, knowing how I like it. "Bless the person who discovered sugar."

"You can thank my ancestors for sugar. India originally started crystallizing sugar during the Gupta dynasty," he informs me.

"That's around the time you were born, right?"

"Don't forget that our culture knows how to discipline ruffians." He chuckles, his laugh slightly wheezy. "I am not afraid to get out the wooden spoon."

My smile is wide. George always makes me feel at ease. He hands me my tea. "What do you need me to do today?" He sent me an SOS text with no explanation.

"My shower drain is blocked, and the kitchen sink isn't working." He turns on the faucet and it makes a sputtering sound. It releases a small droplet of water and then goes dry. That must be why he used bottled water for the tea.

"Okay, let me see what the problem is. Could you get your toolbox for me?" I pull off my hoodie and throw it over one of the chairs at the kitchen counter. I open the cupboards under the sink to see if there is a problem with the pipes.

"This Anne girl," George says, walking back into the kitchen again with his toolbox. He lowers it onto the floor with another wheeze. "You like her?"

I get down on my knees. "We're friends." It's a strange, flirty friendship, but that's all it will ever be.

"Good, because there is no fraternizing with co-workers."

"I know."

Although I still have to ask Sabrina on a date. That's going to be . . . interesting.

•••

Bystanders turn to stare as I drive home from George's house. Motorbikes aren't that common in this small town. That's one of the many reasons why a large city, where I can do whatever I want without people knowing, would be better.

"Hunter?" my father calls as soon as I step into the house. I cover my nose with my shirt to block the bitter smell coming from the living room. He's smoking something a lot more potent than cigarettes. I haven't seen him since our last fight.

"Yeah?" I need to get upstairs to get ready for the party tonight.

People have been talking about it for weeks. Everyone is going to be there—except Anne.

"Come in here." He is in his usual spot on the couch. The room is clouded with smoke and his eyes are red. For once he doesn't look angry. "Sit."

I hesitantly walk closer and take a seat beside him. He holds out the blunt for me, between his pudgy fingers. "No, thanks." Smoking weed with my father is the last thing I want to do, even if the only time he is not horrible to me is when he is high.

"How was your day? Did you go to work?" I wait for him to add some snide comment, but he doesn't. That's a first.

"Yeah, I went to work early this morning and again after school. I tried making macaroons for the first time and customers loved it, so I will probably make them again. If you'd like to try some, I'd be happy to make a few for you."

Maybe, for the first time in his life, my father will tell me that he is proud of me.

He takes a long drag. "Your mother would be so disappointed in you." There it is. The worst part is that right now, I don't think he is trying to be mean. I think he genuinely believes that. "I work hard and make good money for us. Do you think baking cookies is going to be able to provide for your future family the way I provide for you?"

The first time my father told me that my mom would be disappointed in me, it felt like someone had reached their hand into my chest and completely shattered my heart. He liked seeing the pain his words caused me. I'm used to it now.

"Yes, I'm good at—"

"You're never going to go anywhere in life if you continue on the path you're on."

"That's not—"

"Macaroons." He scoffs and takes a long drag of his blunt. "Get a real job." He watches me through the white puff of smoke he releases from his cracked lips.

"I'm going out tonight." Standing from the seat, I practically sprint upstairs, wanting to be as far away from my father as possible. Every time his gaze is on me, I feel like the wax of a candle being melted by a flame.

I fall back onto my bed and phone Daniel.

"Hey," he answers.

"Can I get ready at your place?" He was clear that I'm always welcome, but he might have a girl over, so I wanted to confirm first.

"Hell yeah. We can do each other's makeup, and I'll put some glitter in your hair and then we can talk about all the girls who—"

"Daniel." He doesn't notice the way my voice shakes slightly when I say his name.

He chuckles. "Of course, come over."

One of the hardest parts of how my father treats me isn't his words; it's the guilt and shame and belief I place in his words. I hate him, but I hate myself more because I can't bring myself to tell anyone—not even my best friend. It wouldn't help me if Daniel knew. It might make things worse, and it would humiliate me to have to explain it all.

I pack some clothes and my toothbrush into a duffel bag. Wanting to avoid any interaction with my father, I climb out my window. My feet thump against the grass below. I glance back, thankful for the high wall and shrubbery that divides Anne's window from mine.

Heading around to their front yard, I trudge up the driveway and into their house.

"Hey," a soft voice calls out as I step through the door.

Anne lies across the couch in the living room with her notebook open. She leans up on her elbows, emphasizing her impressive chest.

I lean against the wall. "Hey."

"I'm going to the party tonight."

"Did my unwitting charm convince you?"

"Of course. I simply can't say no to you."

"Good to know." Although I already knew that.

I was secretly hoping Anne wouldn't come. Tonight is when I'd planned to ask out Sabrina. I have a feeling it is not something she wants to be around for.

She sits up straight. "What is that supposed to mean?"

"Don't you worry, Annabelle." I wink and walk up the wooden stairs. They creak with each step I take. Pushing Daniel's bedroom door open, I find him standing butt-naked and staring at himself in the mirror.

He has scratch marks all over his body. "Holy shit." He turns to face me, and I quickly look away. "This girl—"

"Dude!"

He chuckles and holds his arms out. "What? We used to shower together. You've seen everything already."

"That was over *seven years ago*."

"And I'm still sexy as fuck."

"Can I borrow some bleach to soak my eyeballs?" I close his bedroom door and sit on his bed, facing away from him. "What's with the scratch marks?"

"I hooked up with this girl. She was wild, man! She showed me things I didn't even think were *possible*. She put her—" I make gagging noises to hope he'll stop explaining. "Yeah, that, too."

"Who was she?"

He is silent for a while, which is strange. Usually, he is happy to tell me the details of his . . . adventures. "Promise me you won't tell Anne?"

"Sure, whatever." I stare down at the carpeted floor.

"Clary."

"Are you *insane*? That would be like me sleeping with Anne."

"You can turn around. I'm decent," he says. I turn to face him. He is now wearing a pair of jeans, but no shirt. "And it's not the same thing. Anne isn't as close to Clary. Plus, it was a one-time thing."

"They have been friends since kindergarten. I don't think Anne will be happy about this."

He shrugs. "She doesn't have to know."

"How did it happen?"

"She always comes into the music store, but never buys anything. Sometimes I can feel her watching me. It's . . ." He *blushes*. "Sort of cute. The other day she came in, wearing this stupid shirt with hundreds of cats printed on it. She kept flirting with me so"—he shrugs again—"I gave in and fucked her." He pulls on a black button-down shirt but keeps half of the buttons undone to show off his efforts in the gym.

"You should stop thinking with your dick."

"Why? It knows what it wants, and it goes for it." He adjusts the chain hanging around his neck. "What are you going to wear tonight?"

"I was considering going in the nude."

He starts unbuttoning his shirt and pulls it off. "All right. If we go down, we go down together."

I chuckle and pull my clothes out of my bag. It's a nude-colored hoodie and matching combat pants. "No, I meant this nude." It's a few shades darker than my skin—probably closer to Daniel's skin tone. *"Ba-dum-tsss."*

He deadpans. "I'll pay you to stop your cringy jokes." *Anne likes my jokes.* He falls back on his bed and pulls out his phone. "Are you drinking tonight?"

"Don't know. Are you?"

"No. They moved our football game to tomorrow and I can't play with a hangover."

I lay back and put my arms behind my head. "There is going to be a scout at the game, right?"

"Yeah." He sighs and runs his hand through his black hair.

"Don't think I'll drink, either." It clears my mind, it makes everything feel easier, and I am scared that if I start to enjoy that feeling too much, I won't want to be sober anymore.

I turn onto my side and focus on my breathing. Sleeping has not been easy lately. Whenever I try to fall asleep, I start thinking about my mom. There will never be a day where I don't think about her leaving without me.

Everything feels lucid, as my mother's slightly blurry face comes to mind. With time, the details of her appearance have begun to fade, but I can still see the tears streaking down her face as she asks me to forgive her for leaving.

I don't blame her for leaving, but I hate her for not taking me with her.

She places a hand on my arm, and yet I don't feel it. She's too far now. Everything feels out of reach. Looking down, I see my legs sinking into wet sand. I can't get out. I can't get to her—

"Hunter?" Daniel's voice sounds close and far away at the same time. A pillow slams down against my face.

"Let me sleep." I cover my face with my arm.

"You've been asleep for over an hour. You need to get changed."

That did *not* feel like an hour. I sit up. It's already dark outside. "Maybe I'll just sleep instead of going to the party." The pillows are calling to me.

"Get up or I'll jump on you." Daniel walks into the restroom, so I take the moment of privacy to change. The tank top I'm going to wear under my hoodie makes my arms look good. I flex my biceps in Daniel's mirror and catch a glimpse of my tattoo.

The reversed Ten of Swords. A man lying on the ground with ten swords piercing his back.

The first time I read about it, it hit me hard. It felt like something I wanted as a part of me, a reminder. The Ten of Swords card represents betrayal and failure, but when reversed, it represents surviving and perseverance. A reminder to keep fighting, even with ten swords in your back. It keeps me strong when I don't feel it.

Daniel walks out of the restroom. "You look good."

"I know." I don't, but I can pretend I do.

He playfully punches my arm. "Hell yeah! That's what I like to hear."

I know Sabrina won't say no when I ask her out. She's made it very clear that she wants this. But I'd like to look good for her when I do. I can usually tell, in a girl's eyes, when they like what they see.

I pull on my hoodie, spray some of my cologne on and head downstairs. Anne is still on the couch with her notebook. She has changed into white shorts and a graphic T-shirt with a small, animated penguin on it.

"Ready?" Daniel asks her. She nods and stands up. She looks cute.

Daniel walks out the front door. Anne shoves her notebook and pen into her bag and walks out with me.

Fifteen minutes later, Daniel parks on the side of the road, behind several other cars that line the street.

"Are you nervous?" I ask as we walk toward the house. Anne hasn't been to a party in a long time.

"No. If there's anyone I'd want to walk into a popular party with, it would be you two idiots."

"Did you just call it a popular party?"

"Yes." She lowers her gaze to the pavement. I want to reach out and tuck her hair behind her ear. "You and my brother make the party a popular party. I'm pretty sure most people are here because they know you two are going to be at the party."

I throw my arm over her shoulder. "Damn, you're fucking cute, you know that?" Her eyes widen and she turns to look up at me, her lips parting.

Daniel clears his throat and removes my arm from around her. "Distance, please."

The house is dimly lit with rotating strobe lights. Whoever hosted this has money. Loud music pumps into every corner of every room, causing the floor to vibrate. There are people everywhere. Some doing shots, others doing their boyfriend's best friends. Everyone's voices are somehow louder than the music. As we make our way through the house, a couple of people come to greet Daniel and me. Most of them reek of alcohol or smoke.

I turn to look for Anne. She is standing out of the way with her arms wrapped around herself. Her eyes are glued to two girls who are making out on top of the pool table. I'd give good money to know what's going through her head. *Would she join them?* I shake the thought away.

Clary sneaks up from behind and scares Anne. Her eyes widen and she almost swings her fist at the redhead. Satisfied in knowing she isn't alone, I walk off with Daniel. He has already found a small group of girls who are following along with us, all four of them in tiny matching miniskirts. I've never met any of them; they must be from another school. They'd probably choose Daniel over me, if they had the choice. I wouldn't blame them. He's the captain of the football team. He has a future.

I'm just a chef. Apparently not a good one.

My mood immediately dips until one of the girls slides her hands up against my biceps. She's hot, with long legs and dark brown-gold hair like mine. It's wavy and it must feel as soft as it looks. Her long nails sparkle in the moving light. "What's wrong?" Her voice is feminine and soothing. It makes me want to lean in and tell her everything.

That right now I wish I was someone else; someone who feels comfortable and good enough. Someone who doesn't feel the need to run from himself.

"Baby, are you okay?" she coos over the music, leaning in close, her hand sliding down my arm. She steps in front of me, causing us to immediately lose Daniel and the three other girls to the crowd of drunk dancers in the living room of this huge house.

I've noticed that whenever I'm around huge groups of people, I realize how little everything matters. It's so much easier than being alone—than being in my house.

"I, uh." I brush her hair back behind her ear, leaning down to talk. She's so short that I almost have to break my back to get close enough. She steps closer, nodding.

She has beautiful eyes. They shine in the color-changing lights that occasionally slide past. My hand lifts to cup her cheek.

"Have you been drinking?" I ask. *Great flirting, Hunter.*

She hides her smile by biting her lip. "Yeah, we're at a party."

"But you're still . . ." I can see that she can walk straight and forms coherent sentences. Maybe I'm stalling. Maybe I don't care about kissing random girls.

"Able to tell you to kiss me? Yes, I am." She grabs the part of my hoodie just below my neck and pulls me closer.

I put my hands on hers, pulling my face away. No, I like feeling in control. I don't want her to just grab me. "Stop."

I already have to ask out Sabrina. She's going to try and take control and do something with me. Something that I should want; that every guy wants, right?

Her eyebrows draw together. "I don't understand. You—"

A hand comes down on my shoulder. It's Daniel. He nods his head in the direction of sliding doors that go out into a garden. "A few of us are playing outside. Come join?" He glances at the girl, then back to me. "*Oh.* Oh, shit. Sorry."

"No, yeah, let's go."

The girl goes first, with Daniel and I behind. He slaps my back, a wide grin on his face. "*Nice.*"

Is it?

"I thought you would have been upstairs with two of them already. Maybe three."

He throws his head back with laughter. "Isn't that what party games are for?"

Outside, there is a growing group of people adding white plastic chairs to a circle on the porch. The chairs squeak and scrape against the wooden porch. There are a few couches, too, the fabric worn from years of being outdoors. All of the spaces to sit are cramped with people trying to be a part of the games, or observers who do not want to miss what might happen.

Anne sits on one couch, tucked tightly into a corner with her focus on her notebook. The soft glow of lights hanging above cast a warm, golden hue across her face. Her eyebrows are furrowed in concentration.

Reaching the couch, I fall into the small space beside her. The cushions sag slightly under my weight, and my thigh presses against hers, the warmth of her skin sending a shiver through me. The familiar, comforting smell of violets makes me want to wrap her up in my arms. If there are two scents I'd call my favorites, they're the smell of the bakery and the smell of her.

Everything is loud—the chatter and laughter and music, all turning into an indistinct roar. When I am beside her, the sounds seem to fade into the background.

She warily glances up from her notebook. A heart-stopping smile crosses her face when she realizes it is me. *Oh, man, that is sweet.*

I tilt sideways so my body is pressed against her. "What are you doing?" I ask over the music pumping from inside.

She leans closer to my ear. "I am trying to write. I have outlined everything." Her eyes are bright, her body on the verge of dancing.

"Oh yeah, you writing your PG Disney romance?" I tease.

She gently hits my arm. "I'm retelling a story that is important to me."

"Am I in it?" I tease. I hope not. I don't think I'd be very likable.

Even in the dark, I notice her blush. She tilts her chin up. "I'll have you know, there is some romance included. It is *not* PG."

"Oh, really?" If there were any way I could get closer to her, now is the time that I would. But we are already pressed together.

It immediately hits me that what I am doing with Anne is flirting. It feels so much easier with her. I don't even have to think about what to say.

Thankfully, Daniel is distracted by females, messing around with them as the group settles.

The girl from earlier, the one I had intended to flirt with comes to sit on my other side. She places her hand on my knee Anne notices and immediately retreats into her shell. She closes the notebook, looking at everything and everyone in the garden but me.

It makes my heart tighten. I didn't want that to end. In fact, I was having fun.

"All right, Hunter," Elias cheers. His eyes focus on the way the girl is touching me. "We haven't even started playing yet and you're already winning. I think that means we have to start with you." His bright blond hair seems to glow under the light of the moon.

He smirks. "Truth or dare?"

If I choose truth, people will be disappointed. "Dare."

"I dare you to kiss the girl to your left." The girl with the miniskirt who flirted with me earlier. Maybe I should learn her name. "Or to your right." *Anne?*

Well, miniskirt-girl's hand is already on my leg. She didn't even give me a chance to flirt or take control. I thought she could distract me but she's only making me feel worse. I want control. The kind of control that I feel when I'm kneading dough into the table at work.

So, I take control and turn Anne's face toward me. I hear the hurt hiss of the other girl as she pulls her hand back; the sound of Elias whispering "Oh shit," like he knew—and was hoping—he'd cause drama.

The skin of Anne's cheek is so soft. I brush my hand farther back until it slides into her hair, making it easier to pull her closer. My fingers hook onto her, knowing what I want and acting out of impulse.

"Hunter," she breathes. The whisper of air brushes against my lips.

"I like doing things I shouldn't," I say only to her.

A small whimper leaves her lips, and she nods, giving me permission. Her hand comes up to my jaw, her thumb brushes gently against my skin. It makes me feel like a man.

Her eyes are on my lips, her breath shaking. This kiss would calm her, and I could immediately capture her mouth with mine, but I desperately want to savour this moment. She can barely hold herself together and it is unbelievably hot.

I am smiling when my lips lower to hers. Every inch of my body is heating up. She is addictive. This is everything I have wanted to feel. Why have I never thought about doing this before?

"Are you fucking kidding me?" Daniel's voice booms. "Get away from her right fucking now!"

Right, that's why.

Chapter 7

ANNE

I immediately pull away, realizing how stupid this is. In front of my brother? Did I think that he would just lean back and watch? No, I didn't think about anything other than that Hunter chose *me*. He was going to kiss me. That was a stupid move—but logic flew out the window as soon as Hunter turned my face to look at him. He was all I wanted.

Hunter immediately stands, leaving the space where his body was pressed against mine feeling cold. "Let's talk somewhere else, okay?"

"No." Daniel looks like he truly wants to strangle his best friend. "Fuck you! I trust you with my sister and you—"

"Daniel, let's talk." He nods his head to the side. "At least hear me out before you storm away."

Daniel considers it for a moment, his eyes going to me. My cheeks must still be red because they feel like they're came straight out the oven. "You better have a good explanation." He storms off toward a quieter section of the garden.

Hunter and I follow quickly behind. He sneaks a few glances at me, but I can't face him. Not now. What will Daniel say? Did I ruin everything? I tried so hard to avoid this.

Daniel turns to us, still fuming. "Well, talk," he demands.

"Elias put me on the spot," Hunter says. "I wasn't into that other girl, so I couldn't kiss her. She would never leave me alone if I did, so I pretended like I was going to kiss Anne. Obviously, I wouldn't kiss her."

I don't know if he means that, but it's crushing to hear.

Daniel shakes his head. "I don't believe you."

"I was actually planning to ask out Sabrina tonight. You can watch if you want." Daniel rolls his eyes, but I think Hunter is telling the truth. "Come on man, your sister isn't even my type. You know my type." Blond. "I wasn't going to kiss her. I knew you would stop it. It was just a way out, without me being a wuss and not doing the dare."

That sounds . . . true. Logical. Somehow, it still feels like I've been slapped. My eyes sting. I stare up at the starry sky to stop them from watering.

Hunter holds out his hand to Daniel, like a male truce. Daniel takes it and they do that male shoulder-bump hug. When they pull back, Daniel says, "If you're asking out Sabrina, I want see it." He looks at me. "And Anne is going to see it, too."

"What?" Hunter and I say at the same time.

Hunter looks at me, his eyes soft and wary like he knows every shard of glass that is currently cutting through my heart.

"Hunter has proved he didn't want to kiss you. I want to see that you didn't want to kiss him, either."

Hunter is still watching me closely. It is so hard to not break down under the weight of their gazes.

Daniel knows I can't say no, not without giving my feelings away. "Fine," I say through gritted teeth.

Hunter looks at Daniel incredulously. "Daniel, are you s—?"

"Let's go. Now."

Daniel makes an idiotic plan for us to hide in the cupboard. Hunter will bring Sabrina into the same room, so we can overhear. Over and over, Hunter points out how unbelievably ridiculous it is. All I can do is stare at the floor and follow along, my heart aching so badly that it's making my entire body and mind numb.

The door clicks open and I can immediately hear Sabrina's giggles. "Hi." She must be holding on to him like a baby panda clutches bamboo. "Are you trying to make out with me in dark rooms, Hunter?" she slurs.

"You've been drinking. I'm not taking advantage of you."

"It would be *my* advantage."

He chuckles at that. She sucks in a gasp. "Then tell me, how do you want me to kiss you?"

"Wh—" She laughs. "The better question is: *where* do I want you to kiss me?"

This sounds too intimate for anyone to hear.

It is killing me inside. I can barely breathe in this dusty, wooden closet. Daniel's presence is felt right across from me, and all I can hear is his breathing. I knew he would behave like this; he is overly protective. He thinks that breaking my heart now will help me in the long run.

One of the main reasons why I stay in the closet is because I will get my shoe back. I will be able to hold the stories of my mother's life and be comforted by a love that is stronger than romance. That will make it worth this torture.

I'll get my shoe back. I'll get my shoe back. I'll get my shoe back. I try to get my thoughts to distract me from reality.

Somehow, this feels worse than any of the other times I have seen Hunter kiss another girl. I feel like I was manipulated into this situation, by both Sabrina and Daniel.

"I, uh..." I hear Hunter moving. "I wanted to ask if you'd like to go for dinner some time?"

"You're asking me out?" She laughs.

"Yes, I'm asking you out."

"I'll go out with you... if you kiss me." Her voice is flirty. That statement from Sabrina makes me feel dirty and horrible, like I sold Hunter off for my shoe. Surely, he doesn't like this.

The long silence that follows gives away the fact that they are kissing. It makes my stomach churn. This is why people are afraid of the dark—it gives way to imagination. Sometimes imagination can be a *wicked* thing.

Did he slip his fingers into her hair, the way he did with me?

There's a moan. A moan that is too deep to be from Sabrina. Is he enjoying it? My chest squeezes so tight that it hurts. The closet is small, pressing in on me from all sides, making me feel trapped. I want to bend over; maybe that'll make it easier to breathe. I want to slide to the ground; maybe that'll make it easier to get through this. No, what I truly want is to rip open these suffocating doors and pull them apart.

Eventually the pooling tears in my eyes fall, leaving cold, damp trails behind. Every sound is magnified in here—my shaking breath, the soft sound of their lips as they kiss. The only thing that manages to drown it out is my pounding heartbeat, echoing in my ears.

My hands clench into fists, nails digging into my palms, a small attempt to ground myself in the midst of this emotional storm. I want to disappear into the shadows, to escape, but all I can do is wait. I have read about all forms of torture, and this is by far the worst.

Eventually, after seconds that feel like centuries, I hear Hunter ask, "You want to go get a drink?"

A barely audible sigh comes from Sabrina. "Your lips are so soft."

Just like I'd imagined they would be.

Time—everything—feels slow. I wipe my tears before Daniel can open the closet doors. He glances over at me, assessing how I am feeling. I didn't go through that just to give my feelings away, so I pull it down, deep inside. "I'm leaving now, if you'll *allow me*."

"You okay?" Daniel asks.

"Yeah, it was just dusty in there." He doesn't want the real answer. He just wants to know that Hunter and I will never be together.

Hunter might have only agreed to this because he wants to be a good friend to both Daniel and I, but from the sound of it, he enjoyed that kiss. What if he ends up liking her? Did I trade my heart for a lost shoe?

I try to find my way back to the dance floor, hoping that talking to Clary will take this broken feeling away, but I'm so lost in my own thoughts that when I glance up, I have no idea where I am. Each open door in the hallway reveals a different surprise: gaming rooms with flashing screens, bedrooms—some closed with socks on the door, a wine room with rows upon rows of bottles, an indoor garden. It seems endless.

The indoor garden calls to me. It's a large room, filled to the brim with a variety of plants, and a stunning glass ceiling that lets in the soft glow of the moonlight. The music from the party is muffled to a faint hum, creating a peaceful oasis away from the chaos.

The air is rich with the scent of soil and flowers. Bright green plants are arranged neatly, yet some flowers have begun to bend over, most likely because winter is approaching. The stone path beneath my feet leads me in deeper, and I find the storm in my mind easing.

I kneel on the floor and cup one particularly sad and browning rose in my hands. "I feel you," I whisper. Some people go to parties to get drunk. I go to parties to speak to flowers in the dark. This is a particularly low moment in my life.

"Are you okay?"

My heart lurches, my body spinning so fast that I accidentally pull the rose from its stem. I stare down as the petals fall apart in my palms. Oh no, I killed it.

Jaden, the guy with the red-framed glasses from my biology class, stands above me. He sways on his feet. "Enjoying the party?"

I shrug. "I'm not really a party person." I deeply regret coming and will not be making the same mistake again.

"I see that," he says teasingly.

I laugh at how ridiculous I must look, kneeling in a garden with broken rose petals in my palm and dried tear stains on my cheeks.

After an awkward silence, I turn to look back at the garden and then at him. "Whoever owns this house is rich . . . and *brave*. They're going to be cleaning vomit out of every crevice." The thought makes me sick.

"Luckily I've got cleaners to do that, otherwise I would absolutely not do this." He brushes some of his dark brown hair away from his face.

"This is your house? I had no idea you were hosting this party."

"To be frank, I don't want to be here." I'm not surprised. He doesn't exactly look like the party type, but I guess you can't judge a book by its cover. "I host these parties because my parents say I need to make more friends, but it always feels like a waste of time. My number of friends remains zero."

"And you were searching for friends in *here*?"

He shrugs, his silhouette blending with the shadows of the tall plants. "Or I was hiding. It has yet to be determined."

I stand, dusting my palms. "Well, you found a friend."

He reaches out and gently takes my wrist, pulling me closer to him. His movements are slow, making me feel comfortable. "You have something on your . . ." His thumb brushes against my bottom lip, his touch sending a strange tingle through me.

I take a step back, laughing to diffuse the sudden intimacy. That's strange. I thought only Hunter could make me feel things like that. "Nice try, Jaden."

He shrugs, a goofy smile lighting up the space. "It was worth a shot, right?"

"Not now."

"Then a date?" When I'm quiet, he fills the silence. "Or if now isn't the right t—"

"Okay, a date. One date." I enjoyed our conversation in class the other day, and he seems kind and drama-free. This could be a welcome distraction. "Nothing fancy, okay?"

"I have my parents' card."

I shake my head. "Nothing fancy." Extravagance only reminds me of my dad. Of my family when we were whole. Of the ways we used to celebrate with five course meals and extravagant gifts.

"Okay, just coffee then."

Chapter 8

HUNTER

This is exactly what I meant when I said that I don't like women trying to take it too far.

Sabrina's leg brushes against the side of mine, slowly. She's been doing this since I asked her out at the party last weekend—unwanted touches and brushes. Clearly, she wants to kiss me again.

We're at a small Turkish restaurant where they serve a variety of spiced dishes and play beautiful music on large, double-headed drums. The booths are a made of dark wood and topped with colorful cushions, making it very warm and comforting. The temperature has steeply dropped outside, with winter approaching, and the cozy atmosphere in here is great. Sabrina wraps her lips around the straw of the milkshake she ordered, her eyes not leaving mine from the other side of the table.

The kiss at the party was good, I'll give her that. She knows what she is doing. But I feel powerless; I would never do this if she didn't have Anne's shoe, and so every touch and brush and word shared up until this date has made me feel less and less like a man. Like I have no control over the situation. It's only been a week since I asked her out, and I have hated every second of it.

Every second Sabrina gets, she's at my side—not even asking me what I'm doing or how I am doing—simply trying to get me turned on. The frustrating part is that she's good at it. My body is not connected to my brain, it seems, so whenever she slowly trails her fingers over me, I react.

And now, she gives up on brushing her leg against me and moves to my side of the booth, pulling her milkshake over. She drops her hand onto my thigh, a little too high, my hand stops her from sliding it even higher. Flirting can be a good distraction, but not like this. If I'm going to do this, I need to reestablish control. Pushing her hand away, I slip my hand behind her neck and pull her close to my face.

She smiles and looks down at my lips. "Hunter, what are you—?"

"Enough."

She giggles like this is a game to her. "Are you going to punish me for teasing you?"

I close the space between us and press my lips to hers. I'm not sure what kind of chemicals are released in the brain during kissing—oxytocin, I think—but it feels good.

I don't expect much when it comes to kissing. Just soft lips and no tongue-biting. I pull away first, remembering about my pizza that is getting cold. It's so good; it's called a *pide*. They put a cheese on top that stretches as soon as I lift a slice. It's topped with shaved chicken and some flavoring that has to have been made in heaven.

"So, uh . . . have you ever been in a relationship before?"

As soon as I've swallowed, I say, "No." Plenty of the girls I have gone on dates with have indicated they would like to. I've just never felt the need or desire to make it permanent—or maybe it's because it's another person whom I would have to hide my home life from.

"So, I would be your first?" She grins from ear to ear.

I didn't say there would be a second date, but I don't want to crush her smile. The awkward silence settles, and I don't bother to fill it with lies that we will do this again. I'm here for Anne's shoe, and nothing more.

I don't even know why girls want a second date. Look at me. I can barely hold a conversation.

Even though I dislike small talk, I ask, "What do you like to do for fun?" I don't know a lot about her. I've noticed with Daniel, when he is around people, he treats them like an unread book that he can't put down. I'll try that.

She giggles and shifts closer to me; her hand coming to my biceps and then quickly dropping. "Are you flirting with me?"

Why are conversations so difficult? Are people always like this? Maybe if my room were a place that I felt safe in, I'd never leave it. Around my friends, Daniel and Elias and even Anne, it always feels easy and peaceful.

"No, I mean . . . outside of school, what do you do?" I rub my palm against my thigh to self-soothe.

She shrugs, her mood seeming to shift. She leans back and folds her arms across her chest. "I work at the bakery, as you know, and I take care of my dog. He is getting a bit sick. I got him when I was seven and he's nine now. It's like . . . I know he's going soon, but I don't want him to." She folds the end of her straw, trapping it inside the cup. "Sometimes I wish my parents had another kid instead of buying a dog."

That is something I half relate to, but I'm better off as an only child. I wish my dad would let me have a dog.

The door to the restaurant opens and I immediately recognize Daniel's and Omar's voices. Daniel's eyes scan the restaurant and land on me. He had another football game today, and he is still wearing his jersey. I see him pull out his phone to text me.

Daniel, 9:04 p.m.: Thought u were here alone. U 2 dating for real?

After the incident at the party, where I stupidly almost kissed Anne, I have to prove to Daniel that my feelings lie elsewhere.

Me, 9:05 p.m.: Yeah

Daniel, 9:05 p.m.: Should we go?

Me, 9:05 p.m.: No. You're already here.

Thank goodness they're here.
Daniel and Omar walk over, greeting us. Sabrina points at the seats across from us. "Join us?"
Daniel shrugs and slides in. Omar grins and says, "Sorry, bro."
Omar, an exchange student from Lebanon, has formed a close bond with Daniel. Their shared ability to speak Arabic, despite the differences in their dialects, and their mutual love for gaming have brought them together. With their very dark-brown thick hair and dark-brown eyes, they could easily be mistaken for brothers. Omar's hair is short, and likely curly if he'd let it grow any longer than a grain of rice.
"Is the food good? I'm starving." Daniel eyes my now-empty pizza plate.
"Amazing." I kiss my fingers. "Obviously not as good as Lebanese food, though."
"*Obviously.*" Omar chuckles.
I watch Daniel for a moment, sensing that something feels off. He is fidgeting with his fingers, tugging at his hair, and his shoulders

are tense. The strangest part of all is that he doesn't have a girl with him after a game.

He meets my eyes and I nod, trying to get him to speak.

He shrugs, tilting his head toward the men's restroom.

He wants to talk alone. "I'm going to the restroom."

"Same." Daniel stands with me. "And I'm going to order a pide. You want one too, right, O?"

Omar responds in Arabic, nodding.

We walk past the band, who are all grinning and enjoying the melody they produce like it has them in a trance. The restaurant has provided tea for them, which sits steaming in small, curved cups.

As soon as we're alone in the dimly lit restroom, Daniel says, "I need your help."

My protective instincts immediately kick in. He's my brother, so of course I'd help him. "Yeah?"

"Tonight, in two hours, uh, my dad is picking us up." He runs a hand through his hair again. "We're supposed to be going on a family vacation, and I can't do it alone. He said I can invite whoever I want. Can you come?"

"Of course."

"Maybe you could ask Sabrina to come, if you want. The more people the better because I need to speak to my dad as little as possible."

"Sure . . ." I guess that means Sabrina and I are going further than a first date. *Great.*

He shakes his head. "My mom is totally okay with us going, but I wish she weren't. I'm trying to pretend like it's fine for Anne and the twins, but this—I, I just—" He gestures with his hands, not knowing what to say.

"It's okay. You don't have to be okay with it. You won't be alone."

I slap his shoulder. "And I think Anne is mature enough to handle you not being okay with your parents' divorce. You don't have to be perfect around her." It's why I like being around her.

"I'm her older brother," he says, as if that means that he has to be perfect. "I'm already not a great role model. But for this, I need to at least seem like I'm okay with it, otherwise there's no way she'll go."

"I'll be there, don't worry. I've got you."

He grins, pulling me into a hug. He smells like sweat and his favorite cologne.

I hope Sabrina is busy this weekend.

Chapter 9

ANNE

I tug my warm jacket tighter around myself as a cool wind sweeps past. A sleek white limo comes to a stop in front of our driveway. It shines like fresh snow in the midday sun.

My father believes that taking us on a vacation to Canada will help us to bond, and yet he does not bother to show up for the five-hour drive there. I don't think he has ever shown up to our house since he left. He always has other people doing these things for him. Proving my point, a stranger steps out of the limo, ready to help us with our luggage. I would rather have my father drive us in an old, rundown car than have a stranger drive us in some fancy limousine.

I can see Daniel's reflection in the car door as he stands beside me. He doesn't want to go on this trip. He is trying to play it cool but gives himself away by obsessively running his hands through his hair, which he only does when he is stressed.

My stomach ties into knots when I hear Hunter's motorbike nearing us. But those knots tighten and triple when I notice there are two people on the bike. *Sabrina*. She wears Hunter's helmet and a big smile.

Did she touch him slowly when wrapping her arms around

him? Did she enjoy the way his body feels against hers? Did she—"Daniel?" I hiss under my breath. "You did this?"

Though he may have caught on about my feelings for Hunter, he has no idea that Sabrina has my shoe. I should have told him, but I thought it would have all been solved after *one* date.

Not this. Never this. My body feels like it is slowly sinking into the ground, being swallowed up whole and pulled all the way into the burning center of the Earth.

Huffing, I climb in the limo and push myself into the deepest crook of the leather seating, pulling out my tablet so I can write and forget about the world. I have been making good progress with my word count, and have been recalling most of the stories from memory, but I believe this trip might help me with some inspiration.

The car starts moving and—though there is more than enough space—Hunter immediately comes to sit next to me, closer than necessary. He pulls one side of his earphones out and hands it to me. Suggestive R and B music is playing. He trails his tongue over his lips. There's a playful glint in his eye.

My cheeks heat up and I immediately turn away. Hunter mouths the lyrics, his lips forming each word with intimate familiarity. I press my thighs together, a tingling sensation pulsing through me. My heart pounds in my chest, and I can't help but imagine him whispering those words softly in my ear, his breath warm against my skin.

He slides down in the seat and leans his head against my shoulder, watching me type. "How is it going? Have you gotten to the exciting, dirty sex scenes yet?"

If I had a drink, this is where I would spit it out. "Wh—? *No.* I wouldn't even know where to start on writing anything that dirty."

He nods and grins like I gave him an interesting piece of information. "I don't believe that."

"Hi, everyone! Today, we're taking you tooooo . . . Canada!" Adam and Haiz shout in sync to their video camera. They do a panoramic view of the limo. I quickly block my face.

Daniel is lost in the music of his headphones, his eyes fallen shut. I wonder if it is only the nerves of the holiday, or if there are other things that he carries but doesn't share as he tries to fill the big-brother role.

The twins continue explaining where in Toronto we will be staying. My father hasn't taken us to his time share home since before the divorce, which makes me all the more suspicious that there are hidden agendas for this trip. Maybe Daniel knows it, too.

As Hunter shifts closer, my heart nearly explodes. I had forgotten how soft his winter hoodies are. This one is a mint green, the texture so warm and smooth that I want to reach out and run my hands all over him. But he should not be this close. Sabrina is watching us like we're a game she placed all her bets on.

Hunter doesn't seem to care. With his head still on my shoulder, he tilts back so his lips are right by my ear. When he speaks, warm air brushes against me, but it's his words that make me shiver. "If you want, I could teach you some non-PG things."

His words suck the air out of my lungs like a balloon in outer space. I know I shouldn't be taking his flirting seriously, but I have a feeling that there are things he could teach me—and now I'm imagining every single one.

I shift away. "Hunter." Even though every part of my body is saying yes, I shake my head.

His gaze lingers on mine, trying to read me. I should want him far away, but I crave him. When I say nothing, he eventually shifts and goes to sit beside Daniel.

Something feels like it has shifted in the way he flirts with me, and I am not sure how to feel about it.

● ● ●

An empty water bottle drops to the floor of the car as it comes to a stop outside the house, causing me to jolt up. Everyone looks half asleep, and it takes some time for us to successfully get out of the limo. The biting cold outside instantly revives my energy. I layer up with a second jacket.

Canada is not for the weak-hearted.

The brick house that meets us is built for this cold—with four chimneys sticking out of the roof. Despite its size, the house is welcoming, with large windows to let in light and soft green vines growing their way up its sides.

The bleach-blond woman running down the brick driveway, toward us, seems to not know that it is cold in her black shorts and cropped puffer jacket. "Daniel, Haizar, Adam, Arnold!" *Arnold?*

She comes to a halt and throws herself on Daniel. He stiffens. "My goodness, you're almost as handsome as your father!"

"Almost?" Daniel pries her away from him. There's a deep frown etched on his face.

"I'm Cassidy, your father's girlfriend, but call me Cass." She pushes back her neatly cropped, shoulder-length hair and smiles wide.

I clear my throat. "Who is Arnold?"

"It's you, silly!" She laughs and runs her hand down my arm.

She seems to enjoy touching everything. That's probably how she got my dad. "I love your eyebrows. They're so"—she scrutinizes them—"unique. Just like your dad's. Where do you get them done?"

The only thing that I have in common with my dad is . . . my eyebrows? That is a win for me.

"My name is Anne, not Arnold."

Her eyes land on Hunter, and it's as if she immediately forgets I exist. "My word," she breathes, "what is your name?"

It's giving me the impression that she is the human version of a vibrator that doesn't turn off. Again, probably how she got my dad.

"Hunter." He smiles and holds his hand out politely.

Instead of shaking his hand, she holds on to his biceps. "Aren't you gorgeous."

"Thanks . . ." He shifts away awkwardly, glancing at Daniel.

The twins record this moment, both snickering. "Jailbait," Haiz says under his breath, faking a cough to hide his words.

Cass turns with a huff, her hair swishing as she does, and then catwalks up the driveway.

I catch Daniel staring and nudge him with my elbow. He chuckles, looking down at me. "What?"

I could point out that she is the person my dad chose over my mom; over us.

"Come, come," she calls. "Your father is dying to see you."

"If he is dying to see us, why didn't he come out with you?" Adam asks, still recording.

"I'm sure you are all very hungry," she says, ignoring Adam's question. "Let's go to the dining room. Your father is waiting there."

The interior design of the house is inspired by the Victorian era. Beautiful, intricate artworks line the walls. Chandeliers hang from high ceilings. It makes me want to put on a ball gown and dance with a prince. The dining room is no exception. A long wooden table with candelabras, vases of flowers and place settings for about twenty or more people. There is a gigantic portrait of a woman with a huge frilly dress who doesn't seem to have the ability to smile—I wouldn't either if I had to sit in that uncomfortable gown on a chair for hours while some man painted me.

My father rises from his seat at the far end of the table, patting the corners of his lips with a napkin. His beard and hair have started to whiten with age. "Alors, come, come, it's good to see you all here," he says, his voice laced with a subtle French accent.

His small, deep-set brown eyes soften for a moment as he admires us and gives each of us a tight squeeze and a kiss on both cheeks.

He stops in front of Hunter, ready to give another warm hug, but Hunter steps back and folds his arms across his chest.

"Don't be scared, *mon garçon*," my dad teases. "I do not bite."

Hunter gives a tight-lipped smile and shakes my dad's hand instead. "It's nice to see you again, sir."

A girl with brown-to-blond ombré hair cut past her shoulders sits at the table. She doesn't bother to look up from her phone. "Jessica, meet Hunter, Daniel, Adam, Haizar, and Arnold. Your future family," Cassidy introduces us. "Everyone, this is my baby, Jessica."

"Anne, not Arnold," I correct again.

Jessica lifts her head. Her eyes linger on Daniel and Hunter. She seems maybe a year or two younger than me. "Hi." Almost immediately, her fingers start tapping away on her phone again.

"Which room is mine?" I ask, feeling overwhelmed and needing space. It's been a while since I've seen my dad. He seems so . . . normal. Like he used to be. He has carried on like nothing has changed, but everything is different.

"First come first ser—" Cassidy can barely finish her sentence before we're all grabbing our bags where they were left at the door and racing up the creaky wooden stairs.

I make it up first, because I had the smart idea to pack light, and dash for the room with the biggest door. Haiz almost knocks me out of the way, but I make it in first and drop my bags, claiming it. Unwilling to waste time sulking, he immediately dashes out to find another.

The room has a cozy feeling, with wooden floors covered in Persian rugs. A fluffy bed sits at the far end—

"*He trails his fingers along the curves of my body, exploring me. His touch is certain. He has said nothing, but I know we want the same thing.*" *Huh?* I turn to look at Hunter, who leans against my doorframe. "*My back hits the cool glass of the window and I gasp, but he captures the sound with his . . . lips.*" Hunter's eyes tear away from my tablet to find me. I don't miss the way his gaze lingers on my lips. "Is this what you like?" His voice is husky.

I can't think. I can't speak. "Uh . . ."

In the car, after I said that I don't think I could write anything steamy, I decided to try it. It has nothing to do with my story, but it was easy to write—especially because in my mind, Hunter was the one I was imagining.

Stepping inside, he shuts my door and leans back against it. He glances over to the right side of the bedroom, where the entire wall is a gigantic glass floor-to-ceiling window lined on both sides with burgandy curtains. "Well, I found a window." Is he offering to role-play what I wrote?

He looks so relaxed, his curly hair brushing against his forehead. His hoodie looks so warm and cozy that, with the cold outside, I wish I was wrapped up in it. Or better yet—wrapped up in his arms. I walk up to him, hoping that if I get close enough, he will hug me. When I'm within arm's reach, he takes me by the shoulders and pins me so that I am against the door. His arm comes up beside my head.

"You like pushing me against things." He does it a lot, especially against the lockers at school when Daniel isn't around. "Does it make you feel strong?" I'm genuinely curious.

I tug at the string of his hoodie, unable to look into his eyes after he read that part of my story. He smells like cologne now. It's warm and earthy.

"Yeah, I guess so," he admits sheepishly. His cheeks redden. He is so close that I can see the rise and fall of his chest, most likely because it is in my line of sight.

He steps back, but I grab a fistful of his hoodie and pull him closer. "I, uh . . . I like it." It comes out sounding more like a question than a statement. Oh my gosh, I think my heart is beating so fast that it is audible.

"What else do you like?" he asks, his voice lowering again.

I can barely breathe, let alone speak. Instead of saying anything, I reach out and take his hand in mine. His skin is warm and rough.

What am I doing? What am I doing? What am I doing?

He stares down at our hands. His lips part, but he quickly presses this into a thin line.

"What?" I ask.

He's going to reject me.

"Uh, nothing." He puts space between us, turning to assess the room.

I immediately crave the warmth that his body had brought. He falls back into the plush bed that is layered in blankets. The golden headboard has small, detailed patterns sewn in with a shimmering material. A single crystal chandelier bathes the room in warm light.

Hunter rests his arms behind his head, causing his hoodie to ride up, revealing the dark hair of his happy trail and part of his abdomen. My door swings open, knocking against me. I move out the way and Sabrina steps in, her gaze trailing from me to Hunter who lies comfortably on my bed. She still hasn't mentioned anything about giving me back my shoe. I'll have to ask her again later.

"I'm going to tell Daniel that you two have been alone in here this whole time." She turns to leave.

"Wait," Hunter calls, stopping her from taking another step. He slides off the bed and walks to her. He is a head taller than her. "Do you . . . ?" He hesitates. "Do you want to go to your room?"

That crushes me. *Oh.* It makes sense. He is trying to distract her, to stop her from saying a word to Daniel.

He wouldn't have sex with her. *Right?*

This is why I can't take his flirtation seriously. He will play with me and then go a kiss another girl. The flirting means nothing.

She steps closer, placing her hand on Hunter's chest. "For what?"

He wraps his arm around her, smiling down at her. *That's what it is.* The way he looks at people, like they're the only person in the world that matters. He simply gives people his full attention. "Come find out," he says.

I don't want to watch them like this, but they're standing in my doorway and I can't look away.

As soon as they leave, my imagination runs wild, picturing everything they might be doing together—every place he might be touching or kissing her. To distract myself, I change and shower, then head downstairs, hoping to find something to discuss with my father. Maybe we'll discover we have more in common than just our eyebrows.

On my way down, an impulse makes me message Jaden. Maybe I need a sweet, simple connection with a tall, dorkish guy; someone who is consistent and considerate. Jaden seemed like he would be, and he was clearly interested in me at the party he hosted.

"Ah, Arnold! Come, come!" Cassidy is with her daughter in the kitchen.

For heaven's freaking sake! Arnold? Do I even look like an Arnold? Does she not know that the man she is dating would never name his *daughter* Arnold. You know what? If she insists on calling me a name that's not mine, then she is no longer Cassidy to me. I'll call her ... Cabbage.

The kitchen they stand in is warm and inviting. There are several windows above the sink, looking out at the view of a lake and the setting sun. I would love to go out, but the water has frozen over, and I'm not in the mood to lose feeling in my body. The temperature difference between Michigan and Toronto is major. It's the kind of cold that makes bone turn to ice.

"We're making lasagna," Cabbage's daughter says. What was her name? Jessica? Her voice is slightly croaky and her *a*'s are longer than necessary. *We're maaking lasagnaaa*. It sounds more like a question.

"Can I help?"

Cabbage's eyes light up. "Well, we're almost done with the lasagna. It's about to go in the oven. Maybe you could make a dessert for us, of your choice? We went on a huge haul before you and your brothers arrived, so all of the ingredients should be here."

Alone? No pressure. But I'm not going to turn her down on that. I can do this.

I lean against the counter, watching them as they place the final sheet of pasta and grate the cheese. They seem close. Cabbage keeps giving encouragement to her daughter, even for simple things like sprinkling garnishing on top. In another life, this could have been my mom here with our whole family together. It could have been me baking lasagna with *my* mom.

As soon as Cabbage and Jessica put the lasagna in the oven, they tidy up and give me space to make my dessert, heading outside with layers of blankets to watch the last moments of the sunset together.

Alone once again, I start taking out all the ingredients to make tiramisu. It's a great comfort dessert—perfect for this weather and the hurt that I am feeling. As I tear the packet of lady finger biscuits open, strong arms wrap around me. Glancing down, I immediately recognize the bare forearms that hold me.

"Boo," Hunter whispers in my ear. His body is pressed entirely against mine. His skin is warm.

I lay my hands over his arms. I want to lean back into him. "My knight in shining tinfoil," I tease.

"You know, tinfoil can hold a lot of meat."

A wildfire spreads across my cheeks. I try to step forward, away from his embrace, but I am pinned forward against the counter. "I meant, my knight in shining parchment paper."

"Well, it's a good material to spread things on," he says. He uses his hands on my waist to turn me to face him. It's only then that I realize that his lips are swollen and reddened from kissing Sabrina. It leaves an aching, empty feeling in my chest.

"What?" he asked, his brow knitting together and his eyes searching mine with a mix of worry and confusion. *Am I that easy to read?*

I shake my head. "Nothing, just surprised."

"What are you doing?" Hunter asks, glancing at the ingredients behind me.

I can't stop staring at his lips. "I'm making—"

His eyes light up. "Tiramisu? I have a really good recipe. I can—"

"No, I'm doing it myself."

My mom showed me a good recipe years ago, so I can manage. If I need to, I'll use the internet, but I can't have Hunter giving me instructions. Seeing how good he is in the kitchen will only make me want him more, which will only hurt me more. He nods slightly and steps away, taking a seat on the other side of the counter. I continue, preparing the coffee, but he watches my every move.

When I put a spoonful of coffee into a bowl and pour in the boiling water, his lips part and he sucks in a breath as if he wants to say something, but decides to stay quiet. He keeps doing it, even as I separate the eggs and again when I mix the castor sugar with the yolks. His silent observation adds to the tension, making me hyper-aware of every step I take.

As I toss in the mascarpone, just about to start mixing it in, he suddenly exclaims, "Wait." A look of concern crosses his face and he quickly puts his hands up, defensively, like he means no harm.

"What?" I huff. I'd like it if he and his soft, swollen, pink lips could leave.

"Look, it's just that this part is really important." He comes around the counter, grabbing a different flat-spoon thing and handing it to me. "You can't mix the mascarpone like that. You have to fold it. Slowly."

"Fold it?"

He smirks, leaning sideways against the counter. There is an arrogant I-told-you-so look on his face. "Before I show you, I want you to admit that you need my help."

I roll my eyes, blowing a piece of hair away from my face. "I need you, Hunter."

His gaze changes, darkening. He steps closer. "Hm, say that again." It wasn't a question; it was a command.

One that leaves my heart twisting in my chest. Softening the tone of my voice, I say, "I need you, Hunter. *Please.*"

He turns me toward the bowl and guides my hand, placing it against the edge of the bowl. His hand stays on mine. With his other hand, he guides me. I wish so badly that he were mine. That I could turn around, forget the stupid dessert, and kiss him until my knees go weak. Over and over, he guides my hands to do what he wants. My entire body feels like it is buzzing. I can't handle this, and I know I need to stop it, but—but I can't.

"See, slowly. You can't go too fast or it won't set." He lets me go, stepping back.

Setting the mascarpone aside, I take the egg whites and start whipping them until they look like foam. I am about to mix the egg whites into the mascarpone mix when Hunter clears his throat, cringing hard. I sigh, lifting my hands. "What, Hunter?"

He chuckles at my frustration and steps closer. Again, he guides me and I let him. "*Slowly*, Annabelle." His words vibrate against me.

He folds the mixture together, leaving it lumpy and barely mixed. I feel like a child, with him taking the lead and me simply moving where he wants.

He dips his head down. "Good girl," he whispers against my ear. It melts me down to the core.

I turn in his arms, my desire pulsing between us like a living entity. My fingers find their way to his shoulder, gripping it for support as I lean into him, desperately trying to steady myself. The world around us fades, leaving only the intoxicating closeness of our bodies and the tension that hangs in the air, igniting every nerve in my skin.

His hand cups my face. Again, all I can think about is how I shouldn't do this. To put myself off, I remember his pink, swollen lips.

Moving around so I am all the way on the other side of the counter, I finally feel like myself again. "Okay, uh. . ." I take a deep breath. This must be how Humpty Dumpty felt when he hit his head and was never the same. "Next, I dip the biscuits."

Sabrina and Daniel walk into the kitchen together, laughing at something Daniel said. I'm so glad I put space between Hunter and I, or this situation would be very different.

Sabrina she's . . . she's wearing Hunter's hoodie. *Stupid, stupid.* How could I have looked at Hunter the way I did, probably giving away my feelings, while he is busy giving his hoodies to other girls?

He never gives his hoodies to girls, except me.

It's hard to hold back the tears. Hunter watches me intently, and I can see from his expression that he knows I'm hurting. I force a smile, turning to Daniel. "I'm making tiramisu," I say, hoping the lightness in my voice will mask the truth.

Daniel laughs. "Let me guess, Hunter is here trying to do everything for you."

Hunter grins. "It's what I'm passionate about. If you saw a girl having sex by herself, wouldn't you help her?"

Daniel half coughs, half laughs. "Of course I would. But sex isn't the only thing I am passionate about." He rolls his eyes.

Daniel is ready to continue talking, but then Sabrina says, "So is this your version of having sex with Anne?"

Why is she here, again?

Hunter turns red. I mean, the way he had me pressed against the counter was not far off. "Hey, why did the biscuit go to school?" he asks.

Oh no.

"Why . . . ?" Sabrina is the only one who dares to ask.

"Because he wanted to be a smart cookie." He uses the counter ask fake drums, to add, "Ba-dum-tss."

Sabrina laughs and moves closer to his side to touch him reassuringly. When she looks at me, she rolls up the sleeves of his hoodie on her arms, as a reminder that she won here.

Daniel keeps eyeing the bowl where my tiramisu mixture was made. I lift the bowl and lick it. "Yum," I say, taunting him.

He narrows his eyes at me and calls me "wicked" in Arabic.

"That's for farting on me, *habibi*." No, I have not forgotten. Sometimes I wake up in the middle of the night, haunted.

At that, Sabrina laughs. It's a short, unexpected burst of laughter that makes Hunter, Daniel, and I look at her. She covers her mouth to hide her smile, her cheeks red. "I'm sorry. I don't have siblings. This is fun." Hunter walks over to her, slipping one arm over her shoulder and pulling her close to place a kiss on her temple.

Cabbage and her daughter walk back into the kitchen. Cabbage's eyes light up. "What a full kitchen. Looks like everyone is excited for your dessert," she says to me.

The aroma of the lasagna envelops the room, the spicing of oregano and basil familiar and comforting. We carry it into the dining room after setting the table. My father and the twins only join us once all the work is done—typical.

"Why would we need all of these forks?" Haiz asks with a frown on his face, taking a seat at the table.

Adam rolls his eyes. "One for salad, one for mains, and one for dessert. Easy."

"*Easy?* I can use the same fork for all three of those things," Haiz argues.

"Nobody is stopping you." Adam throws his napkin at Haiz. Haiz flings one of his forks back.

My father makes a disapproving noise. "No throwing forks. That is dangerous."

All nine of us settle down, engaging in small talk amidst the clinking of cutlery. That is, until my father loudly clears his throat and sets his napkin to the side, commanding or attention without a word. "I have an announcement," he says. I was right—there *is* an ulterior motive to this trip.

"Cassidy and I will marry in two weeks. We hope that all of you will—"

"Two *weeks*?" Daniel interrupts, his fork dropping onto the plate. "This is the first time we're meeting this woman properly, and you're telling me that you're—" Daniel takes a deep breath, his hands shaking.

"You're upset?" my dad asks. The idea of his children being upset by this seems incomprehensible for him. "I've given you so much. I bought you a car. *Je ne comprends pas.*"

"Because you—!" Daniel lowers the tone of his voice, his eyes bouncing from the twins to me. "I appreciate the car. It makes a big difference in our lives. But *you* are not around. And if you're getting married, that means you'll show up for us even less."

My dad's eyes go to the twins, who stuff their face so full of lasagna that their cheeks seem inflated, then slide to me. "Is this how you feel, also?" he asks.

Under the gaze of eight people, I fidget with my fingers under the table. "Why do—?" I was going to ask why he even wants to marry her, but maybe this is not the right time. Asking now might make him defensive. "It would be nice to have more support from you. Mom's always at work now." She might not admit anything, but I think it's really taking a toll on her.

He nods, putting a bite of lasagna into his mouth. "How is she?" he asks once he has swallowed.

"I don't know." She's aging faster, working nonstop. I miss coming home and seeing her there; needing to talk to someone and going straight to her bedroom. I miss the stories she would occasionally tell me of what life was like growing up in Egypt; how her mom would discourage her from speaking English.

There are so many things I want to say; so many things that I want to ask, but it doesn't feel like the time. It's never felt like the right time to ask him "why?" It's scary. I want to know why he made the choices he did, what his perspective was on it. My mom tells us her side of the story sometimes, how there were small things he used to do to show his love and then slowly it stopped. It always paints him as the bad guy.

Things always feel shallow around my dad. Even at the beginning of the divorce, when we had to go and visit him every few weeks. It felt like he only did it because a contract told him to.

The rest of dinner is quiet and strained. Everyone devours the tiramisu when I bring it out, and Hunter keeps glancing over at me like there is a secret we share. Maybe he is remembering the ways he touched me and guided me when he was showing me what to do.

After cleaning up, everyone goes out onto the porch. The air outside feels too cold to join them, so instead I head upstairs.

In my room, from my window, I can see Cabbage and my dad and the rest of the family. From afar, they seem normal, even happy.

There's a knock on the door and, without waiting for a reply, Hunter walks in. I see his reflection against the window. "Hey, are you okay? The news, your dad . . ."

I shrug and turn. It would be nice to get a hug from him. I'm sure he would if I asked. My head drops, my gaze lingering on the wooden floor. A part of me had hoped that I could get closer to my dad this weekend, maybe get him to want to be around us more. But an upcoming wedding means he is going to be spending his money and time on a different family. A new one. That thought makes my heart sink.

"It was bound to happen. They have been dating for years now," I say, trying to be reasonable.

Hunter rubs his palms together. "Look, I wanted to say—the thing with Sabrina . . . I saw your face earlier, in the kitchen. I'm doing it for—"

"Yeah, no. No. All good." I nod. I asked him to do this, so I won't be the one to stop it. "Are *you* okay with it?" I still feel bad, like I forced this on him.

He shrugs, giving a half smile. "I'm a guy," is all he says. I don't ask him what that means.

He walks up beside me, pressing one hand against the cool glass of the window, staring out into the darkness. The night sky is dotted with countless stars. My gaze drifts to his hand; his nails are neatly trimmed, his fingers long. I can't help but remember what it feels like to be touched by him, those fingers gently brushing my neck, gripping me, drawing me closer—*no*. I shake off the memory.

When I am around him, I often feel like I am at war with my own thoughts and desires. It can be exhausting.

Then my eyes go to his chest. How is he not cold without his hoodie? If I were to touch his skin, would it be warm?

"Hunter?" My heart is pulsing in my throat.

"Hmm?" He turns to look at me, slightly dazed. His eyes are like a dangerous storm that I want to get caught in—rain drenching me and gray encapsulating me.

Sucking in a breath, I lift my hand to his chest. When I am only an inch away, my brain finally starts working and stops me from touching him.

He assesses me slowly, then glances at the hand that almost touched him. When he reaches out to take my hand, I almost jump back. He presses it against his chest, to the place I was going to touch. He is warm. His other hand grips my waist.

If only my brain could take photos—I would want to save this memory forever. His face is so close now. His eyes are slightly hooded as they stay on mine, straying for a few seconds to my lips.

My heart is beating solely for him. Hun-ter. Hun-ter. Hun-ter. It races in my chest. My lips tingle with the absence of his.

But then he leans in closer. My mind explodes in a million different directions.

I can't do this.

Not because of Daniel, not because of Sabrina, but because it scares me so much. What if he doesn't like the kiss? What if things work out for a little while, and then it ends? I can't not have Hunter in my life. There is too much at risk. I know better.

My head tilts down, then toward the window.

The silence settles heavily. I don't move, with his hand still holding mine against his chest.

"What are you afraid of?" he asks gently.

Change the topic, Anne! This tension is no longer welcomed here. "The ocean." I tilt my head. "Did you know some parts of the ocean can get as hot as seven hundred and fifty degrees? Most people assume the bottom of the ocean would be freezing, but that's not necessarily true."

"Seven hundred and fifty degrees. That's very . . . Pacific."

"Your puns are getting out of sand." I smile and subtly pull away. "A good one, right?"

"You can't call your own jokes good?"

"What?" I laugh. "You do it all the time!"

At that, he grins. That gorgeous, heart-stopping smile. *We could have kissed.*

It's all I can think about, even when he eventually leaves. *He wanted to kiss me.*

Chapter 10

HUNTER

Anne is on top of me.

"Hunter, why is my hair *green*?" She should be sleepy, since it is early in the morning, but instead she looks like she wants to choke me to death.

When I try to get up, she pushes her palms against my chest and keeps me against the ground. "I like this position," I tease.

"Why did you do this?" Her face is flushed, eyes narrowed, and lips pressed into a thin line, fuming over the prank.

"The twins asked. They needed content." They came to me after I left Anne's room last night, and it was too funny to say no. I'm surprised she didn't wake up while I was lathering it in. "Don't worry. It's non-permanent. It comes out after one wash."

Her anger softens and she leans closer, her hair falling forward, framing her face. She slaps my chest.

I fake moan, deep and sexual, to tease her. "Ah, Annabelle, that sort of . . . feels good." I know it'll get her off me. I may be getting turned on, because she keeps accidentally rubbing against me. Her face turns red, and suddenly the position we are in begins to feel a lot more intimate than before.

I haven't stopped thinking about her, about the way we almost kissed last night. I've been so curious—how would she whimper against my lips if I kissed her? Would her nails dig into my skin, desperate for more, if I explored the delicate curve of her neck with my tongue?

Haiz and Adam walk out of their room and find us on top of each other in the hall.

Anne looks up, jumps off me, and takes off after them. They instantly break into a sprint, their shouts and laughter echoing in the distance long after they disappear from view.

The thought of Anne stays stuck on my mind, which is frustrating. I have Sabrina; I could kiss her at any time and in any way I want to. Yet all of the small moments I have experienced in the past with Anne makes me wonder if she has liked me the whole time: the way she holds on to me on my bike, the hurt in her eyes when I flirt with someone else, the way she leans in any time I flirt or tease her.

But if it is true—if she does like me—then why did she reject me when I tried to kiss her last night?

•••

On the way back to Michigan, the rest of the family takes a ride in the limo again. Daniel and I, after getting permission from his dad, race to a stop outside my house in an Aston Martin. It has got the same amount of horsepower as an Arabian army.

We were reckless enough that I am almost certain we arrived an hour ahead of them. With shit-eating grins, we climb out. This must be what taking drugs feels like. The aftereffects of the adrenaline feel like bubbles in my chest. Everything is a lot clearer. Cold air brushes against my cheeks. The sky is pink with streaks of gray clouds.

Daniel aims his phone camera and snaps a picture to send to Anne, who refused to believe we'd make it home first. She now owes us two of her legendary cheese sandwiches.

"Thanks for this weekend," I say. I'd never be able to do anything like this without Daniel in my life. I'm grateful to have a best friend like him.

"I'm glad you were around," he confesses.

The entire weekend, Daniel did not react to or talk about his father's wedding announcement. But as soon as his foot was pressed all the way down against the gas pedal, and everything outside seemed like a blur, he opened up. "I wish he cared about us," was all he said. I know Daniel feels the burden of carrying his family, of keeping them smiling and content like it is his responsibility alone.

"Anyway, I'll see you tomorrow, yeah?" he asks, holding out his hand for our usual handshake.

Instead, I nod and pull him into a bone-crushing hug. I can see that it is tough on him, and I am not sure he will ever vent it all out. From all the dark times that I have been dragged through, I know that sometimes, even as a guy, all I need is a hug.

He eventually pulls away and ruffles my hair in a brotherly manner. Only when he is inside do I unlock my own front door. The house smells like a dive bar. Cigarette smoke fogs the dim air. The only light comes from the television in the lounge. "Where *the hell* have you been?" My dad's raspy voice rumbles through the house.

My grip tightens around the handles of my suitcase. *Shit.* Wood creaks as I step closer to the lounge. He's not in his usual spot. That can't be good.

"Where are you?" I ask.

He stands in the kitchen, wearing only boxers. The sight disgusts me. His stomach, along with his stubble, seems to have grown. He isn't leaving the house anymore, not even cleaning himself up to go to bars to meet women like he used to.

Empty beer bottles litter the island. "I asked you a question, bastard." I wish I were a bastard. Maybe then my father would have left my me and my mother in peace.

"I'm sorry."

"Inconsiderate little rat." He is trying to get a reaction from me. The tone of his voice deepens with every word. His hand tightens around one of the empty bottles.

The adrenaline I had been feeling crashes fast. "You're angry, I get it. I'm sorry."

"Angry doesn't even begin to explain it." His neck and cheeks are turning red.

His voice makes me take a step back. "Please, calm down." I know those three words won't work on him, but they are the only words I can manage to say due to the lump forming in my throat.

"You're as useless and pathetic as your mother!"

I shake my head. "Leave her out of this." For *once*.

"It's your fault she left." The worst part is—he truly believes that. He blames me every single day for the mistake that *he* made.

"No, it's not! You hit her! That's why she left!" I snap.

He grabs a bottle and throws it at me. It hits me in my ribs and then falls to the ground with a loud crash. The air gets knocked out of my lungs. I bend over, clutching onto my side.

"What are you going to do when your looks fade? You're not smart enough, you're not strong enough, you will never be enough! How're your grades? You're probably failing as usual, huh?" He leans forward against the counter.

He doesn't care about my grades; he doesn't care about anything related to me. He is just looking for a sore spot to hit.

I suck in deep, shaky breaths. "Actually, I'm passing." I've been studying hard. I'm going to get away from here.

"The bare minimum. Great." I should have known that nothing will ever be enough for him. "Clean up the glass," he demands, throwing another bottle to the ground. It shatters, the sound ringing through the house. This one is still filled with beer, which splatters all over the floor.

I can feel the energy being drained out of my body, being replaced with a terrifying emptiness. "Dad—"

"Don't call me that! You are no son of mine!" His arms flail in his drunken state. A deep fear, which I have never felt around him before, settles in my chest. He has never acted this way before. "I should have put you up for adoption after your mother left. Keeping you was the biggest mistake of my life!"

His words send pain through every inch of my body, effectively breaking my heart. "You don't mean that," I whisper. "I know I'm not perfect, but—"

"Not perfect?" He snorts. "I wouldn't be able to find one good thing about you, even if I searched for years. I know you better than anyone."

I shake my head, wanting to fight him, but knowing it will lead nowhere. "You're wrong."

"Name one good thing about yourself." He scratches his facial hair. His foot repeatedly taps against the wooden floor, like the ticking of a bomb that is about to detonate.

"I'm a good baker." There are many customers who give me compliments. Who moan when they taste what I've made. They always come back for my cinnamon rolls. Or my éclairs.

"Baking is for girls."

My chest tightens. "I'm good with people. I could probably be a good salesman," I add, my voice softer, uncertain. He will always find a way to make the things I'm proud of seem like nothing, no matter what I say.

"Probably? You *probably* wouldn't be hired with those shitty marks of yours."

"Why would you say that?"

"You need to work harder. You claim that you're such a good baker—where is the money, then? Where is the proof that you are anything less than pathetic?" He can't ever know that. He'd take it from me without as much as a thank-you.

Instead of arguing or defending myself, I get down on my knees and start picking up the glass lying in pieces around me.

Chapter 11

ANNE

The cafeteria buzzes with overlapping conversations and clattering of trays and utensils, creating a constant hum. Every part of me would rather be on a beach—or even a frozen lake—instead of cramming for a test set for last period.

Clary and I search for a table near one of the many windows in the dull, gray cafeteria. Usually, Daniel forces us to sit with him, but today he has a meeting with his football coach.

Clary drops her book onto one of the tables and takes a seat across from me. "All right, I know we agreed to not speak, because we 'have to' study for geography," she says, making quotation marks with her fingers. I knew this was coming. "But it's just—how was your trip? What's Canada like? Did you go skating? Did it snow? Most importantly, were there any cute guys—you know, except your brother?" She bites down on a carrot stick.

"It was . . ." I don't quite have words for it. "Well, my father announced that he is getting married." My chest tightens at that. It will crush my mom to find out.

"Will you go?" She has stopped eating to stare at me with wide eyes.

I shrug. "I do want to, because maybe then I'll get a chance to speak to him more; to have him in my life a little bit more." It's weird, and complicated, and I shouldn't want it, but I do.

Sensing my discomfort on the conversation topic, she asks, "And cute boys?"

"Not really."

I grab the cold cheese sandwich that lies beside me and bite into it, so that if she decides to go all Nancy Drew on me, I'll have time to prepare an answer.

She narrows her eyes. "*Define* not really?"

I could tell her about Hunter. She knows I like him, but she doesn't know how much.

Maybe I should just spit it out. "Hunter almost kissed me. Again."

"Wha—?" Her eyes are almost hanging out of their sockets. *"Again?"*

It feels good to finally tell someone. "At the party, during Truth or Dare, he nearly kissed me. In front of Daniel. It seemed like a, I don't know, it-means-nothing almost kiss. Then Saturday night, he's in my room, holding me against him and leaning in and—"

Clary starts squealing and clapping. "And?"

"I couldn't do it, Clary. Daniel would lose his mind. I ... I would lose *my* mind." I bite my lip. "I have a feeling that once I start kissing him, I won't be able to stop."

Her eyes scan the cafeteria for him but he's not around. He's probably at the bakery. He does that sometimes, during his breaks.

Daniel walks in with a group of girls, making me roll my eyes in exasperation. Clary's gaze locks on to them, her expression carefully neutral, but her eyes betray a flicker of something deeper.

Daniel scans the room and then immediately heads over to our table, leaving the girls awkwardly standing around. "You have lunch, right?"

"Yes, *Dad*. I'm fine."

He grins, his eyes going to Clary for a half a second. "All right, well, Hunter asked me to get you to the bakery after school. They have some special or something, so they need all the help they can get." He shrugs and walks off, back to his flock of girls. They all act like birds in a mating dance when he shows up. It's so strange.

Luckily, the rest of the day goes by fast and, as instructed, I take a walk to the bakery once the final bell rings.

It is filled with people. Too many people. They talk over the soft jazz music playing. It smells, as always, like cinnamon rolls and coffee. A chalkboard sign, which reads BUY A BATCH OF ANY PASTRY AND TRY OUR NEW PASTRY PUFFS FOR FREE!, has been placed against the large wooden counter. George assists customers at the till who are ordering bulk amounts of pastries to take home. He has his thin, wire-framed glasses on. I scurry to the kitchen to avoid the customers.

It's a mess. Every countertop is covered in flour and other ingredients. Cupboards lie open, revealing trays and unused cooking contraptions. Hunter rushes around, finding new ingredients to add to his mixing bowl.

"Hunter . . . ?" I say. When he notices me, it is as if he forgets about all his other tasks. His eyes fix on me, a whirl of emotions trapped within the gray. "Are you okay?"

Without a response, he crosses the room in a few quick strides and pulls me into a hug. It is comforting, and with my cheek pressed against his chest, I can hear his heartbeat. It is everything that I needed after a long school day, and though I don't know what elicited it, I hug him back.

"Your voice is the most beautiful sound in the world," he whispers, keeping his arms wrapped tightly around me.

His strange behavior makes me ask again, "Are you okay?"

Silence. His breathing is shaky.

"Hunter?"

I'm not pulling away from this hug; not if he needs it. Maybe that's all he needs, without any explanation.

"Is there anything good about me?" His voice is barely a whisper. He pulls away from the hug. Vulnerability peeks through his expression. I've never seen him look like this in the seven years I've known him.

"Of course, there is." I want to reach out and touch him, hug him again, do anything to make this look in his eyes go away.

"What?"

"You're funny." I poke his cheek, where his dimple would be if he were smiling. "No matter how I feel, you always make me smile with your cringe jokes." I slide my hand down his biceps. My heart flutters. "You're strong. Really, really strong. Have you seen your arms? You could probably throw me across a room. It makes me feel safe when I'm with you. You'd beat up all the bad guys."

A smile curves his lips for the slightest moment, then falls. It's not a full smile, but it's a start.

"You're an incredible baker. When I picture heaven, I see you baking pastries and cakes for me every day." *Shirtless.* "I've never tasted anything better—"

"Than my cake?" He chuckles. There's that dimple. I push his chest gently.

"You're generous. I remember days when you gave me your food because I didn't have money to buy lunch at school. Or how you'd invite random kids to sit at our table during breaks because they were eating alone. You're amazing in every way, Hunter."

"Thank you, Annabelle." His eyes flutter closed. The soft curve of his lips are tilted up. I'm glad I made a difference in his mood.

"Are those enough? 'Cause I can give a thousand reasons why I love—" My voice gets caught in my throat. That was the stupidest thing I could have said. My lips are left open like a fish out of water. *No, no, no.*

He leans closer to me. "Why you . . . ?"

The distinctive aroma of freshly baked chocolate chip cookies fills my nose. "Where are the cookies?" I look around the kitchen, hoping he won't push to figure out what I was about to say. Though a five-year-old could guess the end of my sentence. I swallow hard, searching his gaze for anything.

He turns and grabs a tray lying on a counter near the oven. It is lined with over a dozen cookies. Holding out the tray, he says, "Be careful. You could get hurt."

"What?" *Is it because of what I said?*

"They're hot."

"Oh." I bring a cookie up to my nose and inhale the smell. It's the perfect temperature, actually. They're the size of my palm. "Can I buy you?" I whisper.

"There's actually a promotion on eBay at the moment. If you buy me, they'll throw in a hoodie *absolutely free.*"

I laugh. "Well I found you on Etsy for half the price, and your clothes were"—my chest tightens at the riskiness of this flirt—"one hundred percent off."

He laughs and starts playing with the end of my braid, so I take it as permission to tug at the strings of his white hoodie. "I thought you weren't allowed to wear hoodies to work."

"I'm not." He winks and moves his face closer to mine. "I'm also not allowed to flirt with employees." His lips are pink and look like heaven to touch.

"Look at you, Mister Rule Breaker." I take a bite of the cookie. *Whoa.* The chocolate chips melt together with the warm, sugary dough. I tilt my head back, moaning. I think I am going to finish the whole tray. "Will you teach me how to make these?"

"Yeah, of course. I can on Friday, after Daniel's game?" He runs a hand through his hair. "If you want," he adds hesitantly.

"Friday sounds good."

"I should get back to work, though. There's no time for breaks today."

"Right, but . . ." I'm not going to directly ask him what's wrong, because I want him to feel ready to tell me. "Are you okay?"

He lifts my hand and places a kiss against my knuckles. It's gentle. "Thanks to you, Annabelle."

Walking out into the main bakery area, I work through each table. Customers order huge amounts of food and coffee, all trying to get the free pastry puffs.

Sabrina is nowhere to be found on the one day the bakery actually needs her.

The drive home from Toronto was extremely awkward. Daniel and Hunter had raced home. I had pestered her for my shoe in the limo while the twins slept, but she kept her earphones in and wouldn't say a word. It was unbelievably frustrating.

After getting all of the orders in, I go back into the kitchen and stick them up on the wall for Hunter. The bakery could easily have a computer system, but George likes it to be old-school. "It gives character," he claims.

Hunter switches on the coffee machine. "French toast? That's not on the menu," he says, reading through the orders.

I tie up my hair when it starts sticking to my face because of the heat from the oven. "Should I tell them to order something else?"

"No, it's okay, I'll do it. It's not hard." He pulls out a cookbook from one of the draws and flips through it.

I lean back against the counter. He gathers everything he needs in one place and starts mixing ingredients into a bowl. "Why do you like baking so much?" I ask. He seems to enjoy every second he spends inside this kitchen.

"It helps me feel like I am in control." He is focused, soaking the bread in his mixture. I shuffle over to the sink to wash some dishes while I wait.

That makes sense. He knows every ingredient, every step, and what the result will be.

"So, you like being in control?"

"Doesn't everyone?" He places the bread into a skillet. "And it helps that I get paid for this. It is actually a lot of fun. I'll show you on Friday." The more I watch him work, the more attracted to him I become. He is great with his hands. "Flip it over," he says to himself, reading off the cookbook. He glances back at me and smirks playfully.

Is he teasing me? After both sides of the bread are browned, he slides it onto a plate. "Could you pass me the maple syrup? It's in the cabinet above your head."

I follow his instructions and hand the bottle to him. "Thanks, beautiful."

"What?"

"I said, thanks, Annabelle."

"No, you said beautiful."

He pops the lid of the maple syrup open and nods. "Same thing."

My heart fizzes like a piece of cotton candy in water. *What?* I'm sure I'm red.

He pours the maple syrup over the French toast and then pours a little onto his finger. Making intense eye contact with me, he slips his finger into his mouth. I press my thighs together, shuffling backward to avoid pulling him close to me.

"Hunter, please."

He knows what he is doing. I can see it in his face; in the way he is trying not to laugh. "Please, what?" He walks over to me and pours a little bit more on his thumb and lifts it to my lips. "Taste," he whispers.

I open my mouth, and he slips his finger in, the sweet, sticky warmth of maple syrup instantly coating my tongue. I take my time, savoring the rich flavor.

He draws in a sharp breath and leans closer, his eyes locked on to me. As he pours more syrup onto his finger, I brace myself for him to offer it to me again, but instead, he smears the golden liquid over his bottom lip. Once again, I find myself hooked on the sudden intimacy of the moment.

Heat rushes through my body. *Is this his way of asking me to kiss him?* He leans lower, angling his lips within reach, but as I am about to close the distance, his tongue darts out, licking the syrup away in a playful, teasing way.

Frustration builds inside, and I snatch the plate of French toast off the counter and walk out. I haven't been teased like that before, but I decided that I don't enjoy it.

I'll have to get him back for that.

•••

IT STARTED WITH A HIGH TOP

There's a knock on my bedroom door. "Come in."

Clary steps into my room, holding a round container. Her sparkling long-sleeved blue dress almost blinds me.

"Where are you going?" I ask. It looks like she is ready for a party.

"Dancing." She started dance classes before she learned to walk, and with the December holiday only two weeks away, she has a string of competitions coming up. Placing the container down at the edge of the bed, she sings, "Guess what I brought."

I shift closer to it and pull the lid off. "Éclairs! You're my hero." I stuff one into my mouth. The combined textures of the dough and the chocolate and the cream make it orgasmic. I thought I wouldn't be able to eat anything after all of the cookies I devoured earlier, but here we are. I swore an oath—five seconds ago—that I would never say no to éclairs.

She sits beside me and picks one out of the container. "Bet I can fit more in my mouth than you."

I pick up two and stuff them into my cheek pockets. Clary leans closer to the container and puts four into her mouth. Not willing to lose, I continue stuffing éclairs into my mouth until it's overflowing.

"Aaaahaaaha ah ahaa aah aahaa aah ah," she tries to speak with her mouth full, nodding her head toward the door.

The éclairs almost fall out my mouth when I laugh. I push them back in with my hand. "Haaah?"

We both sit in silence, trying to figure out how to chew it all. Clary fetches tissues from my restroom and spits it out. "I know you beat me because you basically eat éclairs for a living. How many did you fit?"

"Six." I lick my fingers.

"Nice! Here I was thinking I had a big mouth, always yapping." She laughs at herself. "Anyhoo, I have to get to my dance class. Toodles."

"Bye."

My door swings shut behind her. I airlift another éclair in. These could contain poison that would make me puke for weeks, and I still wouldn't stop eating them.

Closing the container, I slide off my bed, heading to Daniel's room. We haven't spoken about how he feels about my dad's wedding. We have barely spoken since getting back from Toronto; he has been in a shell.

Before I barge in, I notice Clary through the narrow crack of the ajar door. She's in front of Daniel, her hand on his chest. They speak softly to each other.

"Clary? I thought you left," I say.

She glances worriedly at Daniel and then at me. "Oh, yeah, Remi is going into the eighth grade and wants to play football. I was just asking Daniel if he has any advice."

With her hand on his chest?

Remi is a scrawny, anti-social gamer with a hatred for anything sports-related. He would become a hermit if his mother would allow it. Football doesn't sound like something he would want to do. "Okay..."

"Thanks, Daniel. I'll let Remi know what you said. Cheerio." She walks past me, out the door.

I narrow my eyes at Daniel. He shrugs. "What? I was chilling in my room. She came to me."

Whatever. I don't want to make him defensive when I intend to have a heart-to-heart. "Okay, Danny boy." My eyes fill with tears suddenly, so I fall face down against his dark-blue bed sheets to hide it. It smells like him—a cologne he always wears with bergamot and something or the other.

"Don't call me Danny boy," he grumbles. The bed dips beside me.

I chuckle against the sheets. "You call me little booger!" I accidentally look up at him, and he notices my drying tears.

"What's wrong?"

That question, and the concerned look on his face, immediately releases all the tears I've been holding back. *Damn it!* I tuck my face back into the sheets. With a shaky inhalation, I say, "I just can't stop thinking about Dad. Why does he get to be happy when he's the one who did the bad thing?" My voice sounds muffled because I am speaking facing down. "Do you know what happened? Why did Dad leave?" I ask.

Daniel sighs deeply and shifts, adjusting my head to lie on his lap. He looks down at me, sighs again, and then tilts his head up to stare at the ceiling as if it might have the answers written somewhere. "Dad was away a lot toward the end of their marriage. I think he was working too much, and when he'd come home, he'd want peace, which he never got with four children and a wife around. He was just looking for an escape, I think, when he"—he looks down at me, playing with my hair—"met Cassidy."

It feels like someone shoved a pillow into my face and is screaming at me to breathe. I can't. I sit up, pulling my legs into my chest. So, Cabbage was the other woman. She is so happy and cheery and sweet that I thought maybe it wasn't true. I thought maybe she wouldn't break a family, because it's not what nice people do. But it's more complicated than that, isn't it?

The tears don't stop even when I command them to.

"I'm sorry, little booger. I know it's hard to hear, and it's something Mom should be telling you herself, but she's hardly around, and since the wedding is coming, and you're asking I thought . . . But I shouldn't have told you."

Daniel doesn't believe in love. After his heart was broken, he lost that hope for love. My heart is breaking now. I'm losing that hope.

"They were happy. All of their stories of passion and adventure. They had a family and a life together. They loved each other and still—" Maybe it's not that love isn't real; maybe it's just that love is not enough in the end.

Love is part of it, but if peace is what my father wanted, and excitement is what my mother wanted, then maybe they simply ended up growing apart.

"Yeah," Daniel whispers, his voice strained. "They got to experience something beautiful together, and just because it is over doesn't mean that the experience was for nothing, you know?"

Seeing him being open and vulnerable makes me ask, "How do you feel about the wedding?"

Daniel falls back against his pillows. It makes a *whooshing* sound. "I don't like love. I don't like drama. This wedding has both. I'm not keen. I don't want to hurt Mom by going, as if I am supporting Dad and his actions."

I feel the same, about the hurting my mom part. I can't imagine how she'll feel, finding out about it. I'm not going to bring it up.

Turning to face Daniel once my tears have dried, I search for a change of subject. "You and Clary. . ."

Daniel jerks his head to look at me as if I'm a zombie that wants to eat his brains. "That will *never* happen. You know that."

His reaction makes me doubt his words. "You sure? You can—"

"Never, little booger. I don't do feelings."

I never mentioned anything about feelings.

Chapter 12

HUNTER

I quietly push open Anne and Daniel's front door, stepping into the stillness of the house. The faint glow of the television flickers from the living room, where the twins are engrossed in a movie. They jokingly toss popcorn at each other.

Hoping Anne is in her room, I make my way upstairs. I can't shake the longing that has taken root since she shared those things that she likes about me. Anyone can offer reassurance and affirmation, but the way she expressed it made me feel deeply loved.

It wasn't just her words; it was the way she looked at me. After my dad had regarded me like I was the world's biggest disappointment, her gaze of admiration lifted me. I wanted to come and thank her for that feeling, for reminding me of my worth.

Inside her room, Anne sits at her desk, typing on her laptop under the soft glow of a small lamp. When I push her door closed, she doesn't notice, her headphones playing music, and her frown set with determination.

I'm not sure how to approach her without scaring her, so I end up going for a light tap on her shoulder.

It doesn't work. She yells and nearly falls out of her seat.

Standing, she shoves her laptop closed and turns to me. "Hunter? What are you—?"

My hand falls over her mouth quickly. Daniel doesn't know I am here. "You are screaming with your headphones on," I say in a hushed whisper.

She pulls her headphones down to sit around her neck and frowns, my hand still covering her lips. "What?" she says, muffled.

"You're talking loudly."

"So?" As I try to come up with a response to that, she licks my hand. I laugh and quickly pull away.

"You taste like cookies." She gives me a once-over, as if the rest of me would taste good, too.

"Can I sleep with you?" I ask.

Her eyes widen. "I-I—no! Don't be disgusting!" She tries pushing me away. I grab her wrists and pin them to the wall beside her desk.

"I mean—" I take in a deep breath, frustrated for some reason. "I mean *sleep* in your room with you. Not have sex with you." My dad came to the bakery searching for me, but thankfully George got rid of him before he found me. I can't go home. I'm . . . I'm scared to.

"Why don't you stay in Daniel's room?"

Because I want you. "Please?"

"I don't think that's a good idea . . ." She bites her lip, a glimmer in her eye as she tries to slip out of my grip. *"Hunter."* The way she breathes my name sends a thrill racing through my stomach.

"Annabelle." My voice is low, playful, as I hold her gaze, but she stares past me into the shadows of her room, her eyes refusing to meet mine. *Look at me.* "Please?" I ask, the word laced in vulnerability.

She huffs. "Okay."

The tightness in my chest eases for a moment and I pull her in for a hug. My chin leans against her head and I take in a deep breath.

"Did Sabrina give you her shoe back?" I haven't seen her around lately.

She looks back up at me, then down at her laptop as if it holds the answers. "No. I . . . I don't think I'll ever get it back." How can I not squeeze her in my arms again, with that look of sadness on her face? "Thank you for going out with her. I'm sorry I made you do that. It wasn't supposed to get so complicated."

"I did it for you. I know those shoes mean a lot to you." Even if I don't understand why.

"Before my mom gave them to me, she told me all of the adventures that went on with them." She goes silent for a while, reflecting. Just when I think she might not want to share more, she says, "I wanted to keep that alive in some way. It's probably stupid."

I squeeze her hand. "It's not stupid. I kept a whole box of things my mom left behind. Things she didn't care to take with her when she left." I kept them because in some ways, I was like those objects; not valuable enough to take with her.

She glances up at me, leaning in closer. "You've never told me about your mom."

"Trade?"

She shifts onto the bed and pats the spot beside her. When I slip off my shoes and sit, she leans her head against my arm, her hair brushing against my skin. It is a small gesture, yet it stirs up something inside me.

"Every night, when I was about eight years old, my mom would sit my brothers and I down and tell us her version of a bedtime story—she called them *hekayat*, which means stories or tales. She used to bring objects with her and tell the stories of the objects. And the shoes had *so many* stories." She smiles to herself. Watching her, I feel an overwhelming urge to shift closer and pull her into my arms, to wrap her in warmth and comfort. "She told the stories of how she wore them when she was traveling to Paris with my dad or how she wore them to the hospital when she had me. They got her through the best and the hardest parts of her life."

I take her hand, trailing small circles on her palm while she talks.

"I remember sneaking downstairs one night, after hearing the soft sound of jazz music playing. In the garden, my parents stood in the pouring rain, dancing and smiling at each other. She had those shoes on. I just *knew*, in that moment, that soulmates did exist."

"So, you're scared that by losing one of those shoes, you're losing those memories?" The realization hits me. That's why she cares, even though the shoes are old and worn.

"Your turn," she chimes, ignoring my question.

I don't think I've spoken to someone about my mom in ages. It's never easy. Even thinking about it sometimes shatters me. "She was beautiful, my mom." She had my curly, dark, sand-colored hair and the brightest green eyes I have ever seen. "And she had the kindest soul in the world. My dad would go to work, and she would stay at home with me. We would cook and clean and do absolutely everything together. Saturday was my favorite, though, because my granny would come over and all three of us would cook and bake together."

"*That's* why you love baking." Her eyes sparkle with the realization. One of the reasons, yes.

"I miss them, and baking makes me feel like a part of them has stayed with me. That way I never feel completely alone."

I continue, "She was always gentle and considerate." My heart clenches. *Always*. Maybe she shouldn't have been. "She used to give me candy in secret and would tuck me in every night before bed. In my completely unbiased opinion, she was the best mother in the world." Until she left without looking back. "For years, I couldn't fall asleep with her gone." She was no longer there to wrap the blankets around me and press a kiss to my forehead. My father would never do it. My breathing shakes and I grip Anne's hand. I am not ready to tell her what happened that made my mom leave.

I scan her dark room for a distraction before she can get the chance to ask any questions. Her notebooks lie open on her desk. "Would you be willing to tell me more about your book?"

"I'll tell you when I have finished writing it. It feels like something that needs to stay my own for now, until this first draft is complete. But I'll give you a teaser. It is related to the things I have been telling you tonight. That is all I am saying about it." I stare at her lips as she speaks. They're coated in something shiny and they look so good. She looks over at me, and I realize she is still talking. "Are you listening?"

Another distraction is needed. I shift closer to her and fix her hair. I want to bottle her scent and keep it with me. She smells like home. Her and Daniel are my home, the place I go when I don't have anywhere to hide.

"I am sorry—I was just distracted by you." I trail my thumb over her cheek. Her soft brown eyes pull me in, even in the dim light, making me want to lose myself in her. "I wanted to thank you, for earlier, in the bakery. I was having a rough day." That is an understatement. "Your words. They meant everything to me. You mean everything to me. I hope you know that."

Her gaze noticeably softens. She shifts in close enough that I could kiss her. Her hand slides up to my chest. It feels dangerous.

I hold my breath. "You mean everything to me," she admits. "And I meant every word that I said earlier. You are kind and smart and so, so wonderful. Truly."

"Could we—?" I am cut off by loud music and deep muffled voices. It must be Daniel having people over. Which means that if I don't go down now, my phone is going to start ringing up here. He will not be happy about this moment I am sharing with his sister. My eyes fall closed for a moment. "I think I have to go down." *But I'd much rather stay here.*

She nods rapidly and pulls away. "All right, I'll just be doing some writing. If you . . ." Her face reddens, so she lowers her head. "If you still want to come back later."

"Thank you, Annabelle." I pull her bedroom door open and light floods in from the hallway.

House music plays from a speaker that vibrates with every beat drop. A group of guys all walk in, some holding hookahs and some carrying food and drinks. "Yo, where should we put this?"

"Take it to the living room," Daniel instructs.

I take the lead and show them to the living room. Luckily, he didn't see me come down the stairs.

They leave all the foods and drinks on the coffee table and take a seat on the couches or on the floor. There are around eight guys; most of them are on the team with Daniel.

"Daniel, why didn't you invite any babes over?" Elias asks. "Speaking of, where's your sister?"

"I'm not in the mood to have girls all over me," Daniel says in a matter-of-fact tone. I'm not sure how much I believe that. I've noticed his eyes constantly drifting to a specific redhead during school, his gaze saying that he'd like *her* all over him. "And as for my sister—that's none of your business."

I take a seat on the couch, beside Daniel. He nods to me in greeting as he takes a pull off the hookah. His short dark hair is pushed away from his face, except for one rebellious strand that brushes against his forehead.

"It's the tongue ring, isn't it? That's how you get the girls," another guy, Tony, asks. He leans closer, in his seat. "Do they like it?"

Daniel smirks. Arrogance shines through his expression and posture. "They fucking love it."

The guys all start playing music and drinking, which causes the volume of their voices to rise rapidly.

Daniel leans in closer. "Why did you just come from upstairs?"

Shit. "I was helping your sister with a project."

His brows draw together. "What project?"

Shit. "I, uh—she's writing a story."

"Yeah, I know. But why did she need your help?" His gaze is intensely fixed on me, making me feel as if I'm under a spotlight in an interrogation room.

"I don't know. She asked, so I went. She's my friend."

He scratches the dark stubble growing along his jaw and tips his head to the side. "You need to distance yourself from her."

"Yeah, yeah. Your whole 'five-meter-distance rule.'" I roll my eyes.

"No." He clenches his jaw and looks away for a moment. "Hunter, I mean that you need to distance *more*. You need to stop hugging her, you need to stop talking to her when you don't have to. You need to put yourself as far away from her as possible. I know she's beautiful, but you *can't*. She'll fall for you."

I think the issue might be that I'm falling for her.

Tony cranks the speaker volume higher, until the beat of the song is reverberating through the wooden floors.

I stand up. "I'm going to find food," I tell Daniel, but he is already lost in another conversation.

Anne stands in the kitchen, her pajama shorts filled with images of little teddy bears. My feet stop in their tracks. She must have used a quiet moment when we were distracted with the music or drinks or conversation, because I hadn't noticed her coming down the stairs.

So much for staying away. I look over my shoulder to Daniel. His smile is wide as he retells a story to everyone.

She turns when she hears me, then notices my expression of concern. "Everything okay?" Her voice is gentle. A contrast against the harsh beat of the music.

Now I feel like I am doing something wrong by talking to her.

My tongue glides over my bottom lip, catching her attention. She follows the motion with her eyes,

There is a can of soda in her hands, already opened. If I kissed her, she'd still have the flavor of it on her lips.

Maybe I could flirt with her one more time. It wouldn't lead anywhere, but it would give me one more chance to be close to her. To have her look at me in that way she does.

This is the last time.

I walk up and stop directly in front of her. "Can I taste?"

She glances down at her soda and then holds it out for me.

"No, I meant . . ." I stare at her lips, then step back a bit. I slide my hand against the kitchen island behind me. "Never mind."

Her face goes red, indicating that she understands what I meant.

"Come here," I say.

She slowly puts her soda down and steps up in front of me.

My fingers tuck her hair behind her ear. Her eyes flutter shut for a moment. I just want to hold her and protect her. That moment we shared in her room felt special.

I don't want this to be the last time.

This is not the time to be flirting. I'm being idiotic and reckless, with both her feelings and my own, and Daniel could come in at any time. There can't be a "last time." It has to stop now. It *has to*.

She runs her fingers through her hair. Looking back to the fridge, she asks, "Do you want a sandwich? I still owe you."

Right, because she was wrong about our ability to race in a sports car. She should have seen it coming.

"I'm not going to say no."

She nods and shuffles over to the fridge, bending forward to pull the ingredients out. My eyes trail down to her shorts.

She spins around to face me and catches me staring. When she starts preparing the sandwich, she chops the ingredients with an unstable, shaky grip.

"Here." I come up behind her. "My grandma taught me this trick for chopping. You press your fingers down against the food like this." I adjust her fingers against the tomato, then take her other hand that is holding the knife. My hands engulf hers. "And then you go in quick, precise movements. Up and down. Up and down, yeah, like that. Sliding the food forward with the other hand as you go."

I shouldn't be this close.

I step back and she continues with a steadier grip. "Thank you, Hunter. You're a good teacher."

I take another step back, even though I want to move forward and wrap my arms around her.

She toasts the sandwich in a pan and then places it on a plate. It smells warm and buttery.

"Your specialty is cinnamon rolls ... mine is this." She holds the plate out for me. I lift the sandwich to my mouth and take a bite.

The flavors melt in my mouth. A moan leaves my lips as I take another bite. "This is so good. Will you make me another one?"

She smiles and nods, grabbing two more slices of bread. "The trick is to add basil and honey," she tells me excitedly.

I moan again as I take another bite. If I could eat one thing for the rest of my life—it would be salted caramel chocolates, but this is a close second.

"Stop moaning."

"Why? Does it bother you?"

"No," she says, knowing I'll do it again to annoy her if she says yes. She flips the second sandwich in the pan.

I move behind her and lean closer to her ear. "Are you sure?" I let out a deep, breathless moan. It sounds even more erotic than I intended.

She turns to me. *"Hunter."* She slaps my arm lightly. "Someone could hear you."

I step back and take a bite of my sandwich, a smile on my face. She likes it. Once she said, during a game of Truth or Dare, that moaning is something she finds extremely attractive.

The more I tell myself I shouldn't be doing this . . . I can't stop.

She lifts up the sandwich from the pan with her hands, and she drops it to the plate, a soft whimper leaving her lips. It is a cute sound. She presses her finger to her lips. "That was hot," she says.

I take her wrist, guiding her to the sink to put her finger under cool water. "Does that help?"

She lets out a shaky breath and nods, looking up at me through her lashes. I want to find out what will get her to make that soft little whimper again.

Daniel walks into the kitchen. "Why are you two alone in here?"

he asks, going to grab a glass of water and not-so-subtly stepping between me and Anne.

He is looking at me—no, glaring at me. Warning me.

"What, do we need supervision all of a sudden?" Anne asks, patting her hand dry with a towel.

"Yes, did you forget that he almost kissed you at the party? I haven't."

"I'm dating Sabrina," I state. That is a lie. I have no idea where she is. Maybe I should check up on her.

I take a bite of the second sandwich. I never thought honey would taste so good in a toasted cheese-and-tomato sandwich.

Daniel stays in the kitchen with us. "You made him a sandwich and not me?" he asks, his jaw hanging open.

"Make it yourself."

"But you promised." He jumps up on the island, sliding back. "Please make me one, little booger?"

"Not if you keep calling me that." She starts preparing another sandwich anyway, chopping all the ingredients the way I taught her. It makes me feel proud to know that I improved her in some way. Even if it is something small.

"I love you," he coos.

She huffs and throws a piece of cheese at him.

It lands on his white ripped jeans. He smiles and lifts it into his mouth. "Extra honey, pleeease."

Chapter 13

ANNE

I grab a denim jacket and my backpack and run down the stairs. Morning sunlight streams in through the windows, painting the walls in gold. "Where are you going?" A voice makes my heart jump out of my chest. Hunter lies on our living room couch.

"Nowhere." I give him a forced smile and reach for the door.

"I'll give you a ride to nowhere, then. Daniel borrowed my bike to impress some girl, so I have his car." He stands, spinning the black car keys around his index finger. The gesture is rather suggestive of something.

I hold my breath. The door swings open, and the chilled morning air cuts through me like a cold blade. "No, no, I'll walk."

"Then I'll drive beside you until you get too cold and climb in." He steps out with me and closes the door.

I spin to him, frustrated. *"Hunter."* The way I say his name is similar to last night, when he moaned playfully—and oh so sexily—in my ear.

He grins. I could stare at his face forever. There is such a kindness to his eyes when he smiles like this. "Annabelle."

"I'm walking."

He shrugs, walking past me toward Daniel's Audi, which is parked in the driveway. "I'm not stopping you. And you can't stop me from coincidentally driving beside you."

He disappears into the car. With a groan, I throw my head back and climb into the passenger seat. The warmth of the car is welcome, though I won't admit it.

Melting back against the leather seats, I turn to look at Hunter and he is already watching me. "*What?*"

He raises an eyebrow. "A location might help if I'm going to be your chauffeur, madam," he says with a fake British accent.

He can role-play, too?

Biting down on my lip, I nervously admit where I am going. "Sabrina's house. She's been MIA, but I want my shoe back. She has to meet her end of the deal." I have one shoe in my backpack. I haven't removed it from there since the other went missing.

"So, we're like, breaking in or . . ."

I turn to him, wide-eyed as he turns his head back to watch where he is reversing. He puts his arm up against my chair and I can't help but notice his black hoodie. "While you look the part, no. I'm going to ask her."

"Has that worked in the past? She doesn't seem like the type to reason."

"Well, what else can I do? We can't break-and-enter."

"Such a good girl," he teases, his voice low. I imagine him saying the same words as he pins me against the wall, in the way that he does, his arm leaning beside my head—

"I'm, uh, yeah." What? "I mean . . ." What?

His megawatt smile returns and he glances at me as he changes gears. "You're looking a bit flustered, Annabelle."

"I'm not—"

"Guess I should add that to the list of things that get you going, alongside moaning and biceps." He takes a right turn with one hand, his palm flat against the wheel. He is mesmerizing when he drives.

"Biceps, I don't..." What?

"Come on, every time I take my hoodie off, I catch you staring."

"No, I just like your tattoo."

"Ah, so shall I add tattoos to that list?"

"No!" I hit him lightly with the back of my hand, making him laugh. It causes a buzzing feeling in my chest.

After a while of silence, I realize he is not asking for directions. "How do you know where Sabrina lives?"

"I picked her up before we left for Toronto."

Ah, that's right.

"How do *you* know where she lives?" Hunter asks.

"Elias." He had her address because she threw a party at her house a few months back.

The silence settles back in for the rest of the ride, and eventually we turn into her cobblestone driveway. "So, what's the plan again? You just going to walk up and ... ask? It's 7:00 a.m."

He's making it sound like a ridiculous idea. Maybe it is.

"Do you have a plan B?"

I turn to glare at him. "Why do you ask so many questions?"

"Look." He pulls up the parking brake when we are stopped outside the iron gates and puts his hands up defensively. "If we end up in the back of a cop car by the end of the night, I just want it be for something I'm aware of beforehand."

I can't help laughing at him. He looks really, really attractive right now—that dark hoodie is doing him favors. I say, "If we end up in the back of a cop car, I promise you, I'll make it worth it."

At that, his eyes widen, leaning forward in his seat. "Yeah, how?"

I grin and open the door to the car, climbing out. "Let's hope you don't find out, right?"

"I'm calling the cops," he states, opening his door.

"Stay here, please. I've already involved you enough. Let me do this myself."

He hesitates but nods and climbs back into the car. "I'm here if you need me." He shuts the car door and switches on the radio.

I buzz the button for the gate. "Hello?" Sabrina answers, her voice sounds dull and raspy, like she's been crying.

"Uh, delivery for Sabrina," I say.

"Delivery of what?"

"Of, uh . . . Anne. It's Anne."

The dial tone goes flat. I ring again. And again. I'm not giving up—"*What?*" she asks forcefully.

"I need to talk to you—"

"No."

"—or otherwise I'll wait out here and keep ringing your buzzer. I have time."

There's a pause and then a heaved sigh. A loud beep is followed by the gate groaning open.

As I walk through the open gate, nervousness twists my stomach. Hunter is right; she could simply say no. What would I do?

A cold wind rustles the trees lining the driveway, their branches forming a canopy that leads up to the hidden house. Landscaped gardens greet me as I continue my way, filled with a vibrant array of flowers and meticulously trimmed bushes. There is a welcoming scent of blossoms. No wonder she barely noticed the house we stayed in during our trip to Toronto; this luxury is normal to her.

The downside to living in this town is that the people here have money. It's tough sometimes, when we are here on scholarships and scraping by, while almost all of the people around us are living in excess. Why does Sabrina work if she has this lifestyle?

The house comes into view. It's something that is straight out of a TV show. Resembling an ancient castle, with carvings engraved into weathering stone. Tall windows line the facade, each decorated with ornate balconies.

Ascending the stone steps, the large iron front doors are already pulled open. It seems like a lot of work to open or close them.

Inside, ceilings rise high, adorned with paintings that belong in a European museum. The floor is a stunning mosaic of marble, each tile meticulously placed. Chandeliers hang from above, each glass pendant seeming to glow. This is crazy.

Sabrina stands in the foyer, her body stuff and uncomfortable. "So, are you going to tell me why you're here?" She folds her arms across her chest.

I do not often think this, but she doesn't look great. Her hair is tied in a knot at the top of her head, looking badly unwashed. Her pajamas are stained, her eyes puffy. "Are you okay?"

She rolls her eyes. "Just tell me what you came for."

I look around the house for a second time, realizing that it is cold and empty. "Are you alone?" She sighs and starts shooing me out. "Okay, okay, I came for my shoe. I followed through with the deal. You got the date with Hunter."

That seems to make her sadder. She tugs at the collar of her pajama shirt. "I, uh ... I don't have your shoe."

The ground seems to open beneath me, nearly taking my balance. "What?" My voice is a mixture of confusion and disbelief.

"I lied." Her words hang in the air, seeming to echo off the walls tauntingly. She cringes, as if she is bracing herself for my explosion.

"No, you have it." My heart pounds like drums in my ears. I had to sit in that closet, listening to Hunter kiss her, for *what*? I refuse to believe that she made it up.

But as I search her face, the truth settles in like a lead weight in my stomach; she's not lying now.

"Why?" I ask. The question escapes me, laced with a desperation that surprises me.

"I didn't know how to get a date with Hunter. I have liked him for so long, but he follows that stupid 'no flirting with coworkers' rule, so I didn't have a chance. But then I watched him flirting with you all the time and I realized he doesn't want me . . . because he wants you."

I shake my head, even more thrown off. "He doesn't want me."

She scoffs. "*All right*, whatever. I spent the entire Toronto trip trying to keep him away from you and still he couldn't. Not even for a day. Not even for an hour."

Oh.

No—no, she's probably lying again.

"I'm sorry," she whispers. All I want is to cry. This is the only thing I have been holding on to; I have been waiting for the moment where she gives my shoe back to me.

I look up again, into the huge, empty house where she lives. I complain about my mom not being around, but I don't think she even has siblings. That must be really tough. "Are you okay? You haven't been at work."

I don't want to ask, or care.

She nods, her gaze lowering. "Yeah, I'm just studying a lot and tired all the time. I mostly went to the bakery to spend time with Hunter, but I know that's pointless now." That makes sense. She clearly wasn't working because she needs the money.

I nod, taking a step back down the stone staircase. "Bye." I don't hear if she says bye back. My head is too busy spinning, trying to figure out who has my shoe if it's not her.

I exit the iron gates, the walk back feeling a lot shorter. Hunter sits in the car, but I walk right past, trying to quell the storm of emotions.

There are tears filling my eyes, and I quickly wipe them away. Crying feels pointless—I need to think. Think! Who else would hate me enough to hurt me this badly? Who would take the one thing that I own that means something.

"Hey, you okay?" Hunter comes around the car, quickly chasing after me. "What happened?"

As soon as he asks, as soon as I see the concern in his eyes, the tears fall. He doesn't give me a chance to say anything, his arms wrapping around me in a tight, comforting hug.

My eyes fall closed. I breathe him in, my body trembling. He has the bakery smell on him. In and out, in and out, I keep taking slow deep breaths until I'm not shaking anymore. My tears eventually stop, but I don't want him to let go.

He doesn't. "What happened?" he asks again, his voice gentle.

"She doesn't have it." The admission only makes me start crying again. He sighs and squeezes me tighter.

He holds me as if he is trying to shield me from the world. His hand rubs my arm, a grounding gesture. I am so grateful that he came with me. I would be falling to pieces without him holding me.

"They just have so many memories that I don't want to let go of. Not only for my mom but for me. Like sitting on the floor in my living room, watching *Lilo and Stitch*, while my parents cuddle on the couch. Coming home from school and being greeted by the smell of the *mulukhiyah* that my mom would always make. I don't want to lose those memories." *It'll never be the same as before.*

"I understand," he says. "Sometimes there are moments we can't capture through photos. You kept those memories through those shoes."

I nod, the negative feelings starting to settle. "Please don't let go."

But he pulls back. "There's somewhere I want to take you. Get in."

"Where?"

"Trust me." He climbs into the car, and I follow.

We drive in silence, and I continually glance over at him, resisting the urge to ask him where we are going. The roads that we go down are not familiar. It starts to look more rundown as we go.

Hunter stops the car outside a small, yellowing building. The walls are crumbling, the windows cracked and broken in places. It looks like the place where someone would come to hide a body. But it's not abandoned. There is warm light pouring out of the windows, through the gaps in the curtains. Voices carry through the broken glass—children.

Climbing out the car, I take a deep breath, letting the crisp air fill my lungs as we head toward the entrance.

As we walk past the threshold, I am hit by the smell of roasted chicken. I smile, knowing that this is the smell of home to these kids, the same way the smell of my mom's food was to me.

The sounds of children playing becomes amplified, their joyous laughter mingling with the sounds of cartoons playing on a small television. On the back wall, a painted mural has started to chip. It reads DOROTHEA'S CHILDREN'S HOME.

The tiniest old lady I have ever seen, wrapped in a pink gown, shuffles up to us with determination. Her gray hair frames her face. The warmth in her eyes makes me smile. "Mr. Denegan, welcome back! It's so good to see you here again. Come in." She takes hold of his arm and leads him farther into the room, ushering him onto a couch.

She looks over to me and assess me in silence. "What's your name, my love?" Her voice is hoarse but gentle.

"Anne."

"Annabelle," Hunter corrects.

"Annabelle, it's lovely to have you here. I'll call some of the children out to greet you. They are helping out in the kitchen. I'll be right back. Could I bring you some tea or water?"

"No, thank you." As soon as she's gone, I shift closer to Hunter on the couch. He leans into me, pressing his arm against mine. "Where are we?" I ask. I see it is a children's home, but I don't understand.

"Sometimes we set our standards too high for our life. Whenever I feel like something is lacking in my life, I like to come here. It reminds me that life doesn't have to be complex. We don't have to find a soulmate, we don't have to be rich or famous, we don't have to be or do or have anything—"

Just then, a group of children run into the room. They seem to be around four to seven years old. Their clothes are torn and disheveled. All of them rush directly to Hunter, their voices cheerful as they greet him. The energy is chaotic and playful, none of them being able to stay still for a moment. It fills my heart with joy.

"Did you bring the bubbles?" one of the younger boys asks, his eyes shining.

"No, buuuut . . ." He pulls out a small bag of salted caramel chocolates from the pocket of his hoodie and they all start cheering.

He places a chocolate in each of their tiny hands. Their delight makes me want to wrap them up in a big hug and shield them from anything that might make them lose this happiness.

"This is Anne," Hunter tells the kids, and suddenly all their eyes are on me. They stay silent, assessing me to see if I am a friend.

I smile and hold out my hand for a high five. A young girl with the cutest, chubby cheeks goes for it and I quickly shift my hand out of the way, making her miss. She giggles and I put my hand up for her to try again.

When she finally hits my hand, she grins. Suddenly, all of them are rushing to me. "Me! My turn! My turn!" Their tiny voices seem to come from everywhere.

Hunter's laugh is a warm rumble that settles inside me. I wish I had a storage locker in my head for that sound.

"Everyone, make a line if you want a turn," Hunter instructs, and they quickly listen.

By the time we leave, it's nearly midnight. After playing with the children, the caretaker insisted that we join them for a meal. It's incredible how the people who barely have anything to give are the most generous. My mood has improved tenfold. I hope I can come back here often. Those children are all filled with an infectious, bubbling happiness.

The car is comfortably silent on drive back to my house. Hunter rolls the windows down, sensual R and B music playing. Cool wind dances through my hair and against my skin.

Looking over, I realize his shoulders are less tense, too. Maybe he needed this just as much as I did. Frown lines are etched on his face, his concentration is on the road because of the lack of streetlamps in some areas.

If I were his girlfriend, I wonder if he would protectively... He notices me staring and grins, reaching over to gently squeeze my thigh. My cheeks flush and I bite down on my lip, excitement fluttering in my stomach.

When we eventually park the car in my driveway, Hunter lifts the handbrakes and pushes the center console backward to remove anything between us. He takes in a deep breath, which inadvertently calms me, and then pulls me into his arms.

Scared of ruining the moment, I don't say a word. My body sinks against him. I feel safe and understood.

"Did that help?" He runs his hand over my hair.

I nod, noticing that the heaviness from earlier is no longer sitting in my chest. "You're right. When we see the challenges others face, we realize that this world and this life isn't about us. It is not about the material things, but about helping where we can and enjoying the people in our lives. I focused so much on the shoe that I forgot what the shoe represented: family and creating memories."

Hunter gently kisses my temple.

My eyes fall closed. "Thank you," I whisper.

He places another slow kiss, a little way below my temple. His lips are warm. His finger tilts my face upward for him to place another slow kiss against my cheek.

"Hunter?" I look up. One look from him and the rest of the world starts to fall away like shattered glass. He is the most incredible person I know. I really, really want to tell him that I love him. I want to say it out loud for the first time in my life and see what happens next, but I won't because I'm terrified of how he might respond.

"Annabelle."

He's looking at me like he can see everything that I am thinking. Maybe he feels it too. Is it possible that what Sabrina said, about him liking me, could be true? The likelihood of it feels improbable, but what if?

My lips part. Okay, I can do it. I can say it. Three, two, one. "I—"

He dips his head and presses his lips to mine. A shockwave goes through me.

My eyes fall closed. Every thought in my mind quiets. All I can focus on is the sensation of his lips, how inexplicably addictive they feel. They are as soft as I imagined. His hand cups my cheek, then slides behind my neck to pull me closer and increase the pressure of the kiss. He groans against my lips, the vibrations reminding me that this is, indeed, real.

Every video I watched on how to kiss flies out the window. I let him lead. He playfully grazes my bottom lip between his teeth. I sigh. *Yes.*

He pulls away slowly, his hooded eyes watching me for a reaction. Immediately, I want him to do *that* again. A soft whimper leaves my lips and I try to lean in for more.

He bites his lip, shifting back to create some distance. With a strained voice, he says, "Daniel is going to kill me. I'm kissing his sister in his car."

Slowly, unable to resist, he leans forward, capturing my lips again.

Chapter 14

HUNTER

There has been a light, playful energy between us ever since I kissed Anne nearly a week ago, but now it's Friday, and, as promised, I am teaching Anne how to make cookies.

The bakery kitchen is clean. We closed an hour ago, and so far, all I've learned is that she should stay far away from the kitchen.

"I didn't know it was salt," she argues. She playfully bats her eyelashes at me.

"And what excuse do you have for burning the first batch?"

"You said bake it for fifteen minutes. I thought sixteen minutes wouldn't be that much of a difference."

I slide my hand over my face. "We're doing this again and you're going to do *exactly* what I say. Got it?"

She grazes her teeth along her bottom lip, causing them to turn darker. "Yes, sir."

We step away from each other. Our eyes remain locked. "Hopefully this time it'll turn out good."

"Yeah, hopefully." Her voice is flat. She looks down at the tiled floor and tucks her hair behind her ear. Something about the way she is acting seems strange.

"Annabelle." I move closer, place my index finger under her chin and tilt her face up to look at me. "Did you sabotage those cookies on purpose?"

Her cheeks flood with color. "No! It was a mistake."

"I think you're lying," I say. She starts backing away, closer to the door. "What are you hiding?"

She holds her hands up. "Nothing."

I grab her wrists and pin her back against the door. This position makes me feel powerful. Her breathing shakes.

I let go of her hands, dip my head down, and press my lips against her neck. I've been wanting to do that the entire day, from the moment she showed up at school with her hair braided, giving me the perfect opportunity to trail kisses along her skin.

Her lips part and she releases a small gasp—maybe a moan. I don't know, but it is so sexy.

Her hand slides up my biceps, over my shoulder and up into my hair as my face aligns with hers. I slowly inch closer to her, unable to resist the force pulling our lips together.

Once could be a "slipup," a lack of control. But twice. Three times. That is a choice.

If I do this, I won't want to stop. I could lose Daniel as a friend. He could find out about this and I'm not sure he would forgive me for kissing the one girl he asked me not to.

Though I want her pressed against the wall, with her lips on mine, I step back. My jaw clenches tight. It takes a lot of restraint to say, "We shouldn't."

Daniel is a brother to me. He has been by my side through the hardest times of my life and has kept me going without knowing it.

"I . . . I know." She closes her eyes and tilts her head back.

"Let's try this again." I point to the bowl that is now coated in different ingredients from the first two batches. "Rinse the bowl, then mix the ingredients, like I showed you."

She bends over to grab the salt and sugar from the drawer, an unnecessary but highly appreciated action. Sliding the ingredients onto the counter, she turns to face me. "I like it when you tell me what to do."

"Stop," I say, my voice strained. She is still beautiful and if she keeps teasing me like this I—

She turns to face me and tilts her head to the side, trailing her fingers gently down the side of her neck. "I-I like neck kisses."

"Yeah?" It stirs something inside me, bringing my thoughts to places they shouldn't be. *"No."*

After rinsing the bowl, she throws the salt, sugar and butter in and whisks it. I take an egg from the carton and hand it to her. "Show me how you do it?" she asks.

"I crack it against the side of the bowl. You've seen me do it a hundred times." I step behind her and hold my hand over hers. "Just bang it," I whisper in her ear. That was probably the worst attempt at flirting I have ever made. What is going on with me? I create some distance between us, not wanting to take this too far.

With a sigh, she cracks the egg. "Next?"

She already knows. "Add a teaspoon of vanilla extract, mix until it's slightly creamy, but be careful not to overmix it." She nods, continuing to follow my instructions.

After making the cookie dough, I place it in the fridge to sit. That always improves the flavor, which results in more sales by the end of the day.

Anne's phone buzzes in her pocket, stealing her attention. There's a smile on her face as she responds, her fingers rapidly tapping against the screen.

I run a hand through my hair, feeling frustrated. "Who are you talking to?"

"Someone I met at the party," she replies.

"Who is he?" I hope she says it isn't a "he."

"Jaden Maddox. He was the host of the party. He asked me out."

"Is he in your class?" *I don't like the sound of him.*

"Is it important?"

I thought our kiss meant something to her... "I don't want you to get hurt. It's my job to protect you."

"That's what I have three brothers for. You don't have to protect me."

I lean down and press my forehead against hers, the action gentle but possessive. "You think that's going to stop me?" My voice is low.

She sighs, her eyes squeezing closed. She places her hands on my chest to try and move me away. "We can't do this to Daniel. That kiss—" She looks up, her big brown eyes pleading with me. "I know flirting means nothing to you. I can see that you regret kissing me. Maybe you did it because you felt bad for me, or it was just the heat of the moment. It's okay, just admit it, and let me move on."

"Move on?" Does she truly believe I regret kissing her?

"Be honest. Tell me you don't want me." Those two sentences are complete opposites.

"But—" *I care about you*, I want to say. Her kindness, her humor, her inability to hide her feelings. She forgives so easily and loves so deeply. When I see her in the stands, cheering on her brother, I get to see what it is like to truly care for someone without reservation. Her eyes are filled with pride and excitement, and in those moments, I wish I could be the one she was cheering for.

And that is why she is asking me to reject her. The love she has for her family is stronger than anything else. I run my tongue over my lips, frowning. I wish I didn't understand her, because then I wouldn't have to say my next words.

"I don't want you." *Can she tell that I am lying?* With a deep, shaky breath, I add, "You're not my type. I just—I felt bad for you. I could see you falling for me, but *this* is never going to happen. I tried, but I am not attracted to you, and I don't see us realistically being together. I'm sorry." I sigh, as if relieved to get it off my chest, but truly it is because everything feels like it is shrinking, and my lungs can't take it.

Her expression crumples, as though I've struck her. Pain and disbelief swim in her glistening eyes. Instantly, I want to take all my words back. I don't want to see her in pain like this, because I know what it feels like to be on the other end of hurtful words. Sometimes they cut deeper than a blade.

My hands ball into fists as I force myself to stay in place and not hug her. She is trying to hide her feelings, but as always, they are as clear as day: I broke her heart.

"Thank you." Her voice breaks. "I needed to hear that."

"I'm sorry," I whisper. I made her cry. "I'm *sorry*." *Can I take it all back?*

"This is good." She nods, forcing a small smile onto her face. It doesn't last longer than a second before falling.

My foot taps restlessly on the ground, not knowing what to do. I don't know how to make it hurt less. Everything happened so quickly, I barely had any time to prepare—and now it is too late to reach out and hold her.

I clear my throat. "The cookie dough should be ready soon."

"I did mess up the first two batches on purpose. I wanted to spend more time with you," she says, her voice a quiet whisper. A tear slips down her cheek and she quickly brushes it away. "I have to go."

I don't understand. She *told me* to do this.

She glances at me once before walking out. The door whines as it swings shut, like it is trying to call her back. I suck in a deep breath, but it feels suffocating.

This is my fault. I kept teasing her and flirting. I should have made it clear from the start that we would never be together. It was never possible between us—and that kiss was the cherry on top of a terrible cake. This was built to fail, right? I simply pushed it over.

The cookies come out of the oven perfectly: warm and soft, and dotted with the chocolate chips. They smell as heavenly as they taste. I can picture the way Anne's eyes light up as she bites into these, her laughter and voice filling the silence. The thought deepens the ache in my chest.

After setting them aside, not wanting the reminder in sight, I clean the coffee machine and the counters. My body moves automatically, my mind checked out in a replay of what just happened. Over and over, I see her face fall.

My dad is right: I am a disappointment to everyone I care about.

I lock up the bakery, the twisting of the key in the door feeling too final.

The roads are silent, aside from the rustling of trees and distant music playing. Laughter carries through the streets, along with the bells of cyclists messing around with their friends. My motorbike roars to life, making me feel a little bit less alone.

When I arrive home, the booming sound of my father's laughter fills the dark entryway. The pungent smell of cigarettes greets me. As soon as the door clicks shut, the laughter stops. The television broadcasts the latest news, lighting up my father's eyes with the imagery of a recent forest fire.

"Welcome home, boy."

"Why were you laughing?" I eye the television. A woman stands on screen, discussing the evacuations that are underway.

"This country. This world. It's all so messed up. It's a joke."

"But there is some good to the world, right?" *Right?*

I need something to hold on to.

"If you want me to say you're the good in my life, stop being an idiot." His words drain me of any energy I had left. "Just for once, I wish you would be the kind of son I could brag about. What can I tell my friends? That my son makes great *cupcakes*?" *He doesn't have friends.*

The painful weight that had been in my chest triples in size, making it hard to remain standing. I nod and close my eyes. "Do you want a bottle?"

"Darn fucking right." I take a beer for my father and a glass of water for myself. "I don't want to see you for the rest of the day."

This is the kind of shitty parenting that creates serial killers. I want to smash everything until I'm sitting in a room that is completely ruined.

Usually, I'd go to Anne or Daniel, but I can't—not after what just happened. I turn and make my way up the stairs to my bedroom with the bottle of vodka in one hand and a glass of water in the other. A low growl leaves my lips. I *refuse* to let him win.

I shut my bedroom door and catch my reflection in the mirror. My head, and my vision, are clouded. All I can see is a blurred shape staring back at me through the tears that I will not let free. I don't want to feel this way anymore. My hand shakes as I drop the glass to the ground.

The water and glass pool around my feet.

Those kids in the children's home help me; their joy and laughter are infectious. They always look on the bright side, yet here I am struggling to see anything but shadows.

His disapproval casts darkness over bright moments, but now—when everything already feels low ... I can't bear it.

I stare at the white wall beside my bedroom door. It's rough and textured. I slam my fists against it. "I." Slam. "Hate." Slam. "You." Slam. I keep going, over and over again, until I can't feel my fists. A low rumble leaves my lips as I breathe through the searing pain. "Ah!"

I stare at my red knuckles, my breathing hard. My phone vibrates, and I pull it out of my back pocket. "Hello?"

"Hey, guess what?" Daniel shouts. "We won the football game tonight and I was approached by a scout. He wants to take me to dinner next week!"

"Nice! We should go out to celebrate."

Daniel chuckles lowly. "Oh, I have two hot celebrations on each arm right now."

I want to ask him to meet me; to tell him about my father and that I might like his sister. Even when I try, the words refuse to leave my mouth.

"Will you be my wingman tonight?" I ask instead.

His line is silent for a while. "Hell yeah, man! Meet me outside." He ends the call.

The connection I had with Anne means nothing now. It could never have been anything more than a good friendship, anyway. I should not feel bad for finding another girl. I let water pour over my bloody knuckles until they go numb, then I slip gloves on them to hide the damage from Daniel.

Slipping the hoodie over my head, an image of Anne pops into my head. She's wearing my hoodie, the sleeves too long for her short arms. The joy in her expression is—stop. This has to stop.

Pain tugs at my heart. Tonight will be good. It will stop me from thinking. That's all I can do until I have enough money to leave this house. It's for the best.

Huffing, I slide my gloved hands over my torso. The black hoodie and dark fingerless gloves make me look like those underground fighters. It feels wrong because I have never fought for anything—not even for myself.

Catching myself in the mirror again, I don't recognize myself. I *hate* what I see. Because the thoughts in my head weren't put there by me.

I climb down the window to avoid my father and the glass on my floor. My foot slips and I fall hard against the ground. Daniel laughs. I rise from the ground and glare at him. He leans against his Audi—where I kissed Anne—wearing a black leather jacket. Two girls stand with him, both smiling at me.

"What kind of girl are you looking for?" He points to the redhead on one side of him. She's got patterned tattoo sleeves up both arms. "Bianca." He points to the other girl. "Annoying."

The second girl, who is around five feet with pitch-black hair, slaps him against the arm. "Shut up," she mumbles, but she's smiling. She must be into him. "I'm Cass."

I'm looking for a girl with long brown hair, bushy eyebrows, stubborn as hell.

I grin and hold my arm out for Bianca, who happily slinks up beside me. In this dark outfit, I feel like I belong next to her. She has a mysterious, attractive aura about her.

When I glance toward the house, a curtain is quickly pulled

closed. Was that her? Did Anne see me with someone else already? Did this push the knife in further? I am a terrible person.

Running a hand over my face, I ask, "How fast can we get to somewhere loud and dark?"

Is this what escaping feels like? I don't like it, but wallowing would be much worse.

"You all right?" Daniel is suddenly concerned, knowing me well enough to sense that something is off.

"Yeah, *yeah*—but dinner with a scout? That is huge. Congratulations." I hope it didn't come off obvious that I am switching the subject. I am not going to talk about it, especially not around strangers.

He beams, not noticing. "I can't believe it."

"I can. You have worked hard for this. I didn't doubt you for a second."

"Thanks."

"My friend is at a party. Maybe we could start over there?" Cass suggests, tugging at Daniel's jacket to try and get his attention back on her.

"Yeah, what do you say?" Daniel asks me.

"Perfect."

My chest feels heavy when we reach the party, the deep bass from the music reverberating through me before I can step out of the car. Daniel manages to find a parking close to the house, and we walk inside together.

This is the perfect escape—dark and loud, the air thick with the smell of sweat and cigarettes. Enveloping me like a thick fog, there is no space in here to think or feel. Lights casts shadows across the walls.

There are so many people, yet I can't help but feel isolated. I wonder if any of them feel the same way I do—empty and aching. It doesn't look like it; everyone seems to be having the time of their lives. Groups are gathered, playing games, and raising their red Solo cups. It only brings back memories of Anne, our *almost* kiss.

She must think I am ashamed of her, not wanting to kiss her in front of anyone and then telling her it means nothing when I kiss her in the dark.

Turning back, I stop in my tracks, realizing I was so lost in my thoughts that I got separated from Daniel and the girls.

Fine, I guess I am on my own. Searching the crowd, I see a blond girl in a skintight pink dress. Her hips sway slowly, mesmerizing. That should be my type, I suppose.

Heading toward her, she turns and catches my gaze. Instantly I am drawn to her bright smile. She seems happy. "Would it be too forward of me to ask you for a dance?"

"You know, I have been waiting for someone to be forward with me all night."

Before I know it, we're body to body, our faces close. She leans up on her toes and kisses my cheek, then smiles at me playfully.

Tucking some of her soft hair behind her ear, I lean down and kiss her cheek back. She bites her lip, telling me she likes it, so I stop dancing and slip my hand behind her neck and kiss her just like I kissed … come on, get out of my head, Annabelle. Please, I can't do this.

Though I should be lost in the moment, this no longer feels right. Pulling back, I am gone before she has the chance to open her eyes. That might make me a terrible person, but it's okay because I have already accepted this about myself.

Stepping out the front door, I lean against the cool brick wall, finally able to breathe again without the horrid smell of cigarettes and alcohol. It reminds me too much of home.

"Are you going to tell me what's up with you?" Daniel stands on the other end of the door, the two girls not around. I hadn't noticed him in the dim lighting.

"What do you mean?" I play dumb. My arms fold across my chest as I try to mask myself.

His dark, angled eyebrows furrow together, casting a shadow over his eyes. "You know exactly what I mean." He steps closer to me, his gaze piercing, like he can read my thoughts.

"Just tired from school, that's all." I shrug, wearing a smile that doesn't quite stick. I am not admitting to anything about my father. I am not ready. Daniel's pity would be too much to bear. He is the only one with an ounce of respect left for me.

My focus turns to a group of people standing outside and laughing together.

Daniel sighs and walks closer to me, blocking my view of the group. He tilts his head, not saying a word. I know what he is doing—he told me about it once. When you stay silent and make direct eye contact, people usually continue speaking out of intimidation or to fill the silence.

Well, two can play that game. I tilt my head and stare, unblinking.

Rolling his eyes, Daniel says. "I only taught you this trick because I never thought I'd have to use it on you." He sits upright. "Come on, man, you can tell me anything."

Anything, *except* that I'm in love with his sister. Anything, except that I've been hiding my living situation from him for as long as I've known him. There are exceptions to his words.

"I've just been having trouble sleeping. My dad has been drinking a lot, so he never stops shouting . . . at the TV." *And I think I broke your sister's heart into a million pieces and it's tearing me apart because I lied about my feelings.* Every time I think about what happened, I realize there is a chance she said those things because she wanted me to fight for her.

"Come stay over at my place, then. You know you're always welcome."

I can't see *her*. "I'm going to stay at George's place, but if things change, I'll come to yours."

He nods. "Well, listen, I don't know if there is more to it, but just know that I have got your back." The corners of his lips lift. "Seriously, you are my brother. I've got your back."

For a moment, those words make me feel at ease.

Chapter 15

ANNE

Leaning against my headboard, I spend my cozy Sunday morning grinning at my phone. After the incident with Hunter on Friday, I've been texting Jaden to distract myself. It worked. We're going on a real date! It will be my first.

Thundering footsteps come toward me from several directions. All three of my brothers stop at the foot of my bed. Their eyes are wide as they silently gesture around with their hands. They are not making any sense.

Dropping my phone to the side, I ask, "What?"

"Mom's here. She found dad's wedding invite," Haiz explains.

"What?" Wedding invite? "How did she get it?"

Adam and Daniel glare at Haiz. His expression is what I would imagine a sulking puppy looks like.

I climb out of bed, ruffle his dark hair and step past him. "How is she handling it?"

"We haven't gone in to find out," Adam admits. "We're not good at consoling people."

All three of them usher me toward the end of the hall, where her bedroom is. The wooden door is closed. There is no crying coming from the other side, which is a good start.

"*Go*," they whisper in unison.

"You guys are idiots," I mumble, knocking on my mom's bedroom door. When there is no response, I push the door open and peek my head in. She is covered in blankets. A cream-and-gold-colored card lies on her lap. "Mama, are you okay?"

"Come in." She sits up against the headboard and pats the bed. I walk inside and take a seat on her bed, folding my legs. "*Yallah!* All of you!"

My brothers come out of their hiding place behind the door, and walk into the room, flinging themselves onto the bed.

"What do you know about my past?"

"You were a stripper in Egypt," Haiz says, not missing a heartbeat.

Adam hits him. "You can't say that!"

"Why not? It's true." He hits Adam back, causing him to almost fall off the bed.

"I was a *dancer*, not a stripper." My mom smiles, the softness of her skin making her smile lines seem deeper. She looks at me. "I would like to tell you a new hekayat." Another one of her stories. "You remember those, *mish keda*?" *Isn't that right?*

Of course I do. I never want to forget them. My brothers seem to feel the same way.

I can't find it in me to tell her about the shoe. Not yet.

My mom places the wedding invitation down in the middle of the bed. "Here is a new one. But before I tell it, I want all four of you to agree to go to the wedding."

"Not a chance." Daniel stands from the bed and starts pacing. He runs a hand through his black hair. "No. No way."

"Your father isn't a bad man. When he was with me, he always made me feel special, but I could tell he was a heartbreaker. He was a lot like you, Daniel. A charmer."

Daniel frowns and leans against the wall near the door. "I'm not like Dad. I would never do what he did."

"Mmmh." She smiles knowingly, leaning her head back against the headboard. "It's a small town. I have young girls recognizing me in the hospital and asking about my handsome son."

"How do you know they're not talking about Haiz?" Daniel retorts.

Haiz nods his head, looking smug. "Can you blame them?"

"I'm nothing like Dad," says Daniel, defending himself.

"He's a good man."

"He—!"

"Fine, Mom, we'll go to the wedding." I give Daniel a warning look, widening my eyes to tell him to stop talking. She doesn't need a reminder of how Dad broke her heart into a million tiny pieces. If she has closed that door and forgiven him, then we can, too. I shift up beside her and lean my head against hers. She smells like rose water. "Tell us the story." She hasn't in a while; she hasn't had the time.

"Your father and I met when I was working as a *dancer*"—she looks pointedly at Haiz—"at an event."

"Event? Was it a bachelor party?" Haiz jokes.

Adam hits Haiz again. Haiz hits him back. Again.

Ignoring them, my mom says, "Your father was with his friend, talking in French about me. I decided to buy him and his friend a drink and serve it to them. Gosh, the way he spoke was sexy and he was so tall and—"

"Mom." Adam cringes.

"Ah, *okay, okay*. He told his friend, in French, that I was 'his' for the night. So, I told him *dans tes rêves*. In your dreams. He almost fell off his chair, because he had spent the whole night saying the dirtiest things about me. Most girls in Egypt could barely speak English, let alone French."

"How did you learn French?" I ask. I barely know English sometimes. Like when I have to spell "necessary."

"Before I left home, I was at a very good school. I'll always be grateful to my parents for that." She takes my hand in hers. "Anyway, back to the story. Your father came back almost every night to see me perform. I was so used to being alone in the world, that having him there with me made me feel so lucky. He never took his eyes off me when we were together. And ah, he was a—oh, right, that's not appropriate." She pulls her bottom lip into her mouth.

Her words remind me of how, at the party I attended, I was sitting outside feeling alone with my notebook as my companion—writing and lost in my own world. Then Hunter came to sit beside me and asked me about it. He genuinely cared. It made me feel important. He has always made me feel special.

The thought makes my heart feel like it's being crushed by a bulldozer.

"There are so many memories that I will always treasure, like the nights when we used to dance in the rain. We had you three and moved to America together. I got to experience what it is like to have a family, thanks to him. He kept me going on days where I thought I couldn't get out of bed. I'm not fibbing when I say your father truly is a good man. He just ended up falling for a tiny blond American girl. But that doesn't mean he didn't give me a lifetime of happiness."

My mother takes in a shaking breath. "I know you're angry. I was, too. But anger hurts you, more than it hurts the person you're angry at. Try to forgive him, please."

A knock comes from downstairs, but I don't move. As long as

my mom is at home, I'm not leaving her side. I have so much to learn from her, and hopefully more stories to hear.

"Probably Hunter," Daniel says, turning to leave.

What? I shift in my spot, moving closer to my mom like that will protect me. I haven't seen him since the bakery.

It's only been a day and a half, but it feels like forever. I miss him. I miss the feeling of knowing he'd come to me if I needed him.

Is he in pain, too? Or is it only my heart that feels like it is bruised and torn apart? Seeing him with his arm around another girl hours after turning me down made me feel certain that my feelings have always been one-sided.

But I'm not leaving my mom's side. He wouldn't come to her room, so I know I am safe here.

My mom watches Haiz, Adam, and me. A calming silence settles over us for a while. "Will you please make sure Daniel goes with you to the wedding? It is important that you keep up a relationship with your father." She presses a kiss to my temple. "And your father gave me the four greatest gifts I could have ever asked for—my babies. For that, I am grateful."

Her words are kind and comforting, but there is pain in her expression. Maybe the wedding will be good—a chance for us to heal old wounds and move forward without carrying this pain any longer.

•••

Daniel's car comes to a stop outside a quaint café, where I am meeting Jaden for our date.

It is nestled on a cobblestone street, quite far from home. Jaden claims it has the best food and coffee for miles. He is a bit of a coffee junkie—bringing his own imported blends to school sometimes—so I trust his opinion on it.

I climb out the car, almost falling onto the ground. The temperature has taken a deep decline. I pull my coat closer around my body. "Thanks, bye." I shut the car door.

Daniel jumps out, watching me with amusement. "Nice try." He follows me toward the entrance. "What is this kid's name?"

"Please don't ruin this date for me."

"What's his name?"

"It's Bitéme." I try to say it with a French accent.

"Tell me his name."

"Jaden."

"Oh, Jaden? The dorky little one. Okay, we don't have a problem." He starts walking back to his car. His hair blows into his face in the wind. "Text me and I'll come fetch you."

The air is warm and cozy inside the café. There is a soft buzz created by voices and keyboards clicking. The strong, bitter smell of coffee hits my nose. Local art has been hung up on the walls.

Jaden stands up and waves from the back of the café, a big smile on his face. His bright red glasses sit on the bridge of his nose. I reach the table and he pulls me into a tight hug, squeezing the air out of my lungs. He smells expensive, hints of wood and leather. "You look beautiful," he says, admiring my cream coat and black boots.

To be completely honest, I had no idea what to wear or how to prepare, and now I have no idea what to say.

"Thanks for asking me out . . ."

The cushions on the chair melt as we take our seats. "Is this your first time going on a date?" he asks.

"Why would you think that?" *Is it that obvious?*

"It's my first time. I wasn't sure what the protocol was, so I came an hour early and I'm pretty sure the waitress thought I got stood up. She brought me a brownie." He points at a chocolate brownie that is topped with melting ice cream. Chocolate sauce has been drizzled over the plate. It makes my mouth water.

"Yes, it's my first time, too," I admit. "I took two showers before coming."

He chuckles. "You smell like flowers."

My heart flutters. The waitress walks up to our table with a friendly smile. "Welcome to Café Ine. Can I take your orders?"

"Order whatever you want. It's on me," Jaden says.

"You don't have to—"

"I insist."

"All right." I'm not going to argue with free food. "Could I get a Hawaiian pizza and a hot chocolate, please?" Hunter pops into my mind. He once joked that he thinks pineapples could easily be weaponized and should not be sold to the public. I teased him, saying that if he ever makes me mad, I am going to throw pineapples at him. *I need to stop thinking about him.*

"I'll get a margherita pizza and a glass of water." The waitress nods and takes the menus. "Thank you." He slides the chocolate brownie between us and hands me a spoon.

"Dessert first?" I take a bite of the brownie. The warm, sugary flavor melts into my mouth. The taste is comforting and sweet. "I like this date already."

"Good, because we will be doing it often." He winks.

I smile and lick a tiny bit of ice cream off my finger. After another bite, I say, "You know, my friend Hunter makes amazing brownies. One taste and you're in heaven." *I have to get him off my mind. I'm on a date with another guy!* "Anyway, what do you like to do for fun?"

"Hunter Denegan is your friend? Oh, right, because of your brother," he says, as if there's no way I could be friends with Hunter otherwise. "I heard he has never had a girlfriend before. I guess girls will continue to dream about being his first. Everyone wants his hoodies. He should open a store—"

"Do *you* have a crush on him?" I tease.

He shrugs. "No." When I don't respond, he keeps talking. "His hoodies do look comfortable, though." *They are.*

"Can we talk about something else?" It was my mistake bringing Hunter up in the first place.

"Yeah, sorry."

The waitress comes and places our pizzas on the table. "Thank you. This looks good." He reaches across the table to hold my hand, making it hard to eat. "Your hands are so soft."

"Thanks." I put a ton of lotion on before I came. I had to after taking two showers. When I pull my hand out of his, the warmth from his touch stays.

Pulling a slice of pizza, the cheese stretches and I bite into it. Italians would hate everything about this, but it tastes so good. The savoury flavor is a strong contrast to the sweetness of the brownie.

The satisfying crunch of the crust occasionally breaks the silence between us. A few children weave through tables, playing catch. A radio station softly plays the latest music.

After finishing the entire pizza, I lean back into my seat, feeling full. "That was *good*."

Jaden talks as he finishes his pizza. Slowly, his words begin to twist a knot in my stomach. "—and we could skip to the part where we sit together and read books like an old couple. We can make out without having to think about whether we're good kissers," he says. "Everyone wants that new, deeply-in-love stage of a relationship, but I want the comfortable, cuddle-on-a-rainy-day stage of a relationship."

He wipes his hand with a wet wipe from the table and moves his chair closer to mine. The chair loudly scrapes against the floor, causing people to look over at us. He awkwardly waves at the people who are staring.

"You're a dork," I tease.

He leans closer to me. His dark hair falls onto his face a little. The hollows of his cheeks are prominent. "Kiss me."

"What?"

"Let's skip the awkward phase. Kiss me," he says. This is weird. Maybe in a good way? It's new having someone so clearly wanting to kiss me without hesitation. I lean closer and brush his hair away from his face. "I know we don't know each other so well, but I'm starting to really, really like you. I'm going to fall hard, I can feel it."

I pull away fast. *"Huh?"*

The thought of a serious future with anyone other than Hunter feels terrifying. The ideas I had of what my future would look like suddenly feel so out of reach. My chest tightens like a cloth being wrung out.

He shrugs, noticing my sudden discomfort. "What?"

It feels like I've eaten a slug and it's gotten stuck in my throat. This was supposed to be a distraction. I didn't think it would feel so real so quickly. "You barely know me."

"I-I know you love the color blue." *Turquoise.* "I know that you like history and theories. I've overheard you speaking to that red-headed girl." *Creepy.* "I know that you're fascinating, and I can't wait to know more about you. I even—"

"Do you have my shoe?"

He leans back, looking at me like there's a spider crawling out of my eyeball. "Your shoe?"

"It went missing from my locker at school. I thought I knew who took it, but now I have no idea. It sounds crazy, but . . ."

He is looking at me like he most definitely thinks I am crazy.

I hold my face in my hands. "I should go." I get up from my seat.

Heart pounding, I rush out without looking back. I had imagined a first date would be awkward, but that . . . gosh. I feel sad and overwhelmed, and now Jaden is going to be another obstacle in the way of a normal school day.

Chapter 16

HUNTER

Anne went on a date yesterday.

My grip tightens on the baking tray in my hands. Daniel was talking about how excited she was when he dropped her off. Her first date. My mind has been on overdrive, wondering what she wore and if it went well and if, maybe, he kissed her. What if she liked kissing him? What if she can't wait to kiss him again? I thought coming to work would help distract me from thinking about her, and her dumb date, but it hasn't. *Whatever.* She can kiss whoever she wants. She's not mine.

Today I am making something that I haven't made in years; koeksisters. I found my grandma's recipe in one of the kitchen drawers when I was still living in South Africa, and I kept it, along with a few other recipes of hers. The last time I tasted it was when I was eight years old. It's a special doughy type of dessert, which is very popular in Cape Town.

I gather all the ingredients needed for my recipe. There's no salt left, probably because Anne poured it all into the cookies she was trying to make.

George steps out of his office. His dark hair is streaked with gray. The brown corduroy pants hanging around his waist seem looser than normal. "Are you okay, George?" He's one of the few reasons I love this town.

"Are you surviving this Monday, kiddo?" George places a hand on my shoulder. His wire-framed glasses sit low on his nose. "I'm paying Sabrina and Anne today. I'll give you your salary next week, all right?" I nod. George likes to pay his employees in cash. He jokes, saying it makes him feel like a drug dealer.

"All right, no problem. I'm heading to the store quickly to get some ingredients," I say. I need to buy salt, but more importantly, I need to get out of here. Anne's shift is starting soon, and I am not ready to see her yet.

I managed to avoid her at school today, but it will be much harder to avoid her here.

In the front of the bakery, the wooden counter is lined with cookies, biscuits, cupcakes, cinnamon rolls, croissants, and more. This weekend, I have spent my time taking all my feelings out on a rolling pin. It is the best way to ease my mind. When I am focused on a recipe, everything feels lighter. I forget the world for a while.

I need to make a pit stop at Sabrina's house on my way to the store. If she is getting paid by George, then she should be working and earning it.

After walking to Sabrina's place, I push the button at the gate several times. I could have taken my bike, but I wanted to walk. I wanted to feel the cold that seeps into my bones. The numbing sensation is welcomed.

"Hello?" her voice comes from the other side.

"Hey, it's Hunt—" The beep of the gate button being pressed

cuts me off, and the gate slides open for me. When I reach the end of the driveway, Sabrina is already waiting for me at the door.

She's wearing a short black dress, her hair tied up. She looks good. "What are you doing here?" she asks.

My eyes slowly trail over her. I take the first step up to her house, watching her without a word. When I take the next step up, and she shifts forward, positioning herself at the edge of the top step so that her face is aligned with mine.

"How are you?" I ask.

She watches me curiously, saying nothing. She usually talks a lot when we're alone.

"Are you okay?" I ask again, questioning myself for randomly showing up here.

She nods but then shrugs, stepping back. "Why are you here, Hunter?"

Did I really come solely to tell her to come back to work? Surely, I could have texted her that, if it was the only reason that I came ... she always makes me feel good, and I need to feel good. "I wanted to kiss you."

"Huh?" Her eyebrows furrow in confusion. She looks like she wants to say more, her lips parting, but she hesitates and remains silent. The air between us suddenly feels heavy.

"You don't want to kiss me?" That strikes a chord, sending a rush of heat to my cheeks. I am standing here and humiliating myself.

"Of course, I do." She lifts her arms, exasperated. "I just don't want you thinking about someone else while you do."

"I'm not thinking about Anne."

She takes another step back, folding her arms. "I didn't say her name, you did—but thank you for admitting it."

Shit. Groaning, I run a hand down my face. Looking at her dress again, I ask, "So you don't want to kiss me now?" She has suspected something between me and Anne for a while, but it has not stopped her before. "What changed?"

She looks anywhere but at me, tucking a few strands of baby hairs behind her ear. "My dad cheated on my mom. He's been in love with someone else for a long time—before my parents even married—and we all knew, but he never did anything about it until . . . now."

"I'm so sorry." I step up to the top step to hug her, and she lets me.

"Whatever, I don't care," she says, though I suspect that might be a lie. "I don't want to end up like my mom. She has been MIA and my dad's gone off with the other woman and I just—it feels like they forgot that they have a kid."

My fists clench, a part of me relating to that feeling of being forgotten. I wonder where my mom is now, if she ever thinks of me, or if I am simply a distant memory in her mind. I blame my dad a lot, but it wasn't only him. "Selfish people shouldn't have kids," I say, the words laced with a bitter tone.

"At some point or the other, we all act selfishly." Her expression turns sheepish, guilty for how she manipulated me and Anne. There is a vulnerability to her words when she says, "The reason I'm telling you is so you choose to be with someone you love before it's too late. Make better decisions than my dad did."

I roll my eyes. "I am not in love with her." She makes it sound so straightforward, but this is real life. It's way more complicated than that. "Daniel would never be okay with it."

"Fight for it, Hunter."

She's actually not so bad. "I need to get back to work. You should come back if you can." At least I know why she hasn't been around.

With everything going on between her parents, it is understandable. "You'll call me if you need a friend, right?"

She grins at that. "I sure will."

On my way back, I stop to get the salt and a few other ingredients as I intended, and then make it back to the bakery before sunset.

The jazz music softly flowing through the bakery and the familiar scent of pastries puts my heart at ease, until I see Anne standing behind the counter, helping two customers. *She's here.* A strange feeling rises within me, tightening around my throat like a rope.

This place that I always come to for comfort is now the same place I want to run from.

"Thank you. That will be seventeen dollars and sixty cents," she says, her tone of voice a lot more polite than usual. The customers pay and exit the shop.

I grab a cookie from the glass jar on the counter, watching her. I bite into it. It tastes fresh and perfectly sweet.

Anne fidgets with her fingers, her eyes darting around the empty bakery, but eventually they find their way back to me. Silence settles between us.

I smile, knowing my teeth are covered in the chocolate chips from the cookie. It causes a small smile to appear on her face. *Jackpot.*

"Where were you?" she asks.

"Did you miss me?" I'm trying to play it cool, but I'm so nervous. I lean forward against the counter.

"It wasn't too busy. Most of the customers wanted coffee and cinnamon rolls. Did you make all of these today?" She gestures to the range of pastries.

I lean over the counter and bring our faces closer together, "You didn't answer my question."

She smells incredibly good. Leaning back, creating space between us, she says, "You didn't answer mine."

"I was with Sabrina," I say truthfully.

She steps back, her expression shifting as my words sink in. "Oh." Her thoughts are written on her face, a mixture of surprise and sadness.

"Now answer mine."

Her fingers fiddle with the hem of her shirt. "No, I did not miss you."

I rub the back of my neck. Not knowing what to say, I mumble, "All right."

A short old lady comes into the bakery, with a toothy grin and smile lines. She is adorable. Anne leads her to a table and takes her order.

Tearing my eyes off Anne, I walk into the kitchen and knock on George's office door.

"Yes, come in!" George calls out. His voice is raspy.

I push the door open. The wood creaks loudly. "George, I know I'm asking for a lot, but could I close up early tonight?"

"Are there any customers?" He pushes his glasses up the bridge of his nose.

"One."

He huffs. "All right, kiddo. Turn the sign and close up once they are gone."

"Thank you! You're the best." I could kiss him for this. This isn't something he would do for anybody. I'm grateful that I have someone in my life who makes me feel like I'm important, even in small ways like this.

Anne walks into the kitchen, beaming. "She's the nicest old lady in the world," she coos, handing me the written order. "I wish I knew my grandparents."

Yeah, I miss mine.

I go to the coffee machine to prepare the drink order. "Hey, listen, can I take you somewhere tonight? Just … to talk, to chill," I ask, turning to face her.

Her hair is loose, one side brushed back over her shoulder. She's in white jeans and a white top—an outfit George asked her to start wearing to the bakery. She looks like an angel.

"I miss you," I admit. It hasn't even been half a week, but being away from her—well, I don't like it.

"But my shift?" She wraps her arms around herself, unsure.

"George said we can close up early." Noticing her body language, I add, "But if you want to go home instead, it's okay. I—"

"No, no." She reaches out to me and then drops her hands. "I miss you, too. I want things to go back to normal." Her cheeks go red, making me smile. When I step closer to her, she quickly moves back. "As friends, right?"

"Is that what you want?" If she says it is, I'll let it go. I'll let Sabrina's stupid advice go and accept this.

She nervously plays with the hem of her shirt. When she doesn't answer, I turn to pour the coffee into a cup, adding in a splash of creamy milk. Once I've done the foam art, a simple heart that I think the little old lady will love, I hand the cup to Anne. The cup rattles in her shaking hands as she stares at the heart.

"Anne?" I whisper. She looks up at me with those big brown eyes and I melt. Words get stuck at the base of my throat. *I love you.* The realization hits me. I know it because I can't go a day without being around her.

She steadies herself and turns, her focus solely on not dropping the coffee. She pushes her hip against the door and disappears into the front area.

The silence gives my heart a chance to calm down. Why is this realization hitting me like a fallen tree trunk on a sunny day? Maybe because it has built up over time; the brushes of skin, the shared laughter, the simple moments that seemed ordinary but weren't.

A hand on my arm makes me jump. "Anne."

She is looking at me with those stupidly cute eyes. They seem to shimmer in the light. "She's gone. Are we going?"

I nod, feeling slightly dazed by my thoughts. "Yeah, yeah." I place my hand on her back, feeling the warmth of her body as I guide her out to my bike. On the way, I grab my leather jacket from beneath the counter, pulling it over my hoodie. The weight of it is comforting.

Anne doesn't fight me this time as I slip my helmet on her head. I throw my leg over the bike and she climbs on behind me, her arms wrapping around me. The sensation is comfortingly familiar, yet her touch is a jolt to my system.

"Are you okay?" she whispers in my ear, air brushing against me. I shiver, my lips parting. I have already told her that I missed her; I missed every moment of us being together, including these small ones.

With my grip tightening on the handles, I start my bike and allow its growl to replace my response. *No, I'm not okay. What are you doing to me?*

The roads are quiet and empty, most people already at home eating dinner. The wind rustles through the trees, but it's drowned out by the sound of the bike.

I take a familiar route toward a lake where we used to go to swim as kids. It is only a ten-minute drive away, and we would spend all our time there. Anne's mom always brought along food for a picnic; enough to feed a village. We'd go home sunburned, full and grinning like animals. If I had more time, I would have planned something better, but I can't wait. I'm afraid that if I do, the words might burst out of me. *I love you.* The thought of it spins in my head.

Anne chuckles when we turn down the dirt pathway, cold air numbing my cheeks. "We're at the lake?"

"Are you cold?" I forgot about that. She has a jacket on, but it might not be enough. The temperature drops as we near the water, the wind picking up.

She shifts her arms closer around me, leaning her face against my back. "A little."

Once we're off the bike, I tug off my leather jacket and hand it over.

"Could I . . ." She bites her lip. "Could I maybe have your hoodie instead?"

I pull it off, my shirt getting caught with it. The cold causes goosebumps on my bare skin. Anne watches me closely in the light of the moon, as I tug my shirt back down. She takes my hoodie and pulls it on.

It's too big, the sleeves going over her hands, just like I knew it would. "It looks good," I say, pulling my leather jacket back on. It's not enough; the ice still seeps through, but it's okay. She's warm.

"Thanks," she whispers, staring down at my hand as if I'm going to capture hers in mine. I want to.

Walking ahead, I lead us up to a grouping of rocks that end in a sudden drop. We sit with our legs hanging off the edge. Anne stares out over the water, the moonlight reflecting in her eyes. Looking at her is a risk; each glance holds me captive.

Daniel would kill me for thinking these thoughts about his sister. If he knew about half the things we do, he'd never talk to me again.

"This is bringing back so many memories." She turns to look at me. "Do you remember when you—?"

"Lost my pants . . . don't remind me."

"—and Daniel tried to drown me. Wait, you lost your pants?"

"No," I say quickly, scrunching my face, making her laugh.

Leaning forward, I brush my thumb against her cheek. Her skin is soft. Tucking my index finger beneath her chin, I gently bring her face closer.

"Why do we keep doing this? What happened to what we discussed, about *not* doing this." She pulls back a little, so I drop my hand.

"Doing what? Nobody has to know. The only witness we have is a sky full of stars."

"I don't want to be a liar." She shakes her head, looking at the stars.

"Then do *you* want to tell Daniel that we made out in his car?"

She sucks in a breath at that, looking at me and then immediately to my lips.

"I just—I can't stop, Anne. I—" My lips press together. My body dips forward so I can look at the dark water below. Should I jump into the darkness? Sometimes not seeing what is coming can be part of the fun.

"You like theories about the multiverse?" I ask, knowing the answer. Of course she does. She likes theories about everything. "Where there are so many different versions of us, all impacted by the choices we make and the choices other people make. There could be another version of me getting hit by a car right now." My hand, which is pressed against the cold rocks beside her hand, shifts so that our pinkies are touching. "Do you think that maybe, in another universe, I could admit that I love you?"

I stare down at our hands because I'm too scared to look at her eyes. "Hunter?" she says breathlessly. "Hunter, *what*? You..."

My heart feels like it's folding up like a paper crane. Being vulnerable is tough. I don't want to dwell too much on what I just said, and what impact it might have on us. This is going to change everything, isn't it? Sitting here in silence, waiting for her response, I imagine all the ways this could go—

She touches my face with her fingers, her touch gentle. She takes in a deep breath, like she's been underwater until now. "I never thought that you would." *Me, neither.*

In her eyes, I see a reflection of my own uncertainty, but there is more—hope.

"Honestly, I had always imagined you leaving this town without looking back; leaving me as a distant memory. That is why I have never admitted I love you."

"A memory? You've always been more than that, and you will always be more than that." Wait—"You love me?"

"I love you." I watch her lips move with the sound of the words.

"Let's just stay in this alternate universe for a while, okay?" I turn so that I am facing her, folding my legs. I want to—need to—kiss her again. "How does alternate-Anne want me to kiss her?"

She grins. "Maybe you could do something that you'd never usually do, like pulling me—"

I carefully place my fingers around her neck, feeling the warmth of her skin beneath my touch. I pull her closer with a gentle but firm motion, our faces inching closer until our breaths mingle.

Her eyelids become heavy. The wind blows, filling my senses with the smell of her. "Then what?" My voice is deeper, huskier. I know many ways I could kiss her, but I want to learn what *she* likes.

Instead of answering, she climbs up and straddles my lap. Her body fits into mine and she cradles my face in her hands. This feels dangerous, sitting on the edge. My one hand holds her waist protectively, while the other stays against the rocks to keep us stable.

She brushes her lips against mine, the lightest feather of a touch. It drives me crazy. I lean in. "Ah, *Annabelle*."

"Uh-uh," she says when I try to pull her closer.

It sounds like both a plea and a warning when I say, "No teasing."

That makes her smile, like she knows exactly what she is doing. She trails her thumb across my bottom lip, then gently down my chin and the front of my neck. I tilt my chin up to make it easier for her to explore me.

Her hand presses against my chest, beneath my jacket, feeling it rise and fall. She's so close, but I want her closer. She tugs my shirt down at the collar, her cold fingers pressing against my skin.

Her breathing is ragged. "Do you really, *really* love me?"

I nod, my hand pressing over hers. "I really, really, love you."

She finally closes the space, her lips meeting mine.

I want this moment to stay frozen in time.

Chapter 17

ANNE

Daniel walks into my room and drops onto my bed. His hair is disheveled. "Hey, little booger."

I reach my foot over and kick him off the bed. "I'm taking you out today. My treat," I say. I need to tell him the truth. It feels wrong to feel this happy while hiding it from Daniel, who has always had my back.

His head pops up from the side of the bed and he quickly grabs onto my ankle to pull me off. "Free food? Why? What have you done?"

My throat constricts at his question. I wiggle my foot out of his grip like a fish out of water. "I got my first paycheck."

He smiles and crawls over to give me a hug. His body crushes me. "You're my favorite sister."

"Don't tell Haiz." I wink, grinning when I imagine how Haiz would pout at me for that.

"Where are we going?" He pulls away from the hug.

"I'm taking you to that Italian restaurant, Scoglio," I say, buttering him up. I'm going to give the rest of my paycheck to my mom. I'm not sure if it will help, but I hope so.

"Fancy." He smirks. "I'll dress real pretty for you."

"You better. We can leave whenever you are ready."

"Aren't you going to change?"

I look down at my graphic T-shirt and jeans. "No."

"Are you going to wear flip-flops, too?" he teases. "I doubt they'll let you in wearing that."

"You know what? The only thing I am changing is my mind. I don't want to take you—"

"Too late," he sings before walking out the door, pulling it shut behind himself. Siblings are annoying, but being an only child seems boring and lonely. I'd choose my brothers every time.

Standing from my bed, I swap my T-shirt for a blue off-the-shoulder top that is buried in the back of my closet.

Daniel swings the door open and leans against the doorframe. He wears dark blue chinos and a nude jacket intricately embroidered with Japanese cranes and plants. With a slow, deliberate spin, he shows off his outfit. Running a hand through his hair, he says, "You get the full Daniel experience."

I sigh and place the back of my palm against my forehead. "Oh, what an honor. I do not deserve your presence."

He nods. "Agreed."

Straightening myself, I mumble, "Fool." Grabbing my handbag, which contains an envelope of money that George gave me yesterday, I make my way downstairs.

●●●

There is not a speck of dirt in Daniel's car, even in the air vents. "Did you clean your car?"

"Yeah." He reverses out the driveway. "I washed her myself. Ain't she gorgeous?"

"How do you have the time for that?"

"I make time. We have to take care of the things we love."

"Can you take care of me by dropping me at Clary's house whenever I want?"

He looks over at me with a bored look. "Don't push it." After a few moments of blissful silence, Daniel switches on the radio. A heavy metal song plays, almost bursting my eardrums.

"Come on!" I raise my voice so he can hear me over the horror music.

"It's so calming." He starts screaming along to the song and I quickly block my ears.

"Is this part of the 'Daniel experience'?"

He nods. "Most girls pretend to like it to get—to, uh . . . be my girlfriend."

"Great cover-up."

It takes around fifteen minutes to reach the restaurant. In a town like this, fifteen minutes is a road trip.

"Do you think I underdressed? I should have worn a bow tie," Daniel asks as we step into the restaurant, which is filled with formally dressed people who are lively with conversation. Teardrop pendant lights hang from a wooden roof, casting a golden color over everything. Heaters are placed around the room, making it inviting.

"Yeah, and a giant red clown nose to go with it."

The kitchen is open in the front, giving everyone a view of the pizza oven and the chefs who frantically prepare the food. This restaurant is three-sets-of-forks fancy. People come from out of town to eat here. Hopefully in time, I'll be able to afford to bring my whole family here.

Our waitress leads us to our table. "My name is Alessandra and I'll be looking after you tonight." Her huge smile falters slightly when she takes a good look at Daniel. Without moving her eyes from him, she places the menus down on the table.

Daniel bites his lip. "Thanks Alessandra. You have a beautiful name." Every girl that Daniel *can* flirt with, Daniel *will* flirt with.

Her hair falls forward over her shoulder as she places a napkin on his lap excruciatingly slowly. "I'll be back in a few minutes to take your orders," she says, her voice laced with a hint of mischief. Daniel's gaze lingers on her, trailing from her eyes to her lips. A playful grin spreads across his face as he runs his tongue slowly over his own lips, his thoughts clearly coming from parts of his body other than his brain.

"Where's ... my napkin?" I ask, but she has already walked away. Daniel chuckles and throws his across the table for me.

My eyes scan over the menu. I check the desserts first, searching for a happy ending to this night. They have a wide range of Italian desserts, from tiramisu to cannoli.

"Everything is so expensive," Daniel says.

"It's on me," I remind him.

"In that case, I'll have three lobsters and one bottle of their oldest wine."

The waitress returns, her lips coated in a dark pink lipstick and a few of the buttons to her uniform conveniently left undone. "What can I get you, tonight?"

"Your number." Daniel smirks. I resist the urge to roll my eyes. "And a large four seasons pizza."

She giggles and twirls a lock of her hair around her finger. "To drink?"

"A peach iced tea for me."

She nods and glances over at me. "I'll have the pumpkin pansotti and the same as my brother to drink, please."

"Sure thing." She smiles and walks away with the menus.

"What do you do when you're on a date and the waitress starts flirting with you?" I ask.

"I let it happen. If the waitress flirts with me, it always makes the girl I'm on a date with want to impress me, so it works in my favor."

"You're disgusting."

"Yes. Don't be like me."

Silence falls between us. The wait staff weaves through the tables, delivering food and a lot of wine to customers. We haven't been to fancy restaurants like this alone. It has always been with my dad.

"I miss having Mom around," I admit.

Daniel nods and picks up a piece of bread that is lying in a basket in the center of the table. "She's pretty badass. I hope the stories I tell my kids are half as cool."

I sigh and twirl one of my forks in my hands. "You want kids? What story would you want to tell the most?"

"Probably that I followed in their grandma's footsteps and became a stripper," he jokes. "Don't tell Mom I called her a stripper. What would want to tell your kids?"

"I would . . ." I pop a piece of warm bread in my mouth to give myself a moment to think. "I would want to show them a book with my name written on the front. I would tell them about all the legacies and beautiful moments that came before them. I would probably also tell them to write down the things about their life that they want to remember—because everything goes by so quickly, and it is easy to lose track of what matters. The memories and the people and the moments that make up our lives. When they're old, it's those moments that are worth putting on paper that will be priceless." I would have loved to show them my shoes, too, but that may never happen.

"I want to change my answer," Daniel says, grinning.

The waitress comes back with the food and drinks. She has carved her number into the crust of Daniel's pizza. *That's kind of cute.*

"Enjoy your meal and let me know if you need anything else." She walks away again.

Daniel takes a picture of the pizza to save her number before he eats it.

I take a bite of my pasta, a warm, buttery flavor exploding in my mouth. The hints of garlic and herb are perfection. We fall silent as we devour our food.

The silence may also be caused by my hesitance to speak. I need to tell Daniel about Hunter. If I do it now, in public, he will stay relatively calm, right? I doubt he will leave without having dessert.

My heart begins to pound in my chest, as reality comes reaching for my throat.

Daniel notices my discomfort. "What's on your mind?"

"I am in love with Hunter," I blurt out. Oh, it is out now. There is no way to inhale them back into my mouth. Daniel stares at me, his face void of expression. "He loves me, too. I know you don't want us together, but I really care about him. I can't date him in secret, so I had to tell you."

"No." He takes a bite of his pizza.

"I know you're not happy about it, and I'm really sorry, but—"

"No, Anne." His voice is strained. Hearing my name come out of his mouth hurts. For some reason I miss his gross nickname.

"There are billions of people on this planet. Choose someone else. Love doesn't fucking last, anyway."

"You don't know that our love won't last."

"Please," he whispers and reaches across the table to squeeze my hand. "You're only going to end up being hurt. I've had my heart broken and I promise you it is the worst feeling in the world. One second you think you can't live without that person, and the next you're picking up the pieces of what's left of you after they're gone."

"I know you've had your heart broken, Daniel. That doesn't mean Hunter will break mine."

"How do you know? Anyone can wake up one day and suddenly feel nothing. I don't want it to happen to you. If Hunter broke your heart, I would never be able to forgive him. Don't mess up my friendship with him. Please don't date him."

I take in a deep breath. "What if it would break my heart to have to stay away from him?" I have been in love with him for so long that I couldn't imagine wanting someone else. He finally wants me back.

"I told you to stay away from him from the beginning. This is exactly why!" he shouts. My lip starts to shake. People turn to look over at our table.

"I'm sorry. I didn't plan on falling in love with him. He's funny and kind and the most amazing person. I didn't have a choice in the matter. My heart sort of decided for me."

"No."

"No?"

"No. He's my best friend. I have done so much for you, please do this for me. You're too young to be with him, anyway. End things now, before anything more happens."

I intertwine my hands on my lap to stop them from shaking. I want to agree, but I can't bring myself to. "I can't," I whisper. "I love him, Daniel."

For as long as I can remember, I have loved Hunter. He has been the person I dreamed of kissing, the person I imagined as the main love interest in any novel I read. We've tried to stop it, but we couldn't.

Daniel slams his hand against the table. "You're so selfish."

Tears make my eyes glossy. I shake my head, whispering, "Don't say that." My heart twists, like it is being stabbed and ripped apart. His opinion of me matters, and his words deeply hurt.

"*Please.*" He leans forward at the table. The desperate look in his eyes breaks my heart. "I tried so hard to make sure this didn't happen. Don't. Date. Hunter. He's someone who I want to keep as a friend, even after high school, and if you get in the way then it will mess everything up."

I don't want to disappoint Daniel. Tears slip down my cheeks. I quickly hide my face in my shirt. *This is so embarrassing.*

Maybe if I can explain how much Hunter means to me, he will understand. "I've been in love with him since I was eleven. I have loved him for so long that not loving him would feel wrong. I tried, and everything felt so empty. When we kissed, it was like—"

"What? You've *kissed* him?"

I hesitate for a second. "It was—yes."

Daniel stands up. The sound of his chair scraping against the floor echoes through the restaurant. His hands are balled into fists. "I hate you," he says. "I hate you so much." His eyes are full of rage. "My friendship with Hunter is something that I got to have outside of my responsibilities for this family and now you're taking that, too."

His words shatter my soul. "Daniel," I whisper, standing up. I didn't think he would say these things.

"If you had listened to me from the beginning and stayed away, this wouldn't have happened," he says through gritted teeth. "You're *reckless and selfish*. Don't talk to me again." He turns and walks out of the restaurant.

My legs suddenly feel like jelly. I quickly sit down to avoid falling. Hot tears fall furiously down my face. I place my hands over my eyes to hide myself from wondering eyes.

The waitress comes up to me and places her hand on my back. "Are you okay? Can I bring you anything? Should I call someone?"

I shake my head, not removing my hands from my face. Reckless and selfish. That's what Daniel thinks of me. He is my brother. I thought he would love me and be here no matter what.

I quickly pay the bill and leave the restaurant, a sense of humiliation burying itself in my chest. As I walk down the street, I stop trying to hide my tears and allow them to fall freely.

Pulling out my phone, I call Hunter.

"Hello?" he answers.

"Where are you? I'm coming to your house." My breathing is shaky.

"What's wrong?"

"I told Daniel."

The line goes silent for a moment. "I'm leaving the bakery now. Where are you? Do you need me to fetch you?"

I nod my head, forgetting that he can't see me. "I'm on Willow Street."

"I'll be there in five minutes." He ends the call. I continue walking slowly, wiping tears off my face.

Hunter's bike hums as it comes down the street. It stops beside me. Without saying a word, he climbs off the bike and wraps his arms tightly around me. He smells like cinnamon rolls. My fingers grip on to his white hoodie. The feeling of his body against me eases the pain in my chest a little. My body relaxes against him.

"What did he say?" Hunter asks.

"He got so angry," I whisper, my heart tightening again. He has never been angry at me before, except when we were younger, and I blew out the candles on his birthday cake. "Can I stay at your place?"

That might make Daniel more upset, but I don't want to go home. I can't look Daniel in the eyes right now and see the disappointment and anger.

In this moment, I think about how badly I want my mom to come home from work. I would be able to turn to her and receive a hug or some comfort from her. Maybe she would be able to help me navigate this mess.

Hunter hesitates for a moment. He glances down the dark, empty road. "Okay . . . I'll have to sneak you in, though. My father can't see you." His dad is extremely strict. That's why he always comes to our house and never the other way around. He is protective of his only son, which is understandable.

Hunter slides his helmet over my head. "You look like a microphone in this helmet." He pushes the screen over my face and starts singing into my head.

I push his chest lightly. "Well, you look like a potato."

He winks, playfully saying, "You mean . . . a stud?"

"It's *spud*." I laugh.

We climb onto his bike. My head feels heavy with the helmet on. Slipping my arms around Hunter, the realization hits me again that he said he loves me. Excited shivers run through my body. It will take time to convince Daniel that Hunter will not hurt me. Then again, who knows? He might hurt me, but that's a risk everyone has to take when they fall in love.

Hunter parks his bike inside my garage before leading me to his front door. "I need you to be *absolutely* quiet. I'll distract my dad while you go up to my room. It's the second one on the left. Got it?"

I nod. "Got it."

The door creaks as he pushes it open. This is the first time I am stepping into his house. It smells strongly of cigarette smoke. Dust has settled over their furniture. This house desperately needs some love and maybe a bit of color, too.

"Hunter?" his dad calls out.

"Yeah?" Hunter turns to me and puts his index finger against his lips, then points upstairs.

"Get in here, you lazy fucker."

I gasp and open my mouth to say something, but Hunter shakes his head rapidly. *Please go upstairs*, he mouths. His eyes plead with me.

He walks away from me, into the living room, where his dad's voice came from. "If you're such a great baker, why do you never make anything for me? I'm starving. Inconsiderate child."

"I can make you something. Is a sandwich all right?"

"A *sandwich*? Are you that talentless? All you have to offer is a sandwich." I curl my fingers into fists. *Why is his dad talking to him like this?* "Fine, make a sandwich. It better be good."

Hunter walks out of the living room. His eyes lock with mine. He looks so different. His shoulders are slumped, and his head dipped as if he has been completely drained of energy in a matter of seconds. I defiantly walk toward the living room, ready to give that horrible man a piece of my mind, but Hunter steps in my way.

"I told you to go upstairs," he whispers.

"But—"

"*Please.*" His expression is so vulnerable. He glances back toward the lounge. "Go."

"Fine."

The stairs groan as I take each step. Reaching the top, I sneak into Hunter's bedroom. It smells like his cologne. I'm used to Haiz and Adam's "room diffusers" known as dirty socks and old plates of food. This room is dark, with blackout curtains keeping all light out. The dark blue walls and wooden drawers are void of pictures or sentimental items. Sitting down on the edge of the bed, I listen for Hunter or his dad's voice. There's an empty silence.

How dare Hunter's dad talk to him like that? It doesn't seem like this is the first time he has spoken this way. Daniel probably doesn't know about this.

Hunter walks in holding a sandwich and a bag of chips. He places them down on the bedside table.

"Please tell me you don't believe your dad's words," I say.

He doesn't look at me, ashamed.

I walk up and place my hand on his cheek. Rough stubble runs along his jaw. Touching him like this feels intimate. It's new and different, in a good way. "Hunter?"

His eyes become glossy. "I don't want to believe him."

"None of it is true. He is only saying it to hurt you."

He turns away from me. His muscles are tensed. The wooden floors squeak beneath his feet. "He's doing a good job."

"Does he always talk to you like that?" Hunter hasn't told me much about his mom. He hasn't told me much about his dad either, clearly. Maybe I am pushing it by asking him about this.

He turns and takes a seat on the bed. "It happened one day, when I got a bad mark in third grade."

I take a seat beside him and intertwine his fingers with mine. Unconsciously, he traces circles with his thumb on the back of my hand. It gives me goosebumps and causes that familiar warmth to fill my body.

"I was so *stupid*." His voice breaks. "My father was so angry, because all his friend's kids were doing so much better than me, and he had nothing to brag about. I didn't think it mattered because I was so young. He'd never cared about my grades before." He roughly runs a hand through his curls. "One night, he got drunk and started hitting me for a small test that I failed, but my mom intervened." He bites down on his lip.

I shift closer to him. It must be difficult for him to recall these memories. The expression of pain and vulnerability on his face makes is difficult to see, but I know this is something that he needs to let out.

"He hit her." His fists tighten. "I don't think he meant to. He loved my mom more than anything. Everyone knew it from the way he looked at her or smiled at her. But after that, she disappeared up to her room without a word." He stares up at the ceiling. A tear slips downs his face, which he roughly wipes off.

I wish I could take his pain away. He doesn't deserve this.

"She returned downstairs with my father behind her, pleading for forgiveness, but she refused to look at him or respond at all. A lot of that day is a blur for me, because I was so young and at that time I didn't want to remember, but I remember one thing: the way she knelt down in front of me and promised she would come back for me." He takes in another deep breath, the weight of the memory crushing him. "My father has hated me ever since. And maybe, in a way, he was right. It was my fault. Maybe that's why she never came for me."

"When people can't control their emotions, it comes back to bite them. Your father lost control and he's pinning it on you. You were a child. There is no way that this is your fault." I rub my hand against his biceps, trying to comfort him. "Do not blame yourself for his actions."

"Yeah, maybe." He is silent for a while. "At least I met you and Daniel after moving here. That is the one good thing that came out of it."

"I could not imagine my life without you." Truly, and that is why I had to tell Daniel.

"Thank you for listening." He presses his lips against my temple. "I love you." His words are like honey to my ears. It warms me up inside.

"I love you, too." I trail my fingers against him. His skin is slightly dry. "You need lotion."

He leans closer to me and glances down at my lips. "Will you rub it on me?" It lightens the heaviness in the air.

He seems to want to move on from the subject, so I let it go.

Flirt back, Anne. I place my hand on his thigh. "Will you show me how?"

"Start slow," he says, his voice getting a little bit deeper. I slide my hand up his arm, feeling his muscles flex. "Then get faster and harder." He pulls me onto him.

I straddle his lap. "Then what?" I ask, staring into his eyes.

A storm is rolling in, turning his gray eyes darker. His face is close. I slide my hand up his chest, to the side of his neck. His body is warm. I can feel the fast pulse of his heart against my fingertips.

Brushing my thumb over the light freckles on his nose and cheeks, I ask, "Why didn't you tell someone before, about your dad?" I'm sure Daniel doesn't know about this, because he would have done something about it.

"I didn't want you to look at me differently," he explains. "I want to be Hunter with the gorgeous smile and nice hair." He winks. "Not Hunter with the horrible father."

"We would have done something if you told us. You should move out and come live with us."

"I practically live in your house already." He smiles and tugs me lightly. "I'm sorry for not telling you. I'm saving up to get out of here. I'll be okay, you don't have to worry."

"Good." I nod and look around his room again. "Could I wear one of your hoodies?"

"Will I get it back?"

"Possibly."

He smiles and nods his head toward his cupboard. "Go choose one."

I pull the cupboard doors open and my jaw drops. More than eighty percent of his cupboard is filled with different colored hoodies. "On this episode of *My Strange Addiction* . . ." I pretend to be the host of the show.

I pull out a soft yellow hoodie and slide it over my head. The sleeves fall past my hands as usual. It has a fluffy material inside it that makes me feel like I am being hugged by a cloud.

"Model it for me."

I shut his cupboard and swivel to face him, putting my arms in different strange positions and pouting my lips. He leans back, entertained, looking unbelievably sexy. Suddenly, I find myself feeling self-conscious, being with someone like him.

I sit on the edge of his bed, playing with the too-long sleeves covering my palms. What if Daniel is right and I lose all of this because I fell for someone way out of my league? My mind begins to fill with all of the ways this could go wrong.

Daniel has always had a better understanding of the world, of people and their antics.

"You all right over there?" I nod, but he comes over and kisses my temple. "What's on your mind?"

"You." I nuzzle my head into the crook of his neck.

Instead of asking what I mean, he asks, "Do you remember the day we met?"

As if happened yesterday. "Of course. What made you think about that?"

"You were wearing a yellow sundress, picking flowers from your garden."

"I was minding my business when suddenly a heavy ball flew out of nowhere and hit my thigh. A young, sweaty, curly-haired kid came running after it."

"I thought you would be angry, but instead you gave me one of your flowers." He places another kiss on my temple and holds me tight against him. "You have always had a heart of gold."

I sigh. "Thank you."

"You don't seem happy to hear that."

"I am, but sometimes I want to go back, because having a heart of gold meant handing someone a flower. Now I have to wonder if love is forever, or if I'll find my shoe, or if Daniel will still want to talk to me after this. Everything feels ... heavier."

"You'll be okay. I can tell that you are still golden. And you don't have to carry this weight alone. I am here."

"What if I don't find my shoe?"

He shrugs. "Then you've got a good story to tell your kids."

Maybe he's right. Not every story has to end with a happily-ever-after.

Chapter 18

HUNTER

I don't feel her in my arms. My eyes fly open and I search the darkened room for a figure, but there's no sign of her. As if she were just a fever dream. My heart jerks out of my chest. I throw my sheets off and run down the stairs. The sound of my footsteps seem too loud for the silent house.

I stop near the arch of the living room. Anne's soft voice comes from inside. "—don't think it is right for you to talk to him the way you do. You're his father, you should love him unconditionally."

No, no, no! I take a few steps back, putting my hands behind my head. If he says *anything* hurtful to Anne, I'll punch him. I've been wanting to do it for a long time, anyway.

"Excuse me? Who the hell are you to tell me how I should treat my son? If you have a problem, call the authorities. Get his stupid ass placed in a foster home." He has said the same thing to me. It scared me silent, the thought of being taken away.

Anne places her hands on her hips. "I don't mean to offend y—"

"Then don't," he cuts her off.

I walk into the room. "Anne," I say. Her head whips around to look at me. "What are you doing?" My heart is racing uncontrollably.

My stomach tightens and twist so much that I might throw up.

My father's eyes are red with rage. "You're complaining to your friends about me?" my father asks, his hands clenching into fists. His voice deepens. "You're so much of a wuss that you have to get a girl to come and stand up for you?"

I shake my head, stepping closer to Anne. She needs to get out of here. I don't want him saying these things to me, not in front of her. *Please.*

Anne points her finger at him, which only makes him angrier. "Stop it! Stop talking to him like—"

"Anne, please go." I put myself between her and my father. Even as I try to push her out the lounge, her feet stay rooted in place. "Now," I demand.

Her brown eyes are full of hatred for my father. As grateful as I am to her for trying to help me, she is only making it worse.

I bite down hard on my lip. She's not listening. "Anne, I need you to *go.*" I nod my head toward the door. "You're not helping."

My breathing shakes as I turn to look at my father. He's going to hurt me for this, not physically, but I know he will find a way to destroy me.

My father walks closer to Anne. "Why was she at our house without my knowledge?" This is him being calm, even though his face is painted red.

"Anne, get out," I say.

"You—" she tries to argue.

"Please, Anne. Don't—I can't. I don't want to." I'm not making any sense. I'm terrified. What will he do to me now? What will he say? "Go. I don't need you here!" If my father hurts me in front of Anne, I wouldn't be able to take it. That's why I've kept it a secret. She'll realize how weak I am.

Hurt crosses her expression. It makes me feel selfish. I don't want her here, but she needed to be here. Why did she have to meddle? I told her not to. "Fine." She turns and walks out. The front door slams closed, trapping me here with him.

"Can't even keep your mouth shut. Fucking pathetic." My father stands tall, his hands clenched into fists.

"I know." My heart caves into itself. As much as I don't want to admit it, I believe my father's words. It feels like everyone is telling a lie and he is the only one being honest with me.

"You're never going to amount to anything. I'm sure your mother is glad she never came back for you." He chuckles dryly and shakes his head. "A baker. How sad that you see that as an achievement."

"I know." Before walking out, my mom ran her hands through my hair, gave me a kiss on the forehead and whispered *I'm sorry, but I'll come back for you.* As much as I want to deny it, she left me, too. She was never planning on coming back. I'm sure she *is* glad about leaving me behind.

"No, you don't know. I wish I wasn't stuck with such a disappointment."

Maybe becoming a baker was a mistake. I might not have a future with it. He's right. "I know." I can barely hear my own voice. I clench my jaw, trying to keep my face as stoic as possible, but the tears brimming my eyes betray me. If I could see myself in the mirror right now, I'd be disgusted.

At least Anne is gone.

My grades are average, too, which means I might not be able to do anything with my life except bake cupcakes. It's pathetic. Everything I've done is worth nothing. My mind begins tearing me apart.

I bite down on my lip hard enough to tear my skin. Maybe if

I make the pain physical, it'll be something I can bear. The metallic taste of blood fills my mouth. My vision becomes blurry. Tears would make my father laugh. There's no doubt he'd only make me feel worse about it.

"I know. I'm pathetic, I'm useless, I'm a failure, I'm a disappointment! I get it!" My face scrunches up in pain. I don't want to believe I am those things. I want to believe I've helped someone, that I'm good at something, that someone is proud of me. The barrier breaks, causing tears to slide down my cheeks. The harder I try to hold them back, the harder they fall. "I'm sorry to be such a burden to you." He broke me without laying a hand on me.

The pain inside me is a lot worse than what the tears running down my face could show. The tattoo on my arm is supposed to represent strength and survival—but look at me.

"Maybe . . ." I grit my teeth. I can stand up for myself. "Maybe if you turn the TV off for once, you might hear the thoughts in your head. The thoughts telling you that I'm not the disappointment. *You are.*" That felt good to get off my chest, like a weight being lifted. But the weight comes crashing back down a thousand times harder when I see the rage in his eyes.

Cracking his knuckles, he says, "Everyone around you would be better if you were d—"

"Stop!" a familiar voice screams. Anne walks back into the room. Her cheeks are red and stained with tears. She doesn't say anything more to him, only tugging at my arm. Her eyes are wide. "Let's go." She looks at my father with complete disgust.

She must have heard everything and seen how weak I am; how I crumbled in front of him. I lead her outside, "What is your problem? I told you to leave," I say as soon as we step out onto the lawn. I'm glad he didn't follow us out.

She stares up at me, her chest rising and falling rapidly. The only thought running through her head must be how much of a coward I am to have lived with him for so long.

"Hunter." Her voice breaks. She wraps her arms around me, leaning her head against my chest. I stare down at her. She grabs fistfuls of my hoodie. "His words are lies. All of them." Her body is shaking like she has been out in the cold for hours.

My body is still buzzing with remnants of anger and shame. She saw it all. She heard it all.

I never should have brought her into my house, or anywhere near my father. I want to grab her and wrap her up. She is too short to hug back properly, and I need a real hug, so I grab her waist and lift her. She hooks her legs around me and I place my hands beneath her thighs to hold her up.

"Maybe he is right," I admit into the crook of her neck. It's easier to say when I don't have to look at her.

She moves her head to look at me and holds my face in her hands. Her brown eyes are fierce. "He is wrong." The certainty in her voice eases the pain a little. "You are good enough. You are smart enough. You put a smile on people's faces every day, including mine. You are incredible, Hunter Denegan. Don't you *ever* forget that."

"Are you sure?" I ask.

She nods and hugs me tight. She's still wearing my yellow hoodie. I breathe in the smell of her, the warm scent of violets calming my racing heart.

"Thank you for not leaving," I breathe against her skin.

She pulls back and slides her thumb across my cheek to wipe away my stupid tears. "I love you."

Those three words mean more to me than she could ever imagine. "I have to go."

"Go?" She slips slightly lower.

"For a few nights, I have to find somewhere to stay."

"What are you talking about?" Her dark eyebrows furrow together. "You can stay with us."

I shake my head. "Daniel won't want to see me. I broke the one promise I made to him."

"He wouldn't make you stay somewhere else. Tell him about your dad and he'll—"

"No." I lower her back to the ground and step back. "Having you know is already too much." Daniel is so protective of everyone, but he treats me like an equal. If he finds out about this, he'll start trying to protect me. That is the opposite of what I want.

"Okay, okay. We don't have to tell him. But you're still staying over. He will deal with it." She takes my hand and walks into her house. Loud heavy metal music comes from upstairs. It makes the floors vibrate.

We walk upstairs and Anne pushes Daniel's door open. "Clary?" She blinks a few times, trying to register what is happening. "What the hell, Daniel?"

He completely ignores Anne and gets touchy with Clary, grabbing her ass in front of us. He runs his other hand over her dark pink bra. She quickly pushes him away and stands up to pull her shirt on.

Taking Anne's wrist, I pull her away from his room and shut the door.

She stares forward, unable to blink. "I can't believe him."

Clary walks out the room, now fully clothed. "I'm so sorry. I didn't know you'd be home."

"Sure, yeah, it's okay."

She's not even going to question it? Of course she'd forgive Clary. She can't stay angry at anyone, especially when they apologize.

She frowns and tucks a few strands of her red hair behind her ear. "No, it's not. I'm your friend. I shouldn't have done it, and I shouldn't have hidden it from you."

I should be saying these words to Daniel.

"Really, it's fine. I know you've had a crush on Daniel forever. Good for you. I hope he doesn't hurt you." She's saying it is fine, but I don't know what is going through her mind.

He is with Clary again. It seems like they're becoming more than just a fling.

Daniel pulls the door open, adjusting the shirt he pulled on. "You have a crush on me?" Clary's face turns the color of her hair. "That's cute."

She laughs. "No. Anne is joking."

Daniel takes Clary's waist and pulls her against him. He dips his head and kisses her with force. A surprised sound leaves her lips. She holds on to his shirt and kisses him back with equal force.

Then he looks at me and Hunter. "Anything to say?" he asks.

Anne looks too surprised to say anything.

Clary looks between us, confused. "What's going on?"

Daniel's jaw is clenched. He's glaring at Anne, refusing to even look in my direction. "Nothing." His voice sounds animalistic, like he wants to claw something to pieces.

"I told Daniel that I . . ." Anne looks at me. "I'm in love with Hunter."

Clary's head whips to Daniel. "That's why you invited me over. You—you wanted us to get caught. Is this some kind of revenge plot?"

"No, Clary—well, yes. I should have told you, but I didn't think you'd agree."

"Of course I wouldn't agree! I knew you found it hard to love but I didn't think you were heartless." Her lips pout and she looks like she is about to cry. She turns to look at Anne. "I'm sorry. I'm really sorry. I—I let my feelings get in the way."

"Feelings?" Daniel parrots. "We agreed that—"

"Don't worry." She runs her hands through her slightly messy hair. They must have been doing a lot in there. "The only thing I feel now is sad for you. You'll never know real love with that cold heart of yours."

"Clary—" he calls for her but she's already storming off down the stairs. He stares after her long after she has slammed the front door closed. Silence floats through the house.

There is a frown etched into his face, his jaw clenched. But his eyes. I can see he is hurt. Maybe he is considering going after her. Breaking the silence, I say, "Daniel, if you want to talk—"

Finally, he looks at me. And I immediately want him to look away. There is rage trapped like dark smoke in his deep blue eyes. His eyebrows pull together. "Fuck. You."

Anne sucks in a breath, having never heard him speak like this before. "Dan—"

"My baby sister? Fuck you. You have no fucking self-control." The veins in his arms are pronounced, his hands are in fists. Would he really take that rage out? Would he punch me or say something that might deeply hurt me? "Pathetic," he growls.

The word hits its target, right in my empty tank of self-worth.

He walks back into his bedroom, shutting the door hard. The sound is loud and final.

The pain in my chest returns tenfold. I purse my lips. That is all I needed to hear to know how Daniel sees me now. How I wish I could shove cotton in my ears to never have to hear these words again from anyone. "Pathetic," I whisper. Even he thinks it. I purse my lips, a frown etched on my face.

Anne gently holds my arm, shaking her head. "He's just angry. He doesn't—"

"No, he meant it. He thought it. He said it." What's worse is the way he said it, like he knew it would break our friendship and that's exactly what he wanted. To never see me again. "Stop lying to comfort me." There is a hole caving in my chest. I want to breathe but it is suffocating me, burying me. *This* is why I couldn't do anything with Anne; it's why I tried so hard not to. I look at her and see the same pain in her eyes. She puts space between us, staying silent. Her head dips, hair falling around her face like she wants to hide from this as much as I do.

As much as I want to run, my feet stay rooted. With shaking hands, I lift my arms to indicate that I want—need—a hug from her. She immediately dives into my arms, nearly knocking me back. Despite everything, I laugh. It lightens the tightness in my chest.

This girl. This beautiful, loving, gentle girl.

Wanting to kiss her, I lead her back to her room. Once her bedroom door clicks shut, I push her against it, not wasting any time. The way I handle her is anything but gentle, but I need this. I need her. My arm snakes around her possessively, the other hand tilting her chin upward. Her lips mold against mine. The feeling is addictive. I melt into her, moaning—and then I tear myself away.

Breathing hard, she stares up at me, lips parted. Her voice is soft when she asks, "Why did you stop?" Her hand is already tugging on my hoodie, craving more.

"I don't want to use you to escape. I love kissing you, but if we do it like this, then I'm using you as a distraction." It's why I was always willing to kiss other girls; girls I didn't care about. I want this to be different.

She nods, understanding. She crawls into her bed and sinks into the soft pillows, gesturing for me to join her.

Her room is old but cute. It smells of her. Her desk is a complete mess, the usual pile of papers and stationery, but the rest of her room spotless—everything neatly away or organized in rows. "How is your book going?" I ask, lying beside her on her bed.

She curls into my side. I slide my arm under her head and she lies against my chest, letting me hold her against me. "Good. I haven't had much time this week. I've been studying for a chem test. Did you know that the symbol for gold is A-U?"

"O . . . kay." Very useful information.

"Well, I want gold, without the A." *U.* She wants me.

I squeeze her. That—She's so . . . uhhhh. I have not felt this way before, and I enjoy it. I press kiss after kiss against her face, her skin warm. It makes her giggle. "I love you." Every time I say it, it feels easier and truer.

"You're staying, right?"

I shake my head. "I can't stay here. It will only make things worse with Daniel. I'm going to stay with George, if he will let me."

She nods. "Before you go, I wanted to ask if you'd be my date . . . for my dad's wedding. It's in a week, as soon as our winter holidays start." Her cheeks turn pink. "I don't think I can get through it with Daniel being mad at me and my future stepmother calling me—"

"Arnold." I laugh. "Sure, I'll come with you." My thumb brushes against her cheek.

My phone starts ringing loudly. I pull it out of my pocket to see the name on the screen. Daniel.

Shit. My heart takes a dive against my chest, unable to escape, its thumping becomes more furious. I search for the button to silence it. Anne's bedroom door flies open. "Why can I hear—?" Daniel's eyes expression switches from confusion to fury when he sees what is going on. His eyes drift between us.

I am on my feet in an instant. "Daniel, I—"

He grabs me by the top of my hoodie. The world blurs. I am shoved down on the floor. "Are you joking?" he screams in my face. He bares his teeth and I instantly know he wants to hurt me again. In his barely contained state of rage, he says, "Get up."

"Stop it!" Anne shouts, standing.

I get back to my feet. There's no justifiable explanation for this. I knew if he saw me here, I'd be dead.

An animalistic sound leaves his mouth. "You think you can just take whatever you want? She is the *one* person I asked you to stay away from." He roughly shoves my chest. It hurts. I stumble back. "You swore you wouldn't! You gave me your fucking word!"

I know. "This wasn't my intention. I tried to stay away from her." Anne nervously bites her lip. She sways on her feet, clearly wanting to jump between us. "I swear to you, I will never purposely hurt her. I will protect her with everything I've got." *I mean that.*

"As if I can believe a word that comes out of your pathetic, unreliable mouth."

My father was rig—no. "Don't ever talk to me like that." I've accepted it from my father. I am not accepting it here. Here, in front of Anne, I can stand up for myself for the first time.

With a tense jaw, Daniel says, "What the fuck are you going to do to stop me?" He is trying to provoke a fight.

I refuse. Violence is never the answer, not with the people I care about. I'd fight to protect Anne, but this is not right. I shake my head. "Nothing."

"Nothing? Huh?" He shoves me again. "You proving to my sister how *pathetic* you are?"

It is like he knows what my weak spots are, and he continuously jabs at them. It stings, but not as badly as the first time. "Stop, Daniel. Enough."

Daniel swings at me, but I duck out of the way. In a second attempt, he sends a right hook straight to my jaw. A searing pain floods my face. I step back on something and slip to the ground, holding on to my jaw.

"What are you doing?" Anne shouts incredulously.

When I look at Daniel again, his expression has changed. His fingers are curled. To my surprise, he holds out his hand for me and helps me up. Does that mean we are okay?

"I want you to leave. Now," he says.

I glance over at Anne and realize that we all need some time for things to settle. Maybe space will be good. It is hard to leave, knowing things won't be the same. I drag myself downstairs and out into the cold, I make my way to the one place where I know the door will always be open to me.

Parking my bike out front, I come face to face with George's familiar oak front door. I rap my knuckles against it. The sound fills the eerie silence.

It is followed by the sound of slippers sliding against the floor. George pulls the front door open. He is in a black robe. His graying hair is disheveled. "Hey, kiddo."

"Did I wake you up?" I drop my hood from my head and run my hands through my hair.

"No, I was making a cup of tea. Come in." He steps aside to let me in. He eyes the bruise forming on my jaw. "Is everything okay? It's almost midnight." I lean back against the wall beside the door while he locks up.

The place smells of chai. "Would you mind if I stay here tonight?"

"You're always welcome here. You know that." His eyes rake over me. There's a frown on his face. "Come, have tea."

I take a seat at the kitchen counter and lean forward, closing my eyes. This is a place of comfort for me. I feel like I can breathe again. Maybe things will be okay with Daniel one day.

George slides two warm buns in front of me, along with a cup of piping hot chai.

"Thank you."

He leans against the counter. "Now tell me what is wrong."

I groan and tilt my head back. "Can we talk about it another time?"

"You come to my house in the middle of the night, asking me if you can stay over—which probably means you don't want to, or can't, go home. I'm going to need an explanation."

I take a bite of the bun. The center is warm and buttery. "Did you make this?" I ask, hoping to change the topic. George's specialty is breads—baguettes, pretzels, sourdough, bagels, ciabatta, naan. He could talk about them for hours. He once competed in Paris and won awards for his skills.

He gives me a pointed look. "Explain, Hunter."

"I had a girl over and my dad got angry." It's true, technically. "I don't want to see him right now."

"Did he hurt you?"

I stuff my mouth with bread. "He didn't hit me or anything."

"Your jaw?"

"Unrelated."

He walks around the counter and places his hand on my shoulder. "Can I give you a piece of advice?" I nod. Even if I said no, he'd still say it. "You won't find happiness waiting for you. Happiness is something you create for yourself. It is an art. I need to ask you, are you happy, Hunter?"

If only it were that simple. Sometimes the actions we take to feel happy have consequences. "Next you're going to tell me to follow my heart," I tease.

He laughs, which turns into a fit of dry coughs. Patting his chest, he says, "No. Don't follow your heart. That would be shit advice. Follow your brain. You know the facts versus what someone is saying to hurt you." His words feel like he knows the truth about what I am going through.

"But what if my dad is right? What if I'm not good enough?" I shake my head, tears brimming in my eyes. It's almost like my entire life, everything I have worked for and earned, has been for nothing.

"Do you think I would hire you if you were not good?"

I shrug. "You're too nice to say no. That's why you avoid everyone's job applications."

"Fine, let me rephrase that. Do you think people would come in every day and pay a good sum of money to eat your pastries if they weren't fantastic?"

I fake a yawn, stretching my arms out. "I'm really tired. I should go shower quickly."

"No," he says. "The answer is no, they wouldn't. You are more than capable. Take it from me, the pickiest eater on earth. I'd eat your pastries every day if I didn't have diabetes."

"Thank you." His words mean a lot more than he could ever know. I am grateful to have someone in my life who will always be consistent and reliable.

"Now, let's get you on that—what's his name? Craig's list looking for an apartment. I'll help you."

I can't help but smile at him. Even though I am unsure about the future and where I might end up, George may be right: moving out and finding peace will be the best first step. It doesn't have to be a perfect place, but it'll be a step in the right direction.

Chapter 19

ANNE

Fairy lights and flickering candles illuminate the building where my father's wedding is being held. The glass walls on all four sides protect us from the cold but give us an incredible view. The building sits on the edge of a cliff—a tall limestone cliff in the Garden Peninsula, which overlooks Lake Michigan.

The early six o'clock sunset has turned the sky different hues of pink and orange. A harp player sends notes of music through the large space, drowning out the gentle hum of guests—people whom I haven't seen in years, or ever.

I'll give it to my father and Cabbage, they really made the event magical. All I can wonder, though, is how my mom feels sitting at home. She must be wrapped up in her blankets, feeling guilty for any time she isn't spending at work. Would she pull out a hidden shoe box of photos from their marriage and cry over it? It is a difficult thing to try and imagine myself in my mother's shoes, and that is why I have so much love and respect for everything she has done for us.

"Hey, Arnold," Hunter greets, taking a seat beside me at the table. He is wrapped in a sleek black tuxedo. My skin immediately begins tingling with excitement, knowing that at some point he might brush his hand across my arm or against my lower back.

This gorgeous guy, with his cropped curls and intoxicating eyes, has his smile directed at me. He is here as *my date*. "Hey, my knight in shining parchment paper." I lift my glass of soda and bring it to my lips. Children I have never met weave between the elegantly decorated tables, trying to keep themselves entertained in a risky game of tag.

Hunter tugs the chair I am sitting on closer to him and presses his lips against my ear. "You look gorgeous, but there's something missing that would look great on you."

"What?"

He holds his fist out, palm down. I open my hand under it, waiting for him to show me what he is holding. He slips his fingers between mine to hold my hand. "Me."

My cheeks turn red, and I'm unable to stop a small giggle from bubbling out. He's holding my hand again. This not-so-small thing that I have been wishing and praying for. It's real.

He bites his lip and tilts my face up. His eyes shine in the dim lighting. "I love you," he whispers.

I press my forehead against his. "I have loved you for five years."

He pulls back, his eyes scanning my face. Did I really admit that without thinking? Is it going to scare him off? I play with the hem of my dress, waiting for him to respond. Hunter holds his pinky finger up, knowing I wouldn't be lying if I made that promise. Pinky promises are serious.

I wrap my finger around his. His eyes widen. "Five *years*?" He trails the tip of his index finger along the rim of his glass of water. "That time when you asked me to be your valentine as a joke..."

Every inch of my body turns hot with embarrassment. I gave

Hunter a rose when I was thirteen and asked him to be my valentine. He laughed and shot me with a Nerf gun. "Wasn't a joke," I say.

"I—huh," he says, looking completely taken aback. "Oh my god. That long, *really*?"

"You thought my face was naturally red all the time?" I smile and hold my cheeks, which are most certainly red now.

He looks around the glass building. "Give me a second. I'll be back." Rising from his chair, he practically *runs* away from me.

Of course, it took me less than a week to mess up something I have waited years for. I rip apart the gold spray-painted flower that had been placed on the plate in front of me.

Someone lightly taps my shoulder. I turn. A little girl with adorable chubby cheeks looks up at me. There is a tooth missing in her grin. "Aunthee Cas-thithi askth me tew call you." She waves her hand, wanting me to follow her. She swirls in her poofy golden dress and walks out the glass doors, toward a Greek-styled building near the parking lot. Green vines wrap around enormous white pillars.

"Do you know what your aunt wanted?" I ask as we walk into the building and up a staircase.

She shakes her head. Her ponytail, which is topped with a little bow, swings.

The door at the top of the staircase has been left open. Women in green and gold dresses are scattered around the room, primping themselves.

"Hello?" I knock on the door even though it is already open.

Cabbage sits at a dressing table in a beautiful silk dove gown. Her hair is pinned up in an elegant updo. She turns to look at me and smiles as the lady beside her paints a shimmery powder onto her eyelids. "Come in!"

I walk through the dressing room, trying to avoid photobombing all the selfies being taken by the unknown women, and take a seat next to Cabbage. "You called me? Did you need something?"

She glances around the room, at the mess of clothes and items on the carpeted floor. "I'm going to need everyone to leave! I want to talk to my future daughter alone!" *Future daughter?* I . . . no.

The woman doing her makeup waves a small brush around likes she's some fairy godmother. "I'm not done with your makeup, ma'am."

"I've waited seven years to marry Rey. I don't think he'll mind—or notice—if I'm not wearing false eyelashes."

"What about your wedding photos?"

"I need everyone *out*." She claps her hands, finalizing it.

Women begin to pile out of the room until it's only Cabbage and me left. The door clicks shut. The room is silent, aside from the soft sound of voices and the clinking of glasses coming from the garden.

"I'm sure you have a lot of questions, right? If you want to know anything about me, feel free to ask."

Well . . . "How does it feel to be a home-wrecker?" I fold my arms across my chest. If she saw the way it broke my mother, she would regret the day she was born.

Her eyebrows fly up. Her gaze wanders slowly around the room, like it is the first time she is seeing it, as she struggles to find an answer. "I fell in love with your father before knowing he was married, and when I found out, I was already in too deep."

Daniel told me that Dad met Cabbage before the divorce. but hearing it from her feels like a punch to the stomach. "That's a terrible excuse."

"It's not an excuse. Your father is a wonderful person. When he would kiss me and brush his fingers through my hair." She sighs, remembering it all. *Ew.* My face scrunches at the image she has painted. "I fell in love with him without realizing it. He is kind, smart, handsome, reasonable, and so—"

"Rich?"

"Funny," she finishes. "He has my heart. I truly never intended for anyone to get hurt." A tear slips down her cheek. She wipes it away with her fingers. A small part of me empathizes with her, realizing that it is similar to how I feel about Hunter. I never meant for it to upset Daniel, it just . . . happened. "When I found out he was married, I told him that we have to stop, but he told your mother about us and ended his marriage. I'm so sorry."

Damn it, why did she have to say sorry? "It's . . . all right." I guess. Or more importantly, it's done and irreversible. Now all we have are small tokens to tell the story of the past, and new memories to make. With or without my father in the picture.

"Really?" There's a hint of disbelief in her voice. "I didn't expect you to forgive me so easily. I can't even get Daniel to speak to me."

Yeah, me, neither. "I have another question. Why do you call me Arnold?"

A small smile finds its way to her face. "I used to annoy my little sister by calling her that. Her name was Arna. She would get so annoyed that she would curl into a ball and refuse to talk to me. I loved it." She runs her fingers over her silky blond hair, smoothing it down although it is already perfect. "I like your reaction better."

"My reaction?"

"Cabbage." She laughs, causing her eyes to crease.

"I didn't think you'd realize," I admit.

"I did." She nods and looks down at her hands, smiling. "You know, I love your father a lot, and I know he cares about you. I want you to feel comfortable with me, so we can build our relationship more. We're going to be family."

"Family? As if you or my father know the meaning of the word."

I trail my fingers over my baby-green satin dress. It's my mother's. She practically shoved me into it when she found out that Hunter is my date tonight. The material is unbelievably soft. It fits against my curves.

"I know your father is a little distant, but—"

"A little? The only time he wants to spend time with us is when it is for his own benefit. I can't remember the last time he asked us if we were okay and actually cared to do anything about it. Because we're *not okay*. We're struggling. My mom can barely afford our school fees, meanwhile you two are jetting off on different vacations every week."

"We are not jetting off every week. Your father spends most of his time at work. I don't see him often, to be completely honest. I am very grateful to him for working hard and giving Jessica and I a good life, but it is not all sunshine and rainbows." Maybe she misses time with him the way I miss time with my mom. "And I didn't know about your school fees. I will talk to your father and correct him for that."

"Thank you."

"You're welcome. Do you have more any questions?"

Too many. "What is he like, when he isn't busy working?" We spent a bit of time with him in Canada, barely seeing him aside from shared meals.

"He's incredible. He is the most kindhearted person I have ever met. He makes mistakes sometimes, but somehow they become irrelevant when I see his charming smile and hear that French accent of his."

"Okay, can I go now?" I'm still uncomfortable speaking to the woman who broke up my family. My mom says she is happy for them, ready to let go of my father and their past, but I don't believe it. It's going to take time.

She nods and puts her hand on my arm. "I want you to know that I am on your team. I will keep reminding your father of his responsibility to you and your brothers. If you ever need anyone to talk to, I'll be here. I will contact you whenever your father is at home, and you can all come over. Our home is yours."

I rise from my seat. "Your dress is beautiful, by the way."

"Thank you." She slides her hand over the material, appreciating it. Her expression shifts to one of thoughtfulness, and more questions pop up, as I realize how little I know about her. Still, I appreciate this conversation.

I pull the door open. All the women who were kicked out rush back in to continue getting ready, like a bull run in Spain, almost knocking me over.

Escaping the noise of chatter, I descend the marble staircase. The moment makes me feel like a princess, especially in my mom's beautiful dress.

The sun has fully set outside, the cold wind blows through my hair and makes my bones feel like they're tuning to ice. I stop walking for a moment, staring at the glass building. It feels like looking into a snow globe. The golden light inside contrasts against the darkness of the night. It looks magical.

Walking back in, I see Hunter and Daniel standing together with a group of people. Clary is there, too. What does this mean? Did everyone make up without me knowing?

Daniel slides his arm around Clary's shoulders, but she pulls away and gives him a playful look. "Sorry, you're not my type."

"Wait a minute . . ." He tilts her chin up with his index finger and squints at her face. "Did your nose get longer?" The corners of his lips tilt up.

"You're not even a good kisser." They stare intensely at each other. She glances down at his lips, then back into his eyes, her expressions saying a million things.

Well, this is . . . weird.

His eyes widen in feigned shock. "Look, it happened again." He presses his index finger to her nose.

"Shut up. I don't even want you." Clary tugs Daniel closer by the lapels of his jacket.

He places a hand over her face, swiping it down, and chuckles. His hand is the size of her entire face.

The rest of the teenagers standing around don't look familiar. It's weird knowing there might be a whole half of my family that I have no connection to.

Hunter smiles and nods at me. Sometimes I forget how tall he is, until I see him beside other people.

"Go get a room," I say to Daniel and Clary who seem like they are ready to jump on top of each other. "J-k!" I have no idea how to act around them. Did they make up? Are they a couple? I am not sure how I feel about it, especially when they so openly flirt and yet I'm not allowed to stand within five feet of Hunter in Daniel's presence.

Hunter shakes his head. "You say 'j-k' out loud? Such a dork." *Oh.* I wrap my arms around myself. Maybe I pushed him away by admitting how long I've liked him. Well, if this is how Hunter is going to act now, then it will be easy to get over h—"I love you so much," he adds.

My breathing falters. A lump forms in my throat, preventing me from talking. He pulls his suit jacket off and rolls the sleeves of his dress shirt up to his elbows. From the smirk on his face, he knows the effect this has on me.

Daniel looks between the two of us, not knowing what to say for the first time. There is no emotion on his face; I can't tell whether he is sad, angry, or confused. He grinds his teeth slightly. Angry, probably angry. I need to get away from his piercing gaze.

Taking Hunter's wrist, I pull him away, around the side of the Greek-style building, where guests won't see us. Luckily, the cold ensures that nobody wants to stroll around out here. A few birds pass by overhead, calling out. Hunter places his jacket over my shoulders, noticing the goosebumps rising on my skin. It smells like his cologne. Woodsy and delicious.

"I thought I scared you off," I admit.

He caringly trails the back of his hand down my cheek. The way he is looking at me makes my heart do somersaults. "If you think I'm going to let you go that easily, you're wrong."

"You *ran* away..."

"I had to talk to Daniel," he explains. "I wanted him to know that nothing is going to change the way I feel about you. He seemed to be less hesitant after our talk."

"Oh." My vocabulary seems to be failing me. I can't find the right words to say.

"Five years, huh?" His hand slides to the side of my neck. "That's a long time to have a crush."

"I tried to get over you, but you're so . . ." I trail off, distracted by his touch.

His fingertips dance across my skin, exploring me. He tilts his head, his eyes hooded. I remember from our conversation about kissing that he likes to be teased. That makes me tug him in closer, pulling at his dress shirt.

I have nowhere to go now, his body pressed directly against mine. Our breaths mingle. His lips part, his face lowering. My fingers press to his lips, and I playfully ask, "What if I didn't let you kiss me?" I ask.

"What?" His eyebrows furrow, his hand tightening on my waist.

"You didn't ask if I *want* to kiss you."

"Ah . . ." He steps back, turning to look out through the trees. "I can play, too, Annabelle. I can tease too." He runs a hand through his hair, his biceps flexing deliciously. I tilt my head back against the wall, instantly regretting trying to play with him and wishing he'd come back. "And the best part is, I don't have to do a thing."

He turns to look over his shoulder and smirks at me. His dimple curves in unison.

I run my hand slowly over my bare décolletage, sighing. "Please," I whisper, my voice soft.

His smirk falls and he turns to me. "Please what?" His voice is strained.

"Please kiss me." I hold on to the jacket he placed on my shoulders, gripping it tightly.

The muscle in his jaw tightens. He walks over to me slowly, each step seeming to take lifetimes, before his brown leather loafers are barely an inch away from my flats.

I tilt my head up, wetting my bottom lip. "You said you like teasing."

He nods, taking my hand and placing it on his chest. "I like a lot of things, my Annabelle." And suddenly I love my name, the way it sounds coming from his mouth. It makes me smile. "You are so beautiful, you know that?" he asks.

My heart softens. "R-really?" A part of me wants to hide, block my face or my smile, but instead I slide my hands up to cup his face and run my fingers through the sides of his hair.

He nods slowly. "Stunning."

I have never been described as stunning before. The word settles like a fallen feather in my chest. I breathe in. "Thank you."

He lowers his head slowly, waiting for me to say anything. When I don't, he presses his lips to mine. They're warm and comforting, like cocoa by the fireplace. I mold against him in an instant, craving every second of the kiss.

Hunter's hands grip my waist firmly, effortlessly lifting me off the ground. His jacket slides from my shoulders, forgotten as I instinctively wrap my legs around his waist, pulling him closer.

Our lips meet again. His hands slide under my thighs, holding me up with a possessive strength that sends shivers down my spine. My fingers weave into his curls, tugging gently, eliciting a deep, throaty sound from him. He responds by teasingly biting my bottom lip.

A breathless whimper leaves my lips. He smiles against the kiss and pulls back to look at me. I can feel the admiration in his gaze, a silent compliment. "I'd like to see how many ways I can get you to make that sound again for me."

A violin starts playing in the distance. "Oh, the wedding . . ." I trail off, not wanting to leave this space with him.

He lowers me back to the ground. I pick up his jacket and we walk back toward the garden together. Daniel and Clary stand outside the glass building. He has a cigarette between his lips. He inhales the smoke and closes his eyes. He usually only smokes at parties. This is probably a lot for him. I wish I could talk to him, connect with him somehow.

Instead, I pull the white roll of tobacco from his lips. "This is a bad habit."

The smoke leaves his lips slowly. He takes the cigarette back.

"We all have things we want, even when we know we shouldn't want them." His eyes stay on Clary when he says it.

"Stop staring at me or you might fall in love," she jokes, her fingers fiddling with the hem of her leopard-print dress.

He drops his cigarette and steps on it. "You don't have to worry about that. I'm making sure I never fall in love again."

"You sure about that?" She steps closer and takes his arms, wrapping them around her.

The wedding song starts playing, so we all rush inside and take our seats. My father, clad in a white tuxedo, stands under a rose arch in the front of the hallway. Then the little girl in the poofy golden dress walks down the aisle, throwing white petals. We all stand when Cassidy comes through the arched entrance. I see my father lift his hand to block his wide smile. A small bubble of happiness forms in my chest, seeing my father smile so wide.

The last time I remember him smiling this hard was the night my parents were dancing in the rain, and my mom had on those turquoise sneakers. I haven't seen my parents truly happy in a long time and, even though my father's actions were wrong, I do want him to be happy.

Cassidy reaches the rose arch and takes my dad's hands in hers. From the way they look at each other, I do believe they love each other, but it will never be the love he shared with my mom. The priest begins to speak, making a speech about loyalty, trust, and being around for one another. Daniel stands from his seat and storms off. Minutes seem to go agonizingly slow as I wait for the priest to finish speaking.

I need to go find him. "I'll be back," I whisper to Hunter and walk into the white building.

Daniel stands inside the groom's dressing room. It is now

clouded with smoke from his second cigarette. The only light comes from a small lamp in the corner of the room. "I tried so hard." He fills his lungs to their capacity with smoke.

"To do what?"

"To make Mom happy. To make you happy. To keep everyone's heart intact. Damn it, it was *working* until this wedding and your stupid decision to date my best friend." He paces the room.

"I thought—Hunter said that you two spoke and that you're okay with it." I fake-cough, hoping he'll put the cigarette out.

He rolls his eyes and stubs out the cigarette in a tray on a table surrounded by black leather couches.

"You shouldn't be dating—you're too young. You're going to get your heart broken, and you won't be able to handle that kind of pain."

He needs to remember that I am not him. Our experiences won't be the same. "Hunter is a good person." I run my hand up and down my arm, trying to reassure myself. "That's why you're friends with him, right?"

"I'm friends with him because he is willing to do dumb shit with me. Yes, he is a nice guy, but girls are obsessed with him. Good people can still do bad things."

I suck in a deep breath. The room falls dead silent. I can tell he is never going to drop this. Maybe I'm never going to win this one. My heart twists. A hot tear slides down my cheek. I quickly wipe it away with my sleeve, sitting down on the leather couch.

Daniel kneels down in front of me. "Can I tell you the truth?" He takes my hand in his, squeezing it tightly. His dark blue eyes soften in the dim light. He stinks of cigarettes and alcohol. "Love is very complicated. Look at Mom and Dad. Love is not a constant thing. We can love many people. If you choose Hunter now, at such a young age, it is bound to fall apart. Do you remember Mia? I believed she was the one, the same way you think Hunter is the one. She had me making up songs about her, writing fucking love letters for her. Holding her in my arms made me feel like I was a *man*." His hands shake, his breathing getting ragged. "She was *everything* to me. Until one day, when she woke up and simply decided I wasn't what she wanted anymore. She left, dragging my broken heart behind her. That's reality. People change their minds in the blink of an eye. You can wake up one day and find out that the one person you'd go to the end of the earth for doesn't feel anything for you. Putting the broken parts of yourself back together after that is the hardest thing in the world. I don't ever want you to experience that."

"I *know* that love is unpredictable. It's up to us to decide who is worth the risk," I say. Hunter is worth the risk. The silence feels heavy. I'm not used to having these kinds of conversations with Daniel; we used to resolve any problems we had through water-gun fights. "Are you going to say anything?"

"You talk about love as if you're not a sixteen-year-old whose only experience of romance is from watching Disney films." He ruffles my hair. The small gesture makes me feel like everything is back to normal between us. It eases the heaviness in my heart. "Okay, little booger. I won't stand in your way if this is a risk you're willing to take."

"Are you . . . sure?" I smile and rise from the stool.

"Hunter is already like a brother to me, anyway." He holds up a fist. "But if he ever—and I mean *ever*—hurts you, I will break him."

"Yeah, right."

"I mean it. You may be a huge pain in the ass, but I love you and I won't let anyone hurt you."

"If anyone is a pain in the ass, it's you, Grandpa." I throw my arms around Daniel. "Thank you, thank you, thank you."

A knock at the door pulls us apart. Hunter leans against the doorframe. His suit jacket is slung over his shoulder. "Sorry to interrupt, but cake is being served and I knew—" Before the sentence can be finished, Daniel is out the door. All Hunter needed to say is "cake."

Hunter walks closer to me. "And . . . ?"

I bite my lip, trying to hide my smile. He slips his arms around my waist, pressing our bodies together. It always feels like heaven being this close to him.

"He said okay."

He smiles. "It was only a matter of time. Daniel would do anything to make sure you are happy. One smile from you and he would agree to anything you want."

"Does that work on you, too?" I tease.

"Depends. What do you want?"

"You."

He smiles, the dimple on his left cheek showing again. "I'm yours."

Chapter 20

HUNTER

A few of my friends and I, including Daniel, sit at a table inside George's bakery. It is vacation time now and because of the cold, the bakery has been filled to the brim with customers, which has been exhausting. It's mostly grandparents bringing their grandchildren in for an extra dose of sugar, which has them trying to swing off any surface they can find.

I'm on a "mandatory" break now. I would have left and walked around the block or something, but right as I stepped out through the kitchen doors, eight rowdy football players, and Elijah, walked through the door.

"I'm going to write a book about how impossible it is to say otorhinolaryngology three times fast," Elias says, leaning his elbows against the wooden table. Everyone at the table immediately starts trying to say it.

Anne leans against the mini fridge filled with a few freshly baked cakes. She glances over at me and smiles. Her shift hasn't ended so she can't come join us. She has been giving customers different pastries and making the coffee herself. I'm proud of her. She's working hard. She told me after the wedding that she has sent the money she earned to her mom, but her mom still hasn't slowed down from working so much. I think it's more complicated than money. Her mom isn't from here, and most likely feels that she needs to overwork to prove herself to her boss.

I knew that feeling, coming to work at the bakery. It's only when I got to know George and feel his kindness and warmth that I realized that this job could be something I enjoy and find freedom in.

"—they took me for dinner and it was insane. It was on a yacht!" Daniel says as he puts his hands against the table, smiling wide with excitement in his eyes. "They said that I'm on a wait list and being considered for a full football scholarship at USC." All the guys light up. It's great. It also means Daniel will be all the way in California next year.

Things are still weird with us. I'd usually be the first person he'd tell, but now he is barely looking at me. I don't know if it'll ever return to what it was. I don't know if he will ever fully forgive me.

Another glance over at Anne makes me feel at ease. She is worth it.

"I can't wait to tell my mom. She'll probably start dancing," Daniel says. I smile. I've seen her strange dance before, years ago when Daniel and I ran home to tell her we got an A on our tests.

I wonder if my mom would have done the same, or what she might have done to show she is proud of me. It tightens my heart for a second, until I remember that it's selfish of me to think that right now. I'm supposed to be proud of Daniel, not wallowing.

"Eh, I don't know if you're *that* good, Danny boy," Elias taunts.

"Ah yeah." Daniel grins. "Is that a challenge?"

Elias stands, shuffling out of his seat. "Let's see if you have anything to back your words then. Fields?"

In an instant, they're gone, heading out to verse each other on the football fields. I could go with them, but I have a cake in the oven. They are already walking off outside without me, anyway.

The bell to the bakery chimes and a dark-haired guy with red glasses walks in, looking around. When his eyes find Anne, he walks over to the counter and starts talking to her. His fingers gently brush her hair behind her ear; they're clearly familiar with each other. *What is this?*

Anne steps back. The action allows me to relax. At least she's not reciprocating. I lean back in my seat.

He moves closer and reaches for her hand. *All right, that's enough.* I'm not going to allow another guy to flirt with her like this.

He must be the same guy that Daniel was telling me about, the one who took Anne out on her first date.

I walk up and step between him and Anne. "What's up, Jason?"

"Uh, it-it's Jaden." He blinks rapidly, watching me like a fly in a spiderweb.

"Why are you flirting with my girl?" I tilt my head to the side.

"Y-y-your . . ." He peeks around me, to look at Anne. "You and . . . Hunter Denegan? I—you—I didn't know."

"Well now you know." I straighten my back, emphasizing the fact that I am more than a head taller than him. "How do you know Anne?"

"We, uh . . ." He looks away, unsure on how to respond. "We're lab partners. For bio. N-nothing more."

"You went on a date with her." I nod slowly.

His eyes widen. He takes a step away as if I am going to hit him. I would never. That doesn't mean I can't embarrass him. "Did you kiss her?"

He stutters. "Wh-what?" His entire body is red. He doesn't say yes or no, but the thought of it makes me—

"Go." I nod my head toward the door.

"But I-I wanted to buy a pastry. I—"

I take a step closer to him and he immediately dodges backward, his sneakers squeaking against the floor. The door swings shut behind him.

A few of the customers seem to be watching, eating their croissants like this is some movie scene.

I turn to look at her, my face sheepish. I know she would have wanted to do that herself, but I didn't want to wait to see how long she'd let that go on for.

Instead of looking mad, she is grinning from ear to ear. "I'm your girl?"

"Of course you are."

Her smile drops when she pulls out her phone and reads the message. Why'd she stop smiling? "What's up?"

"I sent an email out to almost everyone at school, hoping to hear something about my missing shoe, but there still hasn't been a single response."

I place my hand on her shoulder when I notice she is going to burst into tears. "Come to the kitchen."

She follows me through the swinging doors, looking up at me expectantly, like I have an answer or some wise words to give her. I don't. "Hey," I whisper gently. I brush my thumb across her cheek. The look in her eyes leaves a strange feeling in my chest. Her vulnerability makes me want to protect her and make sure she never looks this upset again. "Come here." I can't give her a solution, not yet, anyway, but I can give her a hug. Hopefully that's enough. She sniffles and steps into my arms, and I hold her tight against me. "I've got you." My fingers run through her hair.

"I don't think I'm going to find it." Her voice is muffled when she speaks against me.

If I were being completely unfiltered, I'd tell her that I don't think so, either. Whether someone took it, or she misplaced it, it doesn't seem like it is going to show up any time soon.

The oven starts beeping, indicating that my cake is finished. It breaks the moment. Then she breaks away from me, her cheeks flushed and eyes still watery. She takes a deep breath and goes out into the main area of the bakery, needing to continue working. I want to hold on to her arm; to comfort her more. I wish I could help.

The office door swings open and George walks into the kitchen holding a white envelope. With a warm smile on his face, he holds it out for me. "I've been keeping track of your payments. You have more than enough money to move out, kiddo. I added a bonus to ensure it."

The envelope suddenly feels a lot heavier. "I don't think I'll have enough yet. I'm—" *Scared to be alone. Scared of what is next. Scared of what might happen.* Will I even survive on my own? I know I have the skills to cook and clean and fix a broken sink—but there is still so much I don't know.

He places his hand on my shoulder. "It's more than enough. Consider it a . . . housewarming gift."

I place the envelope down on the counter, my hands shaking. I'm finally going to get away from my father. "Thank you. I don't know how I can ever repay you."

"There's one way, but it's not going to be easy . . ."

"Absolutely. Anything."

He opens his arms wide, inviting me in for a hug. I step forward, wrapping my arms around him with all my strength, squeezing until he lets out a playful grunt. His laugh, warm and a little raspy, vibrates through me as his hand moves gently in soothing circles on my back. This man has saved me more times than I can count, in ways I'll never forget.

"Why are you wearing hoodies to work?" he asks, his tone scolding, as I step back.

"I'm wearing an apron over it." I give him a dazzling smile, hoping it will distract him from the topic. He gives me a flat look, not buying my excuse. "Come on, George. Nobody is gonna know. They won't see me back here in the kitchen."

"What about when you have to put the cake out?"

"I'll take my hoodie off when I go out."

"You better cut me a big slice and bring it to my desk." He turns and walks into his office, shaking his head as he goes.

"Oh, George, I should probably let you know..."

He turns to me with his hand on the door handle. "What is it, kiddo?"

"I'm not wearing a shirt under my hoodie." I took it off when I got home from school.

He snatches a crumpled-up paper ball from his desk and throws it at me. "You're lucky I care about you like a son." Warmth fills me. The feeling of watching sunshine glint off flowing water.

I lift the cake and carry it out to the front of the store. Anne, who is serving a table, turns to look at me and smiles. Maybe this life won't turn out so bad, because I have some truly great people in my life.

An older woman clears her throat. "Could you stop staring at that young gentleman and take my order, please?"

She nods rapidly. "Of course. I apologize. What would you like, ma'am?" She steals one more glance at me.

I cut a slice of the red velvet cake for George and carry it to his office.

He sits behind his desk with a pile of papers in front of him. "Thank you, kiddo." He immediately digs in, closing his eyes as he chews. A small piece of cream cheese gets stuck in his beard, but he immediately wipes it off with his finger. "You have such a talent. Promise me you will never stop, no matter what *anyone* tells you."

Baking is my therapy, my hobby, and my source of income. It would be stupid of me to quit. "I promise." His words still leave my heart feeling like there are butterflies fluttering around inside.

Walking out into the kitchen, I catch Anne eating whipped cream. Her eyes widen and she quickly hides the can, licking her lips. "Nothing."

"Step *away* from the cream."

Sighing, she steps closer to me. "Caught red-handed." She holds her wrists out as if I am going to arrest her.

"Any last bites before I take you into custody?" My shoulders shake with silent laughter.

"Stop laughing at your own jokes."

"But it's comedy gold."

She taps the note she pinned up on the board. "Get to work, Mr. Denegan. You have people waiting for your delicious hot chocolate." She turns to walk out.

I quickly hold on to her shoulders and turn her to face me. "Guess what?"

Her voice lowers to a whisper, like I am about to share a secret with her. "What?"

"I have enough money to move out. I found an apartment. I'm finally getting away from my father."

Her arms envelop me before I even realize what's happening. "You did it!" she exclaims, pulling me into a tight embrace.

She's right, I did it. I won. He can't hurt me anymore.

The kitchen door swings open. Sabrina walks in, devouring a

slice of my red velvet cake. "This is sooo—" Her eyes widen. "No fraternizing with co-workers!"

Anne doesn't pull away from me. "Glad to have you back, Sabrina," she deadpans.

"Trust me, I'd rather be using my teeth to scrape the gum off the bottom of tables than watch you two for a second longer."

"When did you get back?" I ask, but my eyes are trying to say, *How are you feeling?* Loneliness sucks. I'm glad she's back.

She gives me a small smile. "George kind of said my pay would be cut if I didn't come in today, since the bakery is so packed." Shrugging, she turns to leave the kitchen again. "Needed to get out the house anyway."

Anne leans back against the counter to watch me while I prepare the drink orders. The water for the hot chocolate comes to a boil, and once it's ready, I begin crafting foam art in each cup—teddy bears, plants, and all the intricate designs my mother patiently taught me as a child.

Most children wanted to be out on a swing at the park, but I would stick to her side, holding on to every moment.

Once they're ready, Anne reaches for them.

I grab on to her wrist, sucking in a breath. "Watch out. They're hot," I warn.

Her eyes trail down to where I am holding on to her. Her cheeks turn an adorable shade of pink. "I like the way you say *hot*," she admits. She watches me. "Am I allowed to say that?"

She clearly is not used to openly flirting with me yet, but I'll play along.

I pull her to face me. She places her hand on my chest, making my heart beat faster. "*Hot*," I say, making my voice deeper to tease her.

She snickers. I playfully graze my teeth over my bottom lip.

"Hey! Get off each other. I'm not paying you to make a porno in my kitchen!" George shouts. We pull away from each other with big smiles on our faces.

"Sorry, sir." Anne spins around and carefully lifts the hot chocolates onto a tray. She pushes her ass back against the kitchen door and winks at me before walking out.

George glares at me. "You better wipe down every counter in here until it sparkles. Don't let me catch you messing around again." He fetches a glass of water and disappears back into his office.

I start making a few croissants and pastries to set out for tomorrow. As I bake, George's affirmations drift back into my mind. I *am* good at what I do. The number of pastries and desserts I can make in a day is impressive. I no longer need my dad to be proud of me because I am proud of myself.

Anne walks into the kitchen. "I need you to sneak into my room tonight. We're going to celebrate you being able to move out."

I raise my eyebrows, placing the dough for the croissants into the fridge. "Do you mean what I think you mean?"

"If what you think I mean is cuddling and junk food, then yes."

I'm in.

•••

By the time the sun goes down, I've managed to make a good number of pastries. I pack all the ingredients away and start cleaning the counters, as per George's demand.

Anne walks in and leans against the counter, watching me clean. The corners of my mouth lift. How did I never notice her crush on me before? She loves being near me. I love being near her, too.

"The last few customers have left," she says.

"Okay, I'll be done in five minutes." She lifts herself up onto the counter. "I haven't cleaned that counter, Annabelle. You might have flour on your ass."

She laughs and climbs off, dusting her backside.

I bite my lip and turn away, forcing myself to finish cleaning. George is going to kill me if he catches us doing anything more.

"Let's go," I say.

As we step out into the cold, dark night, Anne wraps her arms tightly around herself, her hands trembling. I begin to lift my hoodie off to offer it to her, but she gently pulls it back down. "Don't, I'm fine."

"You're—" *shivering.*

"I like the cold," she says, knowing exactly what I was about to say.

Reaching my bike, I press her back against it. She leans her hands against the leather seat to balance herself. My lips are only inches away from hers.

Her eyes seem to sparkle in the moonlight. I'd believe her if she told me she was an angel sent to earth. Maybe this *is* an alternate universe.

"It's my turn to put the helmet on you," she says.

"Not a chance." She reaches out for the helmet. I grab her wrist. "Not. A. Chance," I say slowly.

"Why? If we get into an accident, you could get hurt. You're the driver, which means you're at a higher risk of injury. I looked it up and over ninety percent of motorcycle drivers are likely to be injured in an accident. You—"

"Stop reading online statistics." I take the helmet and slide it over her head, hoping it would show her that I'm not having it. I will not let her be hurt.

She groans and reaches up to playfully choke me. "Do you know how . . . *frustrating* you are?"

Moving her out the way, I climb onto my bike. "Let's go home and we can take those frustrations out on your headboard." I shoot her a naughty smile.

She climbs onto my bike, and wraps her arms around me, purposely trailing her hands dangerously low on my body. I groan and grab her thighs, squeezing them slightly.

She laughs and presses her head against my back. "I can't believe you're *mine*."

My heart stops in my chest for a moment. That brings a feeling of peace to my heart. Everything I am feeling is new. Today has been filled with personal wins. I can imagine spending every day with her until I take my last breath.

Starting the engine of my bike, it growls to life. With a small smile on my face and a foreign feeling in my chest, I drive down the road. The streets are quieter tonight. The combination of the cold and the holiday means that everyone is trying to get away from this tiny town. It seems like Daniel is, too. I feel the excitement buzzing off Anne when she quickly hops off my bike, onto her driveway, and rushes into her house without looking back.

Stepping into their house, I glance around. It's still dark and there is a strange shuffling sound. Hands land on my chest. "If I said I was scared of the dark, what would you say?" Anne whispers in the darkness.

I hold her closer, trying not to laugh. She clearly wants me to flirt with her and say something cheesy like "I'll protect you." "I would say that you are talking nonsense and have never been afraid of anything in all the years I have known you."

"I'm afraid of things," she argues.

"Like what?"

"The ocean. It's scary ... not knowing what's coming, not knowing how deep it is. I like certainty, and everything about the ocean is, well, unpredictable and unknown."

"Like the future."

She shrugs. "What are you afraid of?"

Myself. Looking in the mirror and seeing weakness and fear and doubt.

My gaze drops. She slides up against me and I grip her waist, trying not to sink too far into my mind.

A warmth rises from my chest into my throat. It takes hold of me, like a tightening noose. Worst of all, I'm scared that I might disappoint the people I love by not being what they expect me to be.

From her answer, she wants things to be clear and known. She wants stability. I don't know if I can be that. I might take this money I saved and move cities. I've wanted to get away for so long and now I have the chance.

An anchor has dropped into the wooden floorboard beneath my feet, tugging me down. I want to scream. My breath shakes, my chest rising and falling rapidly.

Anne places her hand on my chest. "Are you okay?"

"I ... I don't know if I can—" *Am I doing this? Think!* "I don't know if I can do this, Anne."

Think. Think. Think. You'll lose her. Don't do this.

Shadows swarm, waiting to pounce. What do I fear more? Losing her or hurting her?

Tears fill my eyes. Thankfully it's dark. My father's voice booms in my head: *pathetic*.

My head spins. If I lose her, I'll lose the safe space I have. I'd be alone.

Am I counting on her for companionship? What does she count on me for? To stay? To support her?

How are you going to support your family, Hunter, with that girly job of yours? Go bake cupcakes and see if any woman will stay.

I don't know—I run my hand over my face, wiping the thoughts away.

"Do what?" she whispers. Her voice is laced with a new fear. She can feel my body shaking. She knows what.

"This."

"What? Tell me what?"

"A relationship. Us. I—" I shake my head, gripping her waist tighter because I know this might be the last time I'll ever get to hold her.

"You're giving me the 'I can't do this anymore' line? Already?" Her tone, the way she says already, like it is something she knew would come but simply not this soon.

I'm a disappointment. "Yes, already."

She steps back, out of my reach. I immediately hate the space between us. I know I'm the one that is ending this, but I need her closer.

I reach out for her, step closer to her, but she is already too far. She switches on the lights and sees the tears in my eyes.

All I see, through the blur, is sorrow written on her face. A deep, burning sorrow that isn't going to go away anytime soon.

"I'm sorry."

"Sorry?" She sobs, then blocks her mouth with a shaking hand. "Hunter, I know you're scared of this. But come on, we can work through these things. We can talk about it."

"There isn't anything to talk about. I need to know who I am and what I want. All of these thoughts in my head aren't mine, and

I am realizing that I am so scared to sit alone with them—to have to face myself."

"You don't have to face them alone."

"I don't want to let you down. I want you, I swear. And I love you." It's true. She is the most incredible person I know. "I just can't do this." I hold my breath in punishment. I shouldn't be allowed to cause this much pain to her without suffering myself.

Oh, but I know this is only the start of my suffering.

What is going to happen when I see her at school? Or when I call Daniel and he swears at me? Everything will crumble and I'll have to stand with my palms open trying to catch the pieces.

"I'm sorry." That's all I can say. I know it's not enough. I know.

Her expression is broken, barely able to hold the pain. She reaches out then immediately pulls back, taking a step back. Then another. She's retreating, not just physically, but the words that she wants to say are being sucked back in.

She knows it, too, that I'm going to let her down. Better sooner than later. That much I'm sure of.

Because she said it—*already?*—she knew this would happen. "Did you—Were you waiting for me to hurt you?"

Her eyes fall closed. She turns away. "I'd loved you for so long that I knew this was too good to be true. I hoped that you wouldn't, but it's okay. I understand why you did. You never wanted to stay. I'm an inconvenience."

There are many things that I can handle. But the person I love talking down about herself is not it. "No." Tears stream down my cheeks. I step closer. Before she can protest, she is wrapped in my arms. "Please don't say that."

She whimpers, crying in my arms. "It's okay," she says.

"My feelings for you have been the truest things that I've felt in a long time. You're not an inconvenience, you're the best thing that has ever happened to me."

"It's okay, Hunter. You don't have to be the one to comfort me anymore." A knife to the chest. "Just go."

I'd shove broken bottle shards into my chest, and it still wouldn't hurt like this. I want to collapse. There is pressure pulsing from the inside out.

"I'm—"

"Sorry, yes, I know. Me too." *For what?* "Just go."

End of conversation.

I nod, pulling the door back open. The wind that greets me is colder than my father's eyes. Now, I have to go back home and face his words once more.

I'm denying none of it this time.

Chapter 21

ANNE

Stepping into my house, tired from another long day at school. I am greeted by the smell of mulukhiyah. The scent is warm and savory, with hints of garlic and coriander wafting through the air, *Am I dreaming?* "Mama?"

"I am in the kitchen!" *Wait, what?*

The smell intensifies as I step into the kitchen. My mom's back is turned to me as she stirs several pots of food on the stove. She's like Superwoman in the kitchen.

"You're home." I run up to her and hug her from behind. "You're making mulukhiyah!" It has been years since she has made Egyptian food. I missed it so much—and it's not something I can go buy in a restaurant, because it never compares. But more than that, I missed *her*. She's here. She's really, really here.

"Yes, I told my boss that I am not working late tonight because I have to be home." The words I have been wishing to hear from her for a long, long time. I stare at her in momentary shock. Why? What made her choose to do this now?

It's as if she can see the unsaid questions written on my face. "When you sent me that money, I could see what you needed. You needed your mom to be around. I realized what kind of message I was sending: that money is more important than family. It's not. You and your brothers are the most important things in the world to me. I hope you know that," she says with a soft smile on her face.

Her words cause tears to slide down my face. She's here. And now I can finally tell her what happened. "I lost one of your shoes. I'm so sorry. I don't know what happened. I changed for gym class and then it was just gone and I've done everything to try and get it back, and I thought I would, but it's been months now and every day makes me more sure that I will never see it again and I'm so sorry because . . ."—I suck in a deep breath—"because I know how much those shoes mean to you and all the memories you have with them and it's so selfish of me to lose one of them. I'm so sorry. I—"

She brushes it away, with the wave of her hand, like it was nothing; like she had let go them of a long time ago. Pulling me into a tight hug, she says. "It's okay, *omri*." The word lingers in the air for a moment. It makes my heart fill with joy. The word means "my life." "Do you know what I care about more than my shoe—that can never be lost of replaced?"

"What?"

"*Inti.*" *You.*

I pout. "Mama, stop."

That makes her smile. Smile lines form in the corners of her eyes. "It's the truth. You are everything I have worked for, every hardship I overcame, every story I experienced. It was all for you. That's what you should hold on to and never lose, not some shoe."

A weight that I didn't know was pressing down on my chest and shoulders suddenly lifts, and it feels like I could sprout wings and start flying around. "*Shukran,*" I say. *Thank you.*

She gasps dramatically. "You're speaking Arabic? Who are you?"

At that, I laugh. "Come on, shukran is an easy word to know. You use it all the time."

She turns back to the stove. "Hmm, what? I didn't hear. All I heard is my daughter speaking Arabic." When I say nothing, staring at her while she cooks, she adds, "Go start neatening up the house, please. I've invited a few guests over and you can ask that one friend of yours to come. Go, go."

That one friend of mine? *Ouch*.

I step out the kitchen to find Daniel and Hunter in the living room. The couches have been pushed back and a table has been placed in the center of the room.

"No, man, the tablecloth is the wrong way around," Daniel says. His dark hair is falling into his face as he frowns at the tablecloth.

"I told you, you're supposed to *see* the flowers." Hunter points at the daisies on the tablecloth.

My smile is wide as I lean back against the wall. Hunter glances at me, looks away, and glances at me again. His curls look soft, and it causes me to imagine how it would feel to run my fingers through them and mess them all up.

Daniel clicks his fingers in front of Hunter's face. "Hey, hey! Can you keep your eyes off her for a *second*?"

He shakes his head, biting his lip to conceal his smile.

Ignoring the gesture, I point to the tablecloth. "Daniel, Mom hates this one. Use the white one."

He shrugs. "This is fine."

"You're right." I shrug. "I'd like to be the favorite child for once, anyway."

He narrows his eyes at me and rips the tablecloth off the table. Grumbling something under his breath, he walks off to grab the other one.

Not wanting to talk to Hunter, I walk out of the room. I make my way up to my bedroom and text Clary to come over for dinner. My "only" friend. It's true, but it still stings. I fall onto my bed and close my eyes, burying my face into my pillow. Finally, I can rest. My eyes burn with the need to sleep.

Someone knocks on my door and pushes it open. "Oh, you're taking a nap," my mom says. *Right, I was supposed to clean.*

I sit up. "Sorry, I'll come and clean."

She waves her hand. "No, no. That's not what I came here for." Walking in and closing the door, she takes a seat on my bed. "I wanted to know if you want to talk to me about . . . things." *Did she see Hunter and me?* "I know I'm not around all the time, but if you need me, I'll always be your mom."

I lean my head against her shoulder. I've missed her so much. "There's this boy . . ."

She shifts slightly to face me, her eyes lighting up. "Who?"

"It's Hunter."

"Did something happen between you two?" Well, something *did.* Now it is over, I guess. She doesn't seem as surprised as I thought she'd be. "You've had a crush on him for a while, yes?"

"How—how did you know?"

Her head tilts to the side, laughing. "I have seen you staring at him all the time, especially when he'd laugh. You change your clothes whenever you find out Hunter is coming here. You blush when his name is mentioned. Mama knows best."

I am so embarrassed. She must have known for a while.

"Does Daniel know?"

I nod. "He was upset at first, but I think he is okay with it now." He is not going to be okay when he finds out that it ended as quickly as it started.

IT STARTED WITH A HIGH TOP

She reaches out to pull my face close and kisses my forehead. "As long as you two are together for the right reasons. You must feel comfortable with him and have fun. Talk to me if you have questions." I can't find it in myself to tell her that we aren't technically together anymore.

I nod and shift closer to hug her. She smells like the food she's been cooking.

I am so lucky to have a mom like her. Her phone buzzes, and she frowns, pulling it out of her pocket to check her notifications. Her hand goes to her chest, and she stares at the phone like it's a ghost.

"What?" Was she fired or something?

"Y-your father . . ." She looks at me. "He sent me money. A lot. Why?"

It must have been Cassidy. It is possible that deep, deep, deep, deep down she is a good person. "I may have spoken about it, about how I wish you could work less and be home more like you used to be." I can feel my skin getting hot. I am sure she will chastise me for asking him for money.

Tears fill her eyes and eventually slip down her cheeks. "Thank you." I quickly lean forward and brush the tears away with my thumb. Her skin is soft and slightly squishy from age. She laughs through the tears. "It will help me a lot. I'm grateful that he is willing to help with his children after all this time. Maybe that other lady is good for him. She will take that stick out of his—"

"*Mama.*"

"Ear. I was going to say *ear.*" She waves her hand dismissively. *I'm sure.* "Now, come help me clean, please."

• • •

As I look around the table, everything feels like a happy, warm memory in the making. Most of the people at the table are Daniel's friends. My mom invited two of her friends, whom she met when we first moved to Tecumseh, and their young children. My mom places her dishes down on the table. Her head nods animatedly as she speaks to one of her friends. Laughter fills the room. I'd give anything to do *this* every night. It feels as if someone is blowing bubbles inside my heart.

Soft winter sunlight streams through the windows, bathing the room in a gentle, golden hue. This moment feels a thousand times more ... hygge. It's a Danish term that I, strangely enough, learnt in English class. There's no direct translation, but it correlates to the feeling of comfort, of home.

Hunter's chair scrapes against the floor as he shifts closer to me. Nobody else notices. He slides his hand onto my lap, intertwining his fingers with mine.

I look at him with wide eyes. What is he doing? He squeezes my hand.

Clary sits on the other side of me, her gaze focused on the lettuce she is violently tearing apart on her plate. "What did the lettuce do to you?" I ask.

She flicks a tiny piece of lettuce in Daniel's direction. Her eyes narrow. "It's about what the lettuce represents."

Daniel smirks. *Stop staring*, he mouths to her.

She rolls her eyes and continues to mutilate the lettuce. Her hair falls forward to partially hide her face. Her cheeks are redder than her hair.

Omar, one of Daniel's gamer friends, nods his head toward Clary and says in Arabic, "*Am aftakar ennak btehebha.*" I don't know the exact meaning, but something about him loving or liking her. Daniel's eyes widen, his head whipping toward me.

He knows that I have the slightest hint of what Omar just said and might be worried that I'd spill to Clary. If that is true, if Daniel does have true feelings for Clary, then it needs to be him who says it.

I make a zipping motion over my mouth. He nods, taking a sip of water, and steals another glance at Clary. If he doesn't want her to know, then it is not my place to tell her.

Moving away from Hunter, I reach forward and dish out rice and mulukhiyah with chicken. The dish is a deep green reminiscent of a lush forest. My mom doesn't like it with rice, but I love the way it tastes together.

I take a bite of my mother's food and let out a blissful hum, my eyes fluttering shut in delight. "This is really, really good." I'd sell my soul for an endless supply of this. Each bite brings back memories from my childhood.

Hunter's grip tightens on my leg. "Don't do that," he whispers.

Taking another bite, I moan to tease him. Omar overhears and shoots me a playful wink. His dark brown eyes trail down to my chest.

"Wink at her again. I dare you," Hunter says to Omar, causing the table to go quiet. The children continue to laugh, ignorant to the situation.

"Ana asif." I'm sorry. Omar lifts a glass to his lips and gulps his drink down.

The conversation slowly starts again. I place my hand over Hunter's. "What was that?"

There's a fire in his eyes. He leans in. "What I said the other night was stupid. I said it out of fear. I'm working on it, okay? This is my first time being a boyfriend. Please be patient with me."

"Is anything going to change, or will you keep backing out when you get nervous?"

"No backing out. I want you. Let me prove it to you, okay?"

I nod. We are both new to this. I am okay with it not being perfect.

"Hunter, can we talk?" Daniel says nodding his head toward the stairs. *That can't be good.* They both excuse themselves and leave the table.

"Can you show me how to apply *eyeliner*, Anne? I've always seen it online, but I mess it up every freaking time," Clary says, loud enough for everyone to her. She widens her eyes at me.

But the food . . .

I take one last bite and nod, rising to my feet. My mom watches me. I clear the table, taking all the empty plates to the kitchen.

Clary pulls my arm, practically running up the stairs. The wood creaks loudly, causing her to slow her pace.

We press our ears to Daniel's door, curious as to what is going on. "Fuck." Daniel groans. "If I could get her out of my head . . ."

Hunter laughs. "You are falling so hard."

"No, it's not like that. She's just a great kisser. I could kiss her all day if—" He stops himself short, registering his words.

"You were saying?" Hunter teases.

Clary's eyes light up. Her face is directly in front of mine as we keep our ears against the wooden door. *Do you think they're talking about me?* she mouths.

I nod.

"It's not going to happen. It's purely physical," Daniel argues.

"If you saw her with another guy, would you get jealous?"

"Doubt it."

Clary grins. *Oh, no.* "Let's find out," she whispers, hiking up her fire-engine-red leather skirt. She's crazy to be wearing that in this weather. We walk downstairs and out to the back garden.

All of the flowers have wilted. The grass reaches past our ankles, damp with the moisture in the cold air. The bushes that were once coated in marigold flowers are now patches of brown. Four of Daniel's friends stand and smoke together near a pile of twigs.

Clary immediately gets to work, striding over to chat up Elias, the easiest target. He would never say no to her. Or any female. A small black cross earring dangles from one of his ears, catching the light each time he moves. Oblivious to the chill, Elias wears basketball shorts.

With a daring grin, she lifts his arm and slips it around her shoulders, her confidence radiating as she draws him in. Elias smiles, running a hand through his tousled blond hair, his casual demeanor relaxed yet eager. He offers her his cigarette, and she takes it with a playful smirk, placing it between her lips and inhaling deeply. The smoke curls into the air, mingling with the faint scent of winter.

Daniel and Hunter walk out into the garden to join us, their presence demanding attention. Clary's gaze snaps to Daniel as smoke leaves her mouth. But the moment shifts as she starts to cough, the unexpected bitterness of the smoke catching her off guard. Her laughter mixes with the coughs.

Elias chuckles, a teasing glint in his eye. "Was that your first time?" She nods, her face flushed with embarrassment and the cold. He presses his thumb to her bottom lip. "Taking your innocence is oddly . . . *satisfying*." His words hang in the air.

Daniel scoffs. "She is far from innocent."

"Oh, really?" Elias tugs Clary closer to his side, noticing the tension and fueling the fire. "Are you a *bad* girl?"

I cringe at the scenario unfolding in front of me. Popcorn would help. Hunter comes to stand beside me, slipping his hand into mine—the action so simple and comforting, yet it sends a thrill through me as I realize how real this is. His hand is a welcoming warmth.

"Why don't you come with me and find out," Clary replies, tugging at his shirt. Elias caves in, almost falling over his feet at the offer.

Daniel's expression shifts, a mix of anger and disappointment, and he turns to walk back into the house. This is what he always does, receding inward instead of taking what he wants.

I go inside after him, the warmth of the house like a soft blanket. Daniel is already halfway across the passageway. With a huff, I run up to him and take his arm. "Stop running from your problems, Daniel."

He glances back at me, frustration flickering in his eyes. "Are you saying I should leave her?"

"That's literally the exact opposite of what I am saying."

His mouth moves around as he plays with his tongue ring. Maybe it is something he does when he is deep in thought—something I don't see often. Ha. "Go on," he says.

"She cares about you a lot and I don't want you to be—"

His eyes soften, revealing his vulnerability. "She does? It doesn't really seem like it." His gestures dismissively toward the scene unfolding outside. Through the glass doors, Clary is still laughing and playing with Elias.

Not helping my point. "Yes, she does, and I know you care about her, too. We heard you in your room when you said you can't stop thinking about her."

"*What?* You were eavesdropping on my conversation?" His mouth falls ajar. His eyes wander off toward the glass sliding door. "What else did you hear?" His voice is slow and careful as he tries not to reveal how much he cares.

"Why do you think she is out there trying to make you jealous?" I sigh. "Go do something, so you don't lose her. She wants you to fight for her."

"It doesn't feel right having this conversation with you." He smirks, and I can tell he wants to ruffle my hair. I step back to make sure he doesn't.

"Daniel, I get it. Having your heart broken is one of the worst feelings. But you can't be afraid to find someone who will make you feel happy because that's one of the *best* feelings." Even something as simple as the joy of holding their hand.

"You don't get it, because you've never gone through it."

"No, but—"

"No, you don't get it. You don't get that I have constant thoughts about how my heart might be broken again. Will it be cheating, loss of interest, incompatibility, whatever else?" He leans forward, the intensity in his gaze palpable. "I know it is my problem. I fear being hurt, and I'd rather hold on to that fear because it's not nearly as painful as heartbreak. To give your heart to someone and to be vulnerable with them, for them to say they love you, and then to walk away the next day as if everything we shared didn't matter." He looks to the side, his jaw clenched. Tension ripples through his muscles. "I would have done anything for her."

He is talking about his last girlfriend. Mia. He rarely says her name anymore.

"I understand that it can be painful, and yes, you could get hurt. But it could also turn into the best relationship of your life. You have to take the chance." I want this for him. I want to see him happy. "I thought that love doesn't end well, because of Mom and Dad, but each experience is different. Clary isn't Mia."

He exhales sharply, his resolve flickering. "Fine, I'll be brave, because I want to be a good role model for you."

I purse my lips, trying to hold my laughter back. The determination in his eyes tells me he is being serious. That only makes it funnier. My "good role model."

"Thanks, big booger." I reach out to ruffle his hair, but I am too short, so I go for a cheek-pat instead. Turning, I head back outside.

"*Enough*," Daniel says from behind me as he steps out, his voice stern. It's a command, not a suggestion.

He takes Clary's arm, turning her to face him. They stare at each other for an eternity, as if there is a silent conversation going on between them. Clary grins and bites her lip, nodding.

"Couldn't resist, hm?" Daniel teases as he lifts her up into his arms and carries her inside, whispering something that makes her grin from ear to ear.

"What just happened?" Elias asks, looking around at all of us. "Did Daniel just steal my potential hookup ... *again*?"

"Maybe if you stop referring to girls as 'potential hookups,' you'd get laid," says Maison, one of Daniel's other friends.

My mom walks out into the garden, giving dirty looks to Daniel's friends for smoking. I wonder what she would do if she knew Daniel smokes, too.

"Come help me set up for dessert," Mom instructs me. I nod and let go of Hunter's hand, walking back inside. Once away from everyone, she whispers to me in a stern tone, "You better not smoke. *Wallah*,"—*I swear*—"I will kill you before the cancer does."

"I *know*, Mama."

After lecturing me, she stops near the stairs and shouts, "Daniel Asim Déville, come help us with the food—" She finishes the sentence in Arabic, to hide her threats from the guests. I laugh.

I can't be sure, but I think she said "or else you'll be slapped with an acorn on the ass." I love having my mom here. The whole house seems fuller, not just literally but the feeling of it—she has an energy that can fill the emptiest of spaces. I love her more than anything.

Walking into the kitchen, I immediately start to drool. The twins lay out all the desserts that my mom made onto trays—Umm Ali, kanafa, basbousa, and ghoriba. I pinch my leg to make sure I'm not dreaming. Mom has magical powers when it comes to food. My dad lost so much when he chose Cassidy instead.

"Baby, will you take out the trash, please?" my mom asks. She turns toward the stairs.

I nod and walk over to Haiz, patting his head. "Go put on a jacket. I'm taking you out." He narrows his eyes at me and swats my hand away.

"Why do you make Umm Ali?" Adam asks. "It doesn't even taste good."

"Uncultured," Haiz mumbles, stealing a bite from the pudding-like dessert directly out of the serving bowl. He receives a slap on the back of his head from my mom.

"There is a famous story behind this dish," she explains, placing a spoon into the bowl. "It is said that the dish was created to celebrate a murder." Instead of listening to the story for the thousandth time, I pick up the trash and carry it out.

Walking back into the house, I find Daniel and Clary sneaking back downstairs. Their messy hair and the huge smiles on their faces give them away instantly.

My role model, ladies and gentlemen.

Chapter 22

ANNE

It is already Saturday. I sit alone in a café where nobody knows me, surrounded by the sound of clicking keyboards and constant chatter. The smell of coffee is strong and comforting. Days are flying, yet the idea of time passing no longer scares me.

We had an author come to our school this week, and she had some great advice about structuring stories and finding agents. She told me to read the acknowledgments of other books and to send pitches out to those agents mentioned. Doing that, even though I have gotten zero responses, has helped me feel like I am moving in the right direction for my future.

The only thing I am nervous about is Daniel leaving. Everything is going to be different when he goes to USC. How will the twins get home? Will we only see Daniel on the holidays? Who will annoy me in the morning with blasting rock music?

It's a very real, and very hard, part of life to let people and things go. But I'm slowly learning how. Or at least I'm *trying* to. Yet my head feels like it is in overdrive.

My fingers begin to ache, and the café starts filling up near sundown. I pack up my things and head outside into the biting cold. There are four lakes surrounding Michigan, which means that as soon as the cold comes, it hits like a train without headlights. I blow on my numbing fingers.

Lost in thought, of what life will be like next year without Daniel, I find myself at my house in around ten minutes. I push my front door open.

Hunter bounds down the steps toward me. He seems... happy. Surprise takes ahold of my throat, silencing me. He is here, and he is smiling at me. "I have a surprise for you," he says.

"What?"

He gestures for me to go upstairs, so that I can find out for myself.

My bedroom door groans open like an old man needing to rise from his comfortable seat. Disney-themed plushies sit on my bed. Snacks are placed on my desk, from popcorn to pretzels and even éclairs! My mouth waters. I urge to jump and shove one into my mouth, but I hold back.

Slowly walking over to the snack table, feigning disinterest in the chocolate-coated dough that smells fresh out of the oven, I assess the other snacks. A bag of jelly babies says "you make my heart as soft and squishy as these jelly babies." The cupcakes say "cupcakes are good, but your kisses are better." A laugh bubbles out of me before I silence it.

There is a white sheet hung up on my wall, the screen frozen on an animated movie. Is he trying to apologize? There must be something more to this. He shifts his weight, his fists clenching and opening.

Biting down on my lip, I ask, "Hunter, what is this?"

He runs a hand over his face. "I tried to listen to my head

but"—he sighs heavily, shaking his head—"I can't do it. I am completely in love with you and no amount of logic or fear seems to stop it."

I glance up at the screen, holding back tears.

He walks up to me, holding my arms in his hands. Excitement takes its turn dancing with fear and joy. "I did it. I got my own apartment. Here, in Tecumseh. I was really hesitant, because I wanted to leave this town and move to a big city; live a life where every day is exciting and fulfilling. But I realized that I can stay, and be with you, and maybe one day we could go see the world together. Because you're right Annabelle, we're only teenagers. We have time, but I want to spend as much of it as I can with you. I love you, and I love who I am when I am with you."

He leans in, placing a kiss to my forehead. I sigh, immediately craving more. His lips are addictive and he seems to know that he has got me hooked. His hand slides down my arms, then grips my waist, pulling me flush against him.

My lips part. "Is this your apology?"

He nods slowly, his finger lifting my chin up. Lowering his voice, he adds, "But if you want me to put my lips *anywhere* else, and have me whisper apologies there, I'd be more than happy to oblige."

Luckily, he is holding my waist with a strong grip, because otherwise my knees might have given in. Unsure whether to laugh it off or give in, I place my hand on his chest. "And this?" I nod my head toward the screen and the plushies on my bed.

"Well, I couldn't afford to take you to Disney right now, so I thought for our first date I'd bring Disney to you." His eyes scan over his work. He lets me go, gesturing to the room. "I know it's not the same, but I wanted you to feel like a princess and I—"

I throw my arms around him, squeezing him tight. My heart is melting into a puddle in my chest. I've never imagined that anyone would do something this kind for me.

He wraps me up in his arms and keeps me there. When I saw other people in love, I never knew what it felt like. Now I believe it's a million different things. It is complex, and humans might have gotten lazy—encapsulating so many things into one word: love.

The highs and the lows, the confusion, the emotions—all constant and yet changing. That is the beauty of it. "I love you," I whisper, lifting my head to press a gentle, familiar kiss to his lips.

"I love you so much. The truth is, I haven't been able to stop thinking about you," he admits. He lifts me off the ground and carries me to the bed, laying me down. My hair spreads out against my sheets. "You have always been so kind and gentle to me. I don't want to lose you."

I don't want to lose him. "Do you . . . do you really think this is something that will last?"

"I don't know. There is a lot of things that I am scared of, but I am willing to try. Because I want you in my future, through the good and the bad."

I grin, wanting to hide as I feel my face redden. "Could you kiss me now?"

He lowers his face, hovering his lips above mine. Playfully, he says, "I am going to need to hear you say please."

"Please."

"Say 'pretty please with a cherry on top'?"

I want to be stubborn and refuse, but his voice is deep. It's hard to resist. "Pretty please, ah—hey *you* should be saying please—"

He cuts me off with his lips, laughing into the kiss. I pull back, laughing also. There is a familiar warmth in my chest.

"What, I didn't hear you?" he sings. Shaking his head, he leans down to kiss me again. Slower this time. I sink into the bed, enjoying every pleasurable sensation that comes with the way his lips move. His tongue brushes against my bottom lip. He shifts, grinding against me, his kisses moving down to my neck.

I can tell, even with my lack of romantic experience, where this is going. I think a nun could tell where this is going. The warmth of his body, his kisses against my neck, it all swirls together like liquid fire.

A stuffed yellow bear, holding his pot of honey, shows a little too much interest in what is unfolding. I gently push him off the bed, then return my attention to the gorgeous boy who is—*oh*—he is pulling his shirt off.

My hands instinctively brush across his broad shoulders, down his biceps. Something I have been craving so long. His skin is warm. He lowers himself back down, leaning on his forearms to make sure he doesn't crush me beneath him.

His breath, warm and urgent, skims my skin, sending shivers down my spine that pool in my stomach. His lips trail my collarbone, each kiss deeper, more lingering, as if he is taking mental notes of all the spots that I enjoy being kissed. His hands slide over my hips, finding the place where my shirt has lifted. His fingers press into my flesh just enough to make me gasp.

Ah, I need more. More of his scent, his touch, the sound of his breath hitching as he holds me closer. "Hunter, please."

A low rumble leaves his throat. He pulls back, breathing heavy. His Adam's apple bobs as he gulps, trying to control himself. Desire swirls like a storm in those darkening gray eyes.

"Hello, is anybody at home?" My mom's voice comes from downstairs, followed by footsteps coming up the stairs. "Yallah, I come home early and nobody is here," she says to herself.

I try to push Hunter off of me, but he barely moves. I know she will check my room first. *"Hide."* I hand him his shirt, my eyes wide.

He jumps into my closet, wincing as he stands on something jutting out near my shoe stand, and pulls the door closed. I run out of my room, so my mom won't see Hunter's setup, or my rumpled sheets.

I've been waiting for her to get home—still adjusting to the fact that she doesn't have to be at work all the time. But the timing couldn't be worse. Even so, I have a distraction waiting downstairs. "Mama," I call, pulling her into a hug. She is still in her blue scrubs. In her hands is a large cardboard box. "Come downstairs, I have something to show you," I say.

She follows me down, huffing with each step she takes. "Really? Because I have something to show you also." I sit down on the couch with her and pull forward the manuscript that I had hidden beneath the couch. She laughs, pretending to lean down and look under. "What else do you hide under there?"

"Just my stash of coke."

Her face goes serious, clearly not appreciating my humor. Note to self: do not make drug-related jokes with brown parents. "The drink, Mama. The drink."

Sighing, she places her hand to her chest. "It better be." Did anybody else hear the silent "or else"? I hold the bound papers out for her, my heart pounding like it is in my throat. It doesn't help that Hunter is probably still hiding uncomfortably in my closet. "What's this?" she asks.

"My manuscript. I wanted to write a story—your story. I am still searching for a publisher, but I did it. It is all the stories that you have told us over the years."

Her hands shake as she runs her fingers over the title: *In Her*

Shoes. She looks up at me, tears sparkling in her eyes. One teardrop escapes, leaving a wet trail on her cheek. "Omri, shukran." She thanks me, pulling me into her arms and whispering things in Arabic. Her speed makes it hard for me to pick up everything that she is saying, but she is wishing blessings on me for such a kind act. It leaves a feeling of peace and joy in my heart.

She pulls back to briefly flip through the pages, then holds it to her chest like she is hugging it. Tears are falling rapidly from her cheeks, and I can't hold in my own emotions. With a deep breath, she places the papers down and holds out the cardboard box that was beside her.

"What is it?"

She nods her chin toward it. *"Buss."* Look.

Inside the box is a white pair of sneakers. They have thick soles detailed with blue-and-pink flower prints. The shoelaces of the shoes are also blue. "These are so pretty."

"I know they're not the same, but I thought a different kind of high top might be nice. You can create your own stories now, in your own shoes, to tell to your loved ones one day."

I sidle over to her, pulling her into a bone-crushing hug, just as Hunter sneaks quietly out the front door. "Thank you, Mama. Shukran."

"I appreciate everything you have done for this family," she says. "You have made me proud, working hard and asking for what you want. And this"—her hand goes to the manuscript—"I love it. I love you."

Another version of love, again, stuffed into a word that doesn't quite measure up to the feeling. I am so happy she is here, and her words mean everything to me. This moment is what I have been waiting for and working for.

Chapter 23

HUNTER

This is the moment I have been waiting for and working for.

Paint chips off the walls. A radiator buzzes loudly. I run my fingers along the dusty, wooden kitchen counter. I'm standing in *my* apartment. It may not be a beauty yet, but it is definitely worth the price. A simple student apartment.

Every time Daniel takes a step farther into the apartment, the wooden floor groans in protest. I call that sound *safety*, because no burglar will be able to sneak up on me here. "Why do you need an apartment?" he asks, looking around with a frown.

Anne, who is placing what she deems "home essentials" around the house—candles and scented handwash—freezes to look at me. There is the silent question of *are you going to tell him?* written in her eyes.

I'm not ready, and I don't know if I will ever be.

"I got it at a great price, and I wanted space away from home, to give me a sense of independence, since we're going to university next year," I say. The main reason the rent is cheap is because there is a rumor going around that the woman who lived here was buried near the parking lot and still haunts this place. From her photos, she seemed like such a nice old lady. I wouldn't mind if she haunted me. Maybe I'll wake up and there will be cookies that I never made in the oven.

"Going to be bringing chicks over, huh?" Daniel asks.

"Yeah."

We both laugh, until he realizes I am talking about his sister. He gives me the finger and walks off toward the small outdoor garden.

Clary, who is leaning against the wall near the front door, says, "It's a nice apartment." Her eyes scan the place, checking the ceiling for mold. None, I made sure of it.

Daniel nods, walking back toward me. "It gets the Daniel seal of approval. Let's throw a party here tonight. It's perfect. There is nothing in here for people to break."

George should be here soon to bring some of my things from my old house. He refused to let me go back. There still won't be anything valuable in here, anyway.

"Thirty people?" he asks.

"Fifteen."

"You pronounced thirty wrong." Daniel pulls his phone out and starts typing away.

"Fine, but you're helping me clean up, and you're buying the drinks."

"Of course. I've already got everything in the trunk of my car," Daniel says.

There is a knock on the already open, bright red front door. "Hey, kiddo," George says. His left eye is bruised badly. He walks past me and places two boxes down on the floor. "Come and help me carry the rest in."

"Why do you have a black eye?" I clench my fists when I realize what the answer could be. My heart tightens. "Did my father do that?"

He is silent and refuses to make direct eye contact with me. I am filled with guilt and anger at the thought of it. This is my fault. I shouldn't have let him go anywhere near my house.

I crack my knuckles and walk straight out the door, toward my motorbike. Violence isn't the answer—I know that—and yet the rage I feel to get justice for what happened blinds me. My father can crush me until I'm on my knees, but he cannot get away with hurting someone I love. *Not this time.*

George rushes out and steps between me and my bike, ensuring that I can't get past him. He purposely tries to bounce me off his stomach, knowing it will make me laugh. Hands waving rigidly, he says, "Don't go back there. It's over. You never have to see him again."

Daniel walks out to stand beside us, watching the situation. His face is scrunched in confusion. "What is he talking about, Hunter? Why would your dad do this?"

Looking at George, the purple color that his skin has turned where he was hit, makes me imagine every detail of the scenario. He must have knocked at my front door and gone in. My father would be demanding with his questions—where is he? Why are you taking his things? That pathetic boy can't even face me himself? Maybe George answered, and that angered my father even more. The only person in his life wants nothing to do with him. Well, what did he expect?

"I am ready," I say through gritted teeth. I've been wanting to do this for years, anyway. "He fucking hit you!" My breathing becomes unmanageable. Moving around George, I grab my helmet. I've never sworn in front of George before.

"Your father is a horrible man, with bad intentions. No matter what he has said or done, you have never let him win. But when you become angry because of him, it means he has won."

"From the moment my mother left, he has hurt me. I don't care. But I do care when he hurts you."

"Take a deep breath." He breathes in deeply and I follow. "Be grateful for everything that you do have." He points to the apartment and my friends. "And *mera beta*, you always have me." Mera beta means *my son*. He must know the effect those words have on me, how much it means, but it only makes me want to do this more.

I turn to face my bike, still feeling the rage-induced impulse to face my father.

"You believe that you shouldn't hurt someone, no matter what, correct?" he asks. My fists tighten. It's easier said than done, right now. "If you get on that motorbike, you lose yourself."

"Not much to lose, anyway."

Noticing that he is not getting through to me, he says, "Don't do it, or you're fired."

"You wouldn't." It would be such a hassle for him to find someone to replace me.

"I will not have you going back to that house. It will cause you nothing but pain."

My grip tightens on my helmet. I want to throw it to the gravel beneath my feet. Instead, I place it back down on my bike. There is no way I am losing my job. I'm not letting my father mess with my life for a second longer. George knows his threat will stop me from leaving.

"He hurt you." My jaw clenches.

George waves his hand dismissively and points to his eye. "What, this little bruise? You should have seen the pain I caused back in India. Men were terrified. Women wanted more." He lifts his shirt, revealing a skull tattoo on the side of his ribs. "Now take another deep breath." I follow his instructions and inhale. "And out."

I exhale slowly, my eyes locking on to Anne's. She is standing near the apartment door with Clary. I'm so grateful for the people who are here right now—I wouldn't have made it here without them. Taking another deep breath, I say, "I'm okay."

George nods and walks off to his car to get the rest of the boxes.

Daniel pushes me slightly. "How long has your father been a piece of trash?"

"Years." I shake my head. "It's over now, though."

"Did he ever . . . ?" *Hit me?*

Daniel is going to start getting protective and I don't want that. "No," I say, my voice unsteady. I wrap my arms around myself. Daniel knows me too well, and senses that I am lying.

His dark blue eyes blaze with anger. "How did I not notice?" His fists tighten. Anger is written all over Daniel's face. "If you *ever* need to fuck him up, I'll be by your side."

"Shouldn't you be trying to stop me from fighting?"

He deadpans, as if the answer is obvious, "You'd have to hold *me* back if I ever see your father again."

I nod and head over to grab boxes from George. I don't want to think about that, because I wouldn't hold him back.

We manage to finish most of it before the sun sets.

Once everything is unpacked, George pats his hand against my back. I turn to face him and he holds his arms open. "I am going to head home. The sun is setting and my driving skills are not good at night anymore."

"Maybe you could come over for some coffee soon. I need to hear more of these stories from India that you haven't told me." He sounds *awesome*. Plus, I have a feeling that this place is going to feel a bit too empty when nobody else is around. I'll find some way to keep busy—maybe I'll repaint all of these walls.

"One story per cupcake you bake for me." His hands are still held open.

I wrap my arms tightly around him. "Thank you, George. For everything."

"Now if you need anything, even a little bit of salt, you come to me. Got it?"

I am so grateful for him. None of this would have happened if it weren't for him. He even helped me pay for my apartment, since I am still seventeen and can't do it alone.

•••

Only an hour later, I find myself gripping a red Solo cup. Strobe lights, that Daniel *coincidentally* had in his car, light the otherwise dark room. No matter how many parties I go to, no matter how people come over and hug me tight, I somehow always feel out of place. It seems like everyone else does, too, by the way they awkwardly bounce to the booming music. I hope this party doesn't get me kicked out of here before I get a chance to buy a kettle.

The music playing is from Daniel's playlist, so I only had two options: heavy metal or rap. I chose the latter. The beat of every song rapidly follows the rhythm of my heart.

Daniel leans back against the kitchen counter beside me, watching two girls on the other side of the room make out. "This is how you christen a house," he says and pours a shot down his throat.

"How badly do you want to join them?"

He shakes his head and searches the room for a specific redhead. "I'd only want a threesome if Clary is a part of it. She'd do some wild shit like that."

He may as well have confessed his undying love. They seem to be happy.

Clary walks over to us, her outfit a burst of color. She's wearing a thin, polka-dot button-up shirt tucked into a nearly glow-in-the-dark yellow plastic skirt. Earlier, she had a warm coat over it, but she's removed it now that it's warmer inside. It is almost as if her and Daniel knew there would be a party. I shake my head at their plotting.

She tugs at the random shoelace threaded through Daniel's belt loops. "Is this a shoelace? Why are you wearing it like this?" she asks, puzzled.

He wets his lips. "So that you'd come over here and tug at it like that."

She trails her hand down his chest. Turning to me, Daniel asks, "Will you do me a favor and turn off the strobe lights in fifteen seconds?"

"Do I want to know why?"

He nods his head toward the lights before walking toward the center of the room with Clary. "In ten seconds, the lights are going to go out!" he shouts. "What you do in that time is up to you. If you don't have a date, the snacks are over there." He points to the wooden counter that I am still leaning up against. "The only twist is you don't know when they'll turn back on. Tread carefully."

When I switch the lights off, the music seems to pound harder. It is so dark I may as well have my eyes closed. Too nervous about bumping into someone, I stay planted near the lights, my hand pressed against the cool wall.

A hand runs gently through my hair. The familiar smell of violets puts me at ease. "Anne?" I reach out to pull her closer to me. "I know it's you."

She coils the strings of my hoodie around her fingers. "Kiss me."

I dip my head lower, gently brushing my lips against hers. The music pulses through my body. A low moan leaves my lips, but it's inaudible over the music. She presses her lips to mine for a few seconds before pulling away. It's cute that she thinks she is getting away from me. I roughly tug her hips against me and kiss her with as much force as I can muster.

"Let's go to your room?" she says over the music. I'm sure she wants a break from being around people. I'll come socialize later.

I switch the lights back on, not bothering to look at what everyone else was in the middle of.

Reaching my bedroom, she shuts the door. "Do you actually enjoy being around people?" she asks as if the thought baffles her.

I sit on my bed—or rather on the thin mattress that will be my bed for a little while—and shrug. She lowers herself beside me and leans her head on my arm. "I guess I do, because it is a good distraction," I say. A little distraction always helps, especially on days like today.

"That's not healthy, Hunter. You need to speak to someone to get that built-up frustration out. If not a professional, then speak to me or to Daniel."

Everybody is distracted for most of the day, in different ways. Phones, movies, jobs, video games, classes. It's all different forms of getting to the next day. Maybe now, it'll be easier. I'll need fewer distractions, and it'll feel easier to come back to this place that I call home.

"Yeah, I will." I owe Daniel more of an explanation, anyway.

She slides her hand into mine. "Look at how far you've come. You've got your own apartment. You've got a job you love and people who love you. I'm so happy for you."

I squeeze her hand. Her words mean so much. It feels good to be acknowledged. "Really?"

"Of course. But I still want you to come sleep with me sometimes."

I rub my nose against hers. "You want me to get my *frustration* out in other ways?"

"*Yeah.*"

"Wait, are you serious?"

"By 'other ways,' you mean a pillow fight, right?" She takes the single pillow from my bed and gently hits my head with it.

Pushing her down against my mattress, I hover over her and press my lips against hers. I wasn't done with the kiss that we started in the dark. My hand slides up her thigh. Her skin is smooth. She has to be the most beautiful girl I've ever met. Her lips, her wide innocent eyes, her huge heart. No matter how many times I kiss her, it'll never get old; even if we do. She could rip my heart into a million pieces and I wouldn't regret loving her.

The door swings open. "Why did you turn the lights back on so quick—hey! Get the fuck off my sister!" Daniel stands in the doorway, not knowing what to do next.

We sit up. Anne runs her hands over her top and shrugs.

He points his index finger at her then at the door. "Go. I need to talk to Hunter alone."

She glances over at me with a silent question in her eyes. I nod my chin. *Go.*

Standing up, she points at Daniel and says, "I know you're my brother, but if you mess this up for me, I will disown you."

He rolls his eyes and shuts the door once she's gone. Is he going to tell me that he doesn't approve anymore? Or that I shouldn't touch her when he is nearby?

Kneeling down in front of me, his eyes bore into mine. His hands slip into his pocket and he pulls out a joint. "Wanna get stoned?"

There, another form of distraction. An unhealthier one.

"I think—I think I am good. I no longer feel the need to escape."

He nods, lying back against my bed. "Want to talk about anything?"

"You wanted to know if he ever hit me." I nod, holding my hands together tightly on my lap. "Not really, well—not often. Sometimes he'd throw things at me, beer bottles and that, but as I grew up, he realized I could hit back and so he resorted to words instead. God, did he pummel me with those."

Daniel sits up. His expression is stern. My skin turns clammy, the air suddenly too thick. I got used to opening up to Anne, but I'd rather fall off a cliff than cry in front of Daniel. Until I look up and realize that his eyes are glossy. "I'm so sorry I couldn't help you."

That makes my hardened wall crumble. "You *did*. You have no idea how much you did: giving me a place to stay and a lot of needed distractions. Daniel you saved me." It feels weird saying this, but my words are the complete truth.

He throws an arm over my shoulder. "You have saved me, too. That is why I was so scared of your relationship with my sister. You are an incredible friend and such a good guy. I probably would have lost my shit and ended up in juvy without you." He laughs.

Rubbing my arm, I say, "We should make a pact, that no matter where we end up, we'll always make time for each other."

"I like that." He nods, adding, "What kind of pact is it, though? Blood pact? Do we need to spit in our hands and shake on it?" He wiggles his fingers in front of my face.

I laugh, but it sounds more like a cough. "Words will be just fine."

Chapter 24

ANNE

I have been over at Hunter's apartment nearly every night, whenever my mom works her late shifts. I have lit some candles around his living room tonight, because some of the ceiling bulbs haven't been fixed yet. Hunter has been working a lot.

I huff, getting on my toes to try and leave a candle on a single shelf on the wall. Hunter presses up against me, his one hand protectively on my waist while he helps me safely place the candle. When I turn in his arms, ready to thank him, he is trying not to laugh.

"What, you think I'm *short*?"

"Not exactly. I think that you're like . . . a mini prototype of a human," he says.

"Well, you're—" I huff. "You're looking a bit tired. Do you work as a streetlamp during the night?"

"Where do you shop? The children's section?"

"Do birds fly into you when you walk outside?" Now I can't stop grinning.

"How did you escape the M&M packet?" He holds his fingers together with a smirk, leaving a tiny gap between his thumb and index.

I laugh, my head falling back. He bites his lip, clearly wanting to hold me. His attraction to me is palpable, and so sexy. It makes my heart flutter like paper cards in the wind.

"You know, there's a conspiracy about this apartment," he says. *A conspiracy?* He switches on the lamp in the corner, casting a warm golden glow that gently fills the small space. "They say that the old lady who lived here was buried in the parking lot."

My eyes widen with excitement. "You think she is out there now?"

"Look." Hunter points at a bush that can be seen through his sliding door. "Don't you see her watering the garden?"

"But it's freezing outside."

"I don't think ghosts can feel the cold, Annabelle," he deadpans.

"Shut up." I push his arm gently.

Staring outside, into the darkness, his gaze seems to fill with sadness. "I am sorry that I'm a bad boyfriend." He doesn't take his gaze off his own reflection. Lines crease between his brows. "I want to take you on fun dates, skiing or to Disneyland, but I can barely afford my own water bill. I am not exactly a fun person to date right now."

I take his face in my hands, rubbing my thumb across the slight stubble growing along his jaw. It's a little ticklish. "You could take me to the supermarket for a date and I'd be happy, because being with you makes the most mundane things feel like an adventure. *You* make my heart happy."

I lean in closer, my hand going behind his neck to pull him closer to me. His lips meet mine, gentle but firm. They mold perfectly against me. I have imagined kissing him a million times before, but now that it has become a normal part of my day, I find myself having to remember that this is real. I pull back for a second and he shakes his head. "Mm-mmm." He kisses me again, slowly, and the softness and unspoken feelings between us make me realize why these deep, lingering kisses are so intoxicating.

His hand slips beneath my shirt, his cold fingers brushing my back. I can feel his heart racing against mine. *I still have a huge crush on him.* The kiss deepens, his tongue teasing mine. My fingers curl into his shirt, craving more. I tug at his shirt.

"Our old lady ghost is probably watching this and praying." He laughs, his breath warm against my skin. The corner of his eyes crinkle with amusement.

"I'm sorry, ma'am," I call out. Silence settles over us for a moment, and I nearly consider pulling away. But I don't want to. Biting my lip nervously, I ask, "Do you think that this is what love is?"

He pauses, then shakes his head. "Everybody spends their lives trying to define love instead of feeling it." He pushes my hair away from my face, cupping my cheek. "Humans long to capture, to define, to understand. But let love be like a wildfire—unbound and admired."

My boyfriend, the poet. I just wanted him to say *yes*.

It feels scary to let go and not define something which seems so unpredictable. In Hunter's arms, it feels less scary, even when I don't know what is next.

This is my happily ever after, but it is also only the beginning.

Acknowledgements

Books are an escape, for both the reader and the writer. It is always helpful to have a safe space where humans are not causing harm, where loss is gentle, and love is shown in all forms. That's what this book aims to be. It was my safe space and hopefully for a moment it was yours.

When I started writing, it was just me, my English essay, and a gigantic platform that I couldn't navigate. That is why I want to start by saying thank you to my friends on Wattpad—Nikki, Simeon, Kenadee, Rua, Raneem, Marjana, Niles, and every person that made me want to go onto the app and write every day.

Thank you to my beautiful mother. Everything I am, and every dream I chase, is because of you. Thank you for showing me what it means to live fully, and for filling my life with so much warmth and wisdom.

To my wonderful family and friends who have been my constant cheerleaders in this process, I love you and appreciate you so much.

To my editors, Rebecca Sands, Fiona Simpson and Shannon Whibbs, who helped me shape this novel into what it is now. I have learned so much from your expertise. I appreciate all of your hard work.

To #TeamNoSleep—Sydney, Jordan, and Jessica—who sat through hours of writing and editing with me. This book would not be what it is without you. You were the best writing team out there.

To the amazing people at Wattpad HQ. Deanna, you are doing wonderful things; you are making so many new writers' dreams come true. Nick, you made me feel so welcome when I was first joining the writing programs. Thank you to all the amazing people behind the face of Wattpad.

To Ramez, who helped me with all of the Arabic translations in the book. Shukran.

I also want to say thank you to my friend Georgia, who first introduced me to free writing platforms in the ninth grade. Without you, my writing journey would have been very different or may have not happened at all.

To Yusuf, I could write all the romance novels and none of them could compare to the kind of love you've shown me exists in the world. *Te amo, mi rey.*

To my readers—to you—thank you so much. Truly, my passion was fueled by your support. Thank you for showing up for each new book I wrote. Thank you for sending me the kindest messages. I feel so lucky to have the most wonderful readers. I could write another novel, simply naming all the readers who have shown me kindness throughout my writing journey.

About the Author

Laylaa Khan, a South African writer, has reached over 150 million reads across multiple novels online. Her debut work, *It Started with a High Top*, began as a playful short story and has developed into much more. Laylaa's journey as a writer was enriched by her experience teaching English in Madrid and studying for her Master's in Paris. Aside from traveling, her passions include dancing, design, and escaping to fictional worlds filled with love and magic and adventure.

Recipes

I have added some tried and tested recipes to curb any cravings you may have gotten while reading. I highly recommend you try Hunter's popular cinnamon rolls (they taste good with chocolate filling too).

1. Banana bread
2. Ginger cookies
3. Cinnamon rolls
4. Strawberry shortcake
5. Burnt Basque cheesecake

Banana Bread

Ingredients:
- 4–6 overripe bananas, peeled (approx. 2 1/2–3 cups mashed)
- 2/3 cup (152 g) melted butter
- 1 teaspoon baking soda
- 2 pinches of salt
- 1 1/2 cups (300 g) sugar (adjust to taste)
- 2 large eggs, beaten
- 2 teaspoons vanilla extract
- 3 cups (410 g) all-purpose flour

Instructions:
1. Preheat the oven to 350 °F (175 °C).
2. Grease your loaf pan with butter.
3. Mash the bananas thoroughly.
4. Stir in the melted butter.
5. Add the baking soda, salt, sugar, beaten eggs, and vanilla extract, mixing well.
6. Gradually fold in the flour until the mixture is smooth and well combined.
7. Evenly divide the batter into two prepared loaf pans.
8. Bake for 40 minutes.
9. Cool on a wire rack before serving.

Additional Tips:
- Insert a toothpick into the center. If it comes out clean or with a few crumbs, your banana bread is ready.
- If the top is browning too quickly, lightly cover with foil and continue baking.

Ginger Cookies

Ingredients:

- 2 1/2 cups (312 g) all-purpose flour
- 1/2 teaspoon salt
- 2 teaspoons baking soda
- 1/2 teaspoon ground cloves
- 2 1/2 teaspoons ground cinnamon
- 1 teaspoon ground ginger
- 1/4 cup (163 g) softened (not melted) coconut oil
- 1/2 cup (107 g) butter
- 1 cup (220 g) packed light brown sugar
- 1 large egg
- 1/4 cup (244 g) golden syrup
- 1/3 cup (68 g) turbinado (unrefined brown) sugar

Instructions:

1. In a medium bowl, whisk together the dry ingredients: flour, salt, baking soda, ground cloves, cinnamon, and ginger.
2. Cube the butter into small pieces.
3. Cream the coconut oil, butter, and brown sugar together using a mixer at medium speed for 3–4 minutes.
4. Add the egg and golden syrup and continue mixing until well combined.
5. Gradually add the dry ingredients to the wet mixture, half a cup at a time.
6. Form the dough into a ball, wrap it in cling film, and refrigerate for 30 minutes.

7. Preheat the oven to 350 °F (180 °C) and lightly spray a baking sheet with non-stick spray.

8. Roll the dough into small balls, coat them in turbinado sugar, and arrange them on the baking sheet.

9. Bake for 12–15 minutes.

Additional Tips:

- Avoid overmixing the dough. Use a medium setting on the mixer to keep the texture light.

Cinnamon Rolls

Ingredients:
- 2 3/4 cups (375 g) all-purpose flour (keep extra for rolling)
- 2/3 teaspoon sea salt
- 1 cup (8 fl oz) milk
- 1/3 cup (60 g) caster sugar
- 7 1/2 tablespoons (100 g) cubed unsalted butter
- 1 1/8 teaspoons active dry yeast
- 2/3 teaspoon vanilla sugar (or 1 teaspoon vanilla essence)

For cinnamon spread:
- 1/8 cup (25 g) light butter
- 1/4 cup (40–50 g) sugar
- 2.5–3 teaspoons ground cinnamon

For glaze:
- 3/4 cup (150 g) icing sugar
- 2 1/3 tablespoons (35 g) milk

Instructions:
1. In a large bowl, mix the flour and salt.

2. Gently warm the milk until lukewarm, then add the vanilla sugar and caster sugar. Stir until dissolved, then add the dry yeast. Let it rest for 10 minutes until bubbly.

3. Add the yeast mixture to the flour and mix until a smooth dough forms (about 15 minutes of kneading).

4. Gradually incorporate the cubed butter, kneading until smooth. Add extra flour if needed to achieve the right dough

texture. Cover with a damp towel and allow it to rise for 1 hour or until doubled in size.

5. Once risen, punch down the dough. Roll it out on a lightly floured surface into a rectangle, about 3 mm thick.

6. Spread softened butter over the dough, followed by the sugar and cinnamon.

7. Cut the dough into strips 2 inches (5 cm) wide, then roll each strip.

8. Cover the rolls with a tea towel and allow them to rise for 30 minutes.

9. Preheat the oven to 392 °F (200 °C). Bake for 15 minutes or until golden brown.

10. For the glaze, whisk together the icing sugar and milk, then drizzle over the warm rolls.

Strawberry Shortcake

Ingredients for filling:
- 6 cups (770 g) sliced fresh strawberries
- 1/2 cup (100 g) sugar
- 1 teaspoon vanilla extract
- 1 1/2 cups (12 fl oz) heavy whipping cream
- 2 tablespoons sugar
- 1/2 teaspoon vanilla extract

Ingredients for shortcake:
- 3 cups (375 g) all-purpose flour
- 5 tablespoons sugar (divided)
- 3 teaspoons baking powder
- 1 teaspoon baking soda
- 1/2 teaspoon salt
- 3/4 cup (160 g) cold butter, cubed
- 1 1/4 (10 fl oz) cups buttermilk
- 2 tablespoons heavy whipping cream

Instructions:
1. Combine strawberries with sugar and vanilla, slightly mashing them. Let sit for at least 30 minutes.
2. Preheat oven to 400 °F (204 °C).
3. In a large bowl, whisk together flour, 4 tablespoons sugar, baking powder, baking soda, and salt.
4. Cut in the cold butter until the mixture resembles coarse crumbs.
5. Stir in buttermilk just until combined—do not overmix.

6. Drop dough by 1/3 cupfuls (65 g), 2 inches (5 cm) apart, onto an ungreased baking sheet.

7. Brush the tops with 2 tablespoons of heavy cream, and sprinkle with the remaining tablespoon of sugar.

8. Bake for 18–20 minutes, until golden brown.

9. Beat heavy cream with sugar and vanilla until soft peaks form.

10. To serve, slice the shortcakes in half, layer with strawberries and whipped cream, then top with the other half.

Burnt Basque Cheesecake

Ingredients:
- 2.2 lbs (1 kg) cream cheese
- 7 large eggs
- 2 cups (400 g) sugar
- 1 tablespoon flour
- 200 ml (6.5 fl oz) heavy cream
- 1 teaspoon vanilla essence

Instructions:

1. Preheat the oven to 410 °F (210 °C).

2. In a large bowl, use an electric mixer or whisk to combine all ingredients until smooth and creamy.

3. Line a 10-inch (25 cm) springform pan with parchment paper, allowing the paper to extend beyond the edges.

4. Pour the mixture into the pan and bake for 40 minutes. The cake will rise significantly but will settle once it cools.

5. The top should appear burnt, and the center will still be jiggly. Once out of the oven, let it cool on the counter before refrigerating.

6. After chilling for a few hours (preferably overnight), it is ready to serve.

Additional Tips:

- For a creamier texture, consider adding a bit more heavy cream.
- A smaller pan will create a taller cheesecake but may require additional baking time

Printed in the United States
by Baker & Taylor Publisher Services